STEPHANIE ALVES

Copyright © 2022 by Stephanie Alves

All rights reserved.

No part of this book may be distributed or reproduced by any means without the prior written consent of the author, with the exception of quotes for a book review.

This book is a work of fiction. Any names, places, characters or incidents are a product of the author's imagination.

Any resemblance to actual persons, events, or locales is entirely coincidental.

Cover designer: Stephanie Alves

ISBN: 9798839877436

Playlist

In your eyes – The Weeknd ft Doja cat

Wasted times – The Weeknd

Pov – Ariana Grande

Up at night – Kehlani ft Justin Bieber

Hate that I love you – Rihanna ft Ne-Yo

Never knew I needed – Ne-Yo

Honey – Kehlani

Breathin – Ariana Grande

Best part – Daniel Caesar ft H.E.R

As you are – The Weeknd

Every kind of way – H.E.R

Feels – Kehlani

I know a love – Trey Songz

For the people who want someone to see them at their worst and still love them.

CHAPTER ONE

This wasn't happening.

There was no way this was happening.

This had to be some kind of sick joke or a prank. Right?

I blinked, making Zaria's face come into focus. I was barely awake, struggling to keep my eyes open. It was four in the morning, and her phone rang in the middle of the night, permeating my ears, as we shared a wall. I waited for her to answer it, or silence it, but I should have known better, Zaria slept like the dead, which meant I had to wake her up.

We'd been best friends since freshmen year of high school, for ten years we had been inseparable, I loved Zaria and thought she could do no wrong, until now.

"You're joking."

She shook her head. "I'm not."

Her hand reached up, wiping the sleep from her heavy, tired eyes. Hidden beneath her thick lashes, as she looked at me with remorse.

Zaria had always been glamorous. She was one of those girls that you would see on the street and made your head turn, grabbing your attention, making you think of her for the rest of the day. Since the day I met her, I had been fascinated, her style and clothing stood out to me the most, loud, and colorful to match her personality.

Even at four in the morning, she looked absolutely beautiful. Her warm brown, flawless skin glistened from her ten-step skincare routine she did religiously before bed. Her jet-black hair hidden beneath her silk hair wrap she slept in to keep her hair straight and smooth.

Whereas I, on the other hand, inherited my frizzy, wavy hair from my father's Italian genes, along with everything else. I wondered if I had inherited anything from my mother, not that I particularly wanted to, but was I like her in any way?

"What do you mean Gabriel's moving in?" I asked.

Zaria sighed. "He broke up with Lucy last night and asked if he could move into our apartment for a while."

I laughed bitterly. Gabriel and I couldn't spend more than a few minutes in the same vicinity as one another without us going at each other's throats.

Gabriel and I never got along. From the moment we met, ten years ago, he and I have barely tolerated each other. It was bad enough that we argued whenever we saw each other, but now I would have to see him every day. There was no way I could *live* with him. How someone like Gabriel shared DNA with Zaria, I would never understand.

"This has to be a joke, right?" I breathed out.

"Melissa, this feud has been going on for too long don't you think? He needs a place to stay for a while until he can find an apartment to live in." She sighed. "Can you at least *try* to get along?"

I narrowed my eyes at her. "This 'feud' isn't and was never my fault, your brother hates me. He has done since the moment we met." I ran my hands down my sweats as I laughed, dryly. "We can't even be in the same room without insulting each other, how are we going to live together?"

Zaria's eyes softened, and she stepped closer, squeezing my hand, trying to calm me down. She knew me better than anyone else, she knew how much I hated arguing and confrontation, and right now, she knew how anxious it was making me.

The pressure built up in my chest as I reached up, pressing my hand down on my chest trying to ease the ache. He wasn't even here yet and I was already freaking out. I took a deep breath in. I'd be damned if Gabriel broke me. I had to stand my ground, if arguing was what he wanted, the arguing was what he was going to get.

"It's just for a while, okay?"

My hand dropped from my chest. "Wait, how long is a while?" I asked, looking at her with narrowed eyes. It couldn't be that long right? He was a sous chef at an esteemed restaurant —and as much as I disliked Gabriel—he certainly wasn't an idiot. He would have some money saved up.

"About a month?" She started rubbing my shoulder, easing me like she hadn't just dropped a bomb. This was not what I had in mind. I thought he would be gone within the week, and I could have avoided him as much as possible.

Maybe I should implement Zaria's ten-step skincare routine. I could feel wrinkles coming along just from this news.

"A month?" I cried out. "Why would he possibly need to stay that long?" My shoulders stiffened as I stepped back, looking at Zaria with uncertainty. No amount of shoulder rubs could ease the tension in my neck—hell, my whole body right now.

"He just broke up with his girlfriend M. They weren't dating for long, but they had already signed a lease together, so he has to save up a little and find an apartment before he can move in." She shrugged. "He's my brother, family helps family."

I dropped my eyes. Of course, they did. I couldn't relate, the closest thing I had to a family was Zaria and her parents.

"They were dating for less than six months, and they were already living together?" I bit my lip to stifle my laugh. This probably was not the time to be making jokes at her brother's expense.

"I know." She laughed. My eyebrows shot up, I was not expecting that kind of reaction from her, maybe she was more relieved that their relationship has ended than I thought.

"I thought it was way too quick too, but I'm not sure it was Gabriel's idea, you know him, he was never the kind of guy to settle down and move so quickly too." She continued. "Lucy was very eager to move in together, marry him, and have kids. He probably realized that he wasn't ready for that and bailed."

My brows pulled together. "So, he didn't tell you why they broke up?" I asked.

She shook her head. "No, he just said that they broke up and asked if he could stay here." She shrugged. "I'll get it out of him sooner or later." She smiled, cunningly.

I rolled my eyes, of course, she would. Zaria was the type of person that everyone trusted and somehow ended up telling their deepest, darkest secrets to.

Gabriel's relationship caught me off guard when Zaria told me about it. Back in high school, he was a known player which didn't stop when he graduated. Even when he was away at college, people in our high school would still talk about Gabriel Anderson and how he was the hottest man alive.

Okay, I had to admit he was attractive. And as much as I tried, I couldn't deny that I had a crush on him the first time I laid my eyes on him, which quickly deteriorated into detest for him because assholes are still assholes, no matter how attractive they are.

I met Gabriel when I was fourteen, I had become friends with Zaria, and when she invited me over to her house, I was hesitant at first, meeting new people had never been my strong suit, but her house, and family, quickly became my safe space away from everything I was trying to avoid at home.

Her parents were the kindest people I had ever met, they invited me with open arms and made me feel comfortable in their house, which as someone with social anxiety, was the last thing I expected to happen.

I never let anybody get close or let myself open up to people, so to feel so comfortable in her house was special to me, however, with Gabriel, it was a different story.

The first time I laid my eyes on Gabriel, he was descending the stairs. I sucked in a breath at the sight of him. He was so handsome. His chiseled jaw was covered in stubble that was now a short, trimmed beard covering the bottom half of his face. His big pouty lips, which were always glossy from him constantly licking his lips, taunted me as he smirked at me.

I heard about Gabriel Anderson at school, but I had never seen him until that day. I wasn't prepared for what that smirk would do to me, my knees threatened to buckle as his dark brown eyes glistened, looking down at me. He ran a hand through his black hair, cut short enough where he couldn't grab it.

My eyes drifted to his arms, those muscles. Oh god. They made my breath hitch at the sight of his dark skin glistening on the surface of his ripped body, which was now covered in tattoos.

There was no denying the man was unbelievably gorgeous, but would I ever admit that to anyone? Hell no, especially not to Zaria, because knowing her, she would tease me for it indefinitely, or kill me.

"Can you promise me M? That you'll put this feud behind you and get along?" She asked.

How could I forgive him for everything he had said and done throughout the years? It wasn't just the fact that for some unknown reason, he didn't like me, but it seemed like I was the only person that he didn't like.

Everyone loved Gabriel, he was charming, happy, and charismatic. He had a smile that would bring anyone to their knees. But he didn't even try with me, he had no desire of being friendly

At first, he was distant and wouldn't even acknowledge my existence as a person, but as time went on, he seemed annoyed to have me around, like I was a nuisance who he couldn't get rid of, someone he despised and was an inconvenience to him.

I never understood why, and no matter how amicable I tried to be to him, it was always the same response. Indifference, hardly speaking to me, and when he did, it was nothing but insults and jokes. About my hair, my clothes, my celebrity crushes, anything, and everything Gabriel would find an issue with.

I didn't want his friendship after that, if he wanted to hate me, then I'd hate him back. If he wanted to insult me and joke at my expense, then I would dish it back at him. The conflict was something I tried to avoid at all costs, but the only way he would acknowledge me was if I irritated him right back.

I bit my lip and looked away from my best friend. I couldn't tell her any of this, I couldn't tell her that all I ever wanted was friendship with Gabriel, that I wanted him to look at me as something else other than his little sister's best friend, who he couldn't stand.

I sighed. "I can't promise anything Z, I just can't hold back if he starts attacking me"

I had learned my lesson and I wasn't going to make the same mistake twice. I laughed, thinking of a time when I would do anything to impress Gabriel. When I would bring pastries from the bakery any time I would stay over at Zaria's. How I used to try to watch the football games on tv whenever he did, to try and have something in common with him. Not anymore.

Long gone was the naïve girl who did everything in her power for a guy's attention. Especially a guy who had no interest in her kindness.

"Okay, I'll talk to him M, at least promise you'll *try* to be good, please." She pointed at me with her finger and narrowed eyes. "I mean it. You know you're like my sister and I love you, but I can't have a war going on in the apartment"

Zaria was right. He was going to be staying with us for a month, the least I could do was try. I didn't have to go overboard or even be kind to him, I just had to try and not fight with him.

"I Promise." I bit my cheek from the sour taste in my mouth that sprouted those words and breathed out. "…. That I'll try."

Zaria sighed and shook her head. "I'll take it, he'll be here at noon, I'm going back to sleep."

Zaria crashed onto the bed, and I made my way out of her room. I honestly had forgotten what time it was. This had gotten me so stressed I didn't know if I'd be able to get back to sleep. I laid in my bed with the covers pulled over my head.

I hadn't seen Gabriel since Christmas, it had been nine months without so much as speaking to him, and now I was going to be living with him. seeing him every day, the idea was unfathomable.

How were we ever going to coincide with each other, more importantly, how did he feel about this? He sure as shit couldn't be thrilled about spending time in a place where I was going to be.

If he didn't try this new 'friendly' approach, I don't think I could either. I no longer was the happy, trusting girl I used to be. I had been burned too many times to keep living the same mistake.

I groaned and let myself sink deeper into the bed, forcing my eyes shut, I was too riled up and stressed about what Zaria had told me to sleep, but I had to try. Hopefully, a good night's rest could prepare me for what was about to happen tomorrow, maybe it wouldn't be so bad.

Who was I kidding? It was going to be a nightmare.

CHAPTER TWO

He had arrived.

I heard a knock at the door and my breath quickened.

Footsteps fell across the apartment floor as Zaria walked to the door to invite him in.

To live here.

For a month.

Kill me now.

My ears were engrossed on the noise outside of my bedroom. Hearing his heavy footsteps as he walked through the front door. I could hear muffled noise as he greeted his sister.

I couldn't help but think of how he would greet me, with an insult undoubtedly. I groaned as I sat up in my bed, staying there a little longer for no other reason than to delay the inevitable to happen. I was dreading the unavoidable fact that I would have to interact with the jerk.

My palms felt clammy as my stress built up. I hated that I let him get to me so much. Any other person wouldn't be bothered by what Gabriel said to them, but then again, any other person wouldn't have that problem because, for some reason, I was the only one he seemed to have a problem with.

I wiped my palms on my sweatpants as I let out a cross between a sigh and a grunt. I couldn't believe I was going to have to spend a month with Gabriel Anderson.

There was no use in staying here any longer, at some point I'd have to see him and talk to him, might as well get it over with now. I got up from my bed, heading to my bedroom door. I pressed my ear to the door, my face flush with the cold wood, as I tried to listen in to their conversation. I wasn't quite sure why I was still hiding in my room, maybe because having spent so many days and nights around Gabriel, I knew what happened when we even got close, all hell broke loose.

Knowing that we were going to argue as soon as we saw each other made me gulp. Sure, it got easier to throw digs at Gabriel the more the dislike for him grew, but confrontation still wasn't easy for me.

Thinking about having to deal with all of that now, I just couldn't seem to go out there. If I couldn't even muster up the courage to face him, how was I going to survive this month? How was I going to keep my promise to Zaria?

"Thanks for helping me out, I promise as soon as I'm moved out and have saved enough, I will pay you back for letting me stay." The gentle tone he used with his sister was something I had never been on the receiving end of.

I rolled my eyes at myself, why couldn't he ever be that nice to me? What did I ever do to him to be the brunt of Gabriel's insults?

"Don't be stupid, you're my brother, of course, I'd help you." Zaria responded.

I loved their relationship. I had no idea how it must feel like to love a sibling and feel like part of a team. Being an only child sucked, especially when my mother quit being a parent and left me and my dad. I felt alone, abandoned.

"So... where's trevi?" Gabriel asked his sister. I rolled my eyes. *Trevi*. That was Gabriel's nickname for me, a mix between the Trevi fountain, because of my Italian roots and my last name Trevisano — very original — at least it wasn't pizza face or meatball head. I guess it could have been worse.

"Don't." I heard Zaria say. "This is her apartment too, and you two need to find a way to get over this arguing. I talked to her about it too, please try not to kill each other." I smiled at myself, Zaria had kept her promise to talk to Gabriel and I had to try to keep my promise too.

Sucking in a deep breath, I shook my head and got myself ready to face him, my hand reached for the door, and I opened it. As I did, two heads turned to look my way and I forced a smile on my lips as I faced Gabriel for the first time since Christmas. This should be fun. *More like torture.*

"Trevi." He looked me up and down. "Nice outfit. Are you going for homeless chic today?" He grinned as he tilted his head looking down at my outfit once again.

And the games have started.

I glanced down at my lazy Sunday outfit. My pink sweatpants and oversized t-shirt were the first things I threw on, other than pajamas, if I was chilling at home. I wasn't trying to impress him, and I wasn't embarrassed by it, if he was going to insult me, at least insult me well.

My lips pressed in a tight smile and my eyes narrowed at him. "Hey, dipshit. How's the girlfriend? She left you already? Shocker." It was a low blow, given that he had just broken up with his girlfriend last night, but why should I be nice to him when he continued to be an asshole to me?

I glanced at Zaria seeing her roll her eyes as she sighed. I broke my promise to her in less than thirty seconds. She was clearly disappointed with our interaction and her face made me feel guilty.

His expression turned smug as he took a step closer, dropping his suitcase on the floor with a thud. He placed his hands on his hips. "Why? Begging to be my next fuck buddy? Hate to break it to you trevi, but I haven't dropped my standards that low yet." He licked his lips, smirking like the asshole he was.

I narrowed my eyes at him. As if I'd ever want to be like those girls. He clearly still thought of himself as the pretty boy player, who could get any girl he wanted.

"We'd actually have to be *buddies* for that. Besides, your standards are so low already you would let any girl that even just breathes near you, fuck you."

"Not you." He grinned.

My nose flared as I clutched my sweatpants between my closed fists. I begged myself not to react to his words, not to let him affect me, not to let his words get to me, because at the end of the day what Gabriel thought of me didn't matter, it would never change, and I shouldn't dwell on it.

"Like I'd be hopeless enough to be one of your desperate conquests."

He grinned. The asshole actually enjoyed this, what a sadist. "The only one desperate here, is you. Don't be jealous."

I scoffed. "Jealous? You go through girls so fast you probably don't even remember their names, maybe that's why your girlfriend broke up with your sorry ass, cheat on her did you? Never did imagine you to be the loyal type."

"Okay, enough." Zaria stepped in, between me and Gabriel, putting her hands up before one of us attacked the other.

I bit the inside of my cheek, trying to hold back the frown. I hated that I did this, not even five minutes in and we'd already had an argument.

How was I ever going to keep my promise to Zaria to try and be civil with him? He couldn't hold back the insults better than I could. How were we ever going to coincide with each other? This was just a recipe for disaster.

Gabriel didn't even look at me before picking up his suitcase and walking past us towards our home office — which I guess now was Gabriel's room — closing the door behind him without as little as an apology.

I ran a hand down my face. It was way too early to be dealing with this, especially in my own apartment, which was my safe space, the one place I felt comfortable and could relax. Not anymore.

"Well, that went well." Zaria said, her face expressionless.

I groaned. "I'm sorry Z, I told you I'd try, and I bit his head off the first chance I got."

"I get it, he doesn't make it easy, but you've got to handle it better." She shook her head. "Maybe this was a bad idea, I knew you two couldn't stand each other I —"

"No." I interrupted. I couldn't let her take the blame for my mistakes. She decided to help her brother, the least I could do was not argue with him in front of her. "I told you I'd try to not fight with him, and I'll try."

She narrowed her eyes at me, doubting me, I understood why, it wasn't like we'd ever been around each other this long before. "It's just... going to be harder than I thought." I told her.

I had to try. At least dial it back a bit for her sake, she had always been by my side through everything, and I wasn't going to let her down, no matter how hard it was going to be.

She let out a deep sigh. "Honestly, I worry about you guys killing each other whilst I'm not here."

Zaria worked long hours at the hospital, which meant normally, I'd have the place to myself on the nights Zaria worked late, but now I'd have a new roommate… fun.

Gabriel and I would have to spend time together… alone. Most of the interactions we'd had, Zaria was around, intervening when we started to argue, but now, she wouldn't be here to do that.

Gabriel and I had to learn to live together… we could do that… maybe. Okay, it would be hard, but we'd hardly see each other, I came home from work at the school at four pm and Gabriel arrived home from the restaurant at five. If only he worked the dinner shift so I wouldn't have to see him, but unfortunately for me, we'd be home at the same time. So, we'd have to spend around three hours without tearing each other's heads off, could I handle that?

"Are you going to be fine with Gabriel?" She studied my face for any inclination that I wasn't going to be fine.

"I'll try and stay out of his way, I can handle it," I lied. I would definitely try to, but after ten years of animosity between us, I wasn't sure how we could just put it all behind us and start being friendly to one another.

She took a deep breath in and sighed, she knew that was bullshit, but there was nothing she could do about it, especially when she'd be at work, except hope and pray that she didn't come home to Gabriel's head being cut off.

"I know he's not the easiest person for you to get along with, but what you said wasn't you trying M." I knew she was right, and my stomach churned, guilt eating me up.

"I know." I sighed. "He just infuriates me."

She nodded, chucking, "I can see that, your face is so red I'm tempted to check your blood pressure."

I rolled my eyes at her. "Don't get all nurse on me, I'm fine, just flushed with anger." I smiled at her, reassuring her that there was nothing to worry about. But I knew that wasn't true.

My mind played the argument over and over again, overthinking what he had said to me and how much I let it get to me. I never understood why he hated me so much, from the moment we met, he treated me like I was invisible until he couldn't ignore me any longer and instead made sure I knew he thought of me as nothing but an annoying pain in the ass.

I wish I could slap my former self. Getting nervous about coming to Zaria's house, wanting Gabriel's attention. Not only did I have a crush on her stupid big brother, but for some reason he despised me.

"C'mon, let's get some ice cream."

I smiled at my best friend. Zaria knew me so well. I had a theory that ice cream could solve anything. It could heal loneliness, sadness or even heartbreak. But tonight, I needed some comfort, the only kind that a pint of strawberry ice cream could fix.

CHAPTER THREE

"Give me the remote!" I yelled out.

"No, I want to watch the football game."

It had been one day.

One slow, painful day since Gabriel had moved in.

And I was battling with him over the tv remote.

Zaria was working late today, which meant that today was officially the first day that Gabriel and I would have to spend alone. Together.

Last night she had been a buffer between us, as she normally was anytime we were in the same room together. She sat in the middle of us on the couch and any time we would start to argue, or even talk to each other, she would mediate and interrupt the conversation, knowing that we couldn't have a conversation without a fight breaking out.

I hadn't thought about what would happen when Zaria left for work. I would have to spend hours with Gabriel, I couldn't remember the last time I spent so long with him, and alone for that matter.

Today had been different though, Zaria wasn't around to stop this argument from escalating, which it had.

"Ugh." I groaned at him, failing to reach for the remote. "I want to watch my show dipshit."

"Tough shit. You've seen those crappy reality shows a million times before, I'm watching the game. You have a laptop, use it."

When I was fourteen, I would have sat here quietly, watching the game with him, because I wanted him to like me or at the very least tolerate me, but apparently, that was too much to ask of him.

I would be sat on the couch, watching the game and he would ask 'why are you watching this, you don't even like football'. It was clear that he didn't want me around, he just wanted me gone.

But not anymore, I wasn't that same fourteen-year-old. This was my apartment, and he was invading my space by thinking he was in control, acting like he could do whatever he wanted and that I would go along with it.

"You know, this is my apartment. You can't just come in here and demand things go your way." I stood up, standing in front of him, reaching over his head, fighting him for the remote.

I'd had a long day at work and normally, whenever Zaria was around, we'd be watching reality tv shows with some takeout. Our roommate and best friend tradition. But Zaria wouldn't be here most days and so far, my new tv companion wasn't as eager to comply to my evening routine.

"Melissa, I live here too now, I don't know if you noticed." He narrowed his eyes at me before smirking, like he had just thought of a genius idea. My brows pulled as I looked at him confused, wondering what he was smiling about, until he dropped the remote behind his back, sitting on it so that it was out of my reach.

"For one month." I called out, trying to pull him off the couch, but it was no use. Gabriel was all muscle, he must have thought I was a joke, trying to pull him off the couch.

I released his arm and stepped back, groaning. "It can't come fast enough. It's only been one day and you're already driving me crazy." I yelled out, wiping my hand down my face.

He placed his hand on his chest. "What a warm invitation. It just makes me want to stay even longer." He said with a sarcastic tone, not even looking at me anymore. His eyes were glued to the tv, that had the football game on.

I bit the inside of my cheek. I couldn't take a month of this. Gabriel needed to know he was not in control. I backed up, standing in front of the tv, blocking his view. If he was going to act like a child, I was going to return the favor.

"Melissa, get out of the way." He said, calmly. I grew wary of that tone. He was way too calm.

"No." I called out. "You can't just get whatever you want, I was here first, I want to watch my show."

He groaned before standing up from the couch, approaching me slowly. I pressed my lips together and looked up at him, not moving out of the way. My breath started to quicken the closer he got.

What was he going to do? Push me out of the way? Take the tv and put it in his room? I wouldn't put it past him to do anything that petty. I stood my ground and didn't break eye contact with him as he approached, I wouldn't back down.

He stopped walking when he reached me, his bare feet kissing the front of my slippers. My eyes dropped down looking at where our bodies touched and slowly looked up at him, standing tall.

We were so close I could smell him. I breathed in his scent as I inhaled, spicy, musky and leather. I could still smell the remnants of the cologne he put on this morning, citrusy and warm. He smelled so good, I wanted to bury my head in his chest and inhale. I shook my head, erasing those thoughts.

I begged my body not to react to his body being so close to mine. *He's an asshole.* No matter how good he smelled, or how good he looked, he was still a jackass.

His hand wrapped around my waist and my eyes widened. What was he doing? Before I could even think, he lifted me off the floor and picked me up over his shoulder.

I let out a yelp as he picked me up, easily, and held me up like a child. "Put me down." I yelled out to him.

"You're pissing me off trevi, I'll hold you here all night if I have to."

I kicked my feet, trying to escape his hold. "Put me down NOW!" I bellowed.

"Are you going to be a good girl?" He asked.

I stopped in my tracks. What did he just say? I didn't know whether to be angry or turned on. I knew he didn't mean it in the way my dirty mind was concocting but hearing those words come out of Gabriel's mouth made my imagination run wild.

I pressed my thighs together, still over his shoulder, as those visions flushed past my brain. I bit my lip to stifle a laugh and furrowed my brows. I was angry with him, I needed to remind myself of that.

"No." I replied.

"Then you're staying here. I'm comfy, I could stay like this until the game finishes." He said, still standing in front of the tv, whilst I was hanging off his shoulders, with a clear view of his ass. He must do squats at the gym, there were Instagram models who would be jealous of his ass.

I snickered as I let myself admire it for a second, before I shook my head and went back to kicking my feet.

"This isn't funny Gabriel, put me down." I couldn't believe he picked me up and was holding me hostage in his arms. What was wrong with him?

"I'll put you down if you stop acting like a brat."

My mouth dropped open, he just called me a brat for wanting to watch tv in my own apartment? "Don't call me a brat. you're the one acting like a jackass right now. I can't even watch my show in my own apartment because you want to watch a stupid football game."

My feet slowed down as I got tired of fighting it. Gabriel was strong, he was tall and ripped. I didn't doubt he could stay like this all night.

"I'll make you a deal, trevi, if you wait until the game is over, you can watch your show afterwards. Deal?"

No. What the hell? Why was he always in control?

"I'm not making a *deal* with you."

"Why not?" He asked. Was he serious? Why not? He just expected me to go along with his plan and sit around while he watched the game.

I groaned, trying to push myself off him again. It didn't work. "Because. What am I going to do whilst you watch the game? Sit here and knit?"

He laughed, making me shake as his body moved. "It's not like you have anything else to do."

I winced. "What does that mean?" My face burned, maybe because of the embarrassment this whole situation made me feel, or maybe because all the blood was rushing to my head.

"You don't do anything. You don't go anywhere. You stay home more than my grandma."

My eyes started stinging, tears clouding my vision. I quickly wiped them away before Gabriel heard me crying, luckily my head was facing his back so he couldn't see me. I didn't want him to see me cry over something he just said, I didn't want him to know how much that upset me and have the satisfaction of knowing he could hurt me.

"Fuck off." I couldn't think of anything else to say to him. Why did I let him get to me?

Why should I let his opinions about me being a homebody, who had nothing to do except stay home, get to me? I knew what he said was the truth, but that didn't mean it didn't hurt.

I spent my whole life accepting that about myself, the anxiety, the overthinking, my introverted personality, it was all a part of me. No matter how much I wanted to be fun like Zaria was, I wasn't. I was someone who didn't trust, who took a long time to open up and get comfortable with sharing myself with another person.

"Are you mad at me?" He asked. He sounded surprised. Like I shouldn't be livid at the fact he picked me up and threw me over his shoulder.

"Of course, I'm mad, you're holding me over your shoulder like I'm a child." I replied.

He swung me around and put me back on my feet, facing him. His eyes bored into mine as he scanned my face. "No, I mean about what I said. Are you actually mad at me for that?"

Oh.

Right.

I couldn't let him know that his words had affected me. that I agreed with everything he said, and it sucked. Gabriel might make my life miserable and make me angry, but I didn't want him to acknowledge the fact that he hurt me, that he could make my chest tighten and my throat close, I turned my head away from him, facing the tv. I bit my cheek to avoid crying again.

"No. Why would I be mad about that? It's true, right?"

I looked up at his eyes for a second before pushing past him, making my way to my bedroom. I couldn't stay out here any longer, not after that, not after he made me feel so small and insignificant.

I felt a hand wrap around my wrist and turned back to see Gabriel was holding my wrist. My eyes looked down at where he was touching me. his hand was on my wrist, but I felt his touch everywhere. My skin underneath his touch was hot, burning. "Wait, where are you going?" He called out.

"Watch your game, you win." I released my wrist from his hand and walked into my bedroom, slamming the door behind me.

It wasn't like me to let him get his way, but before this Gabriel had only made comments about my hair or my clothes, not about my personality. The biggest thing I felt self-conscious about. The one thing that I knew was a huge, flawed part about myself. The one thing that made me so alone in my life. The one thing I had resented about myself for as long as I could remember.

Gabriel probably didn't know why it bothered me so much, but that didn't change the fact that he said that to get underneath my skin. I had never reacted like that before, never gave up on arguing with him and let him win the fight. I wondered what he thought of my reaction, if he realized, he actually hurt me. Did he even care?

I bit my lip to restrain from crying, but it was no use. My eyes flooded with pools of water, that trickled down my face making its way to the corner of my mouth. I could taste the salt of my tears, the tangy taste making me cry even harder.

I buried my face in the palms of my hand to muffle the sound. It was bad enough that Gabriel had elicited that kind of reaction from me, but now I was crying? I couldn't let him hear that, he would win for sure.

Win what? I wasn't sure, but this arguing had become a competition throughout the years of who was stronger, who could handle the most insults, which one would cop out first, and I never wanted to be that person, the person so weak that I let it get to me.

But now, here I was. Sat in my bed.

Alone.

Crying.

I wiped the tears off my face, aggressively. I couldn't get upset over everything he said, otherwise I would end up going crazy. I needed to grow a thick skin and learn how to deal with Gabriel.

CHAPTER FOUR

A knock struck my door. "M?"

I smiled, hearing my best friend's voice. I missed her. Granted, that was a little pathetic considering she had been at work, it wasn't like she was gone, but those three hours felt like hell without her here.

I had lost all hope in this living situation. I didn't know how to interact with Gabriel. Before this, we barely talked, we had no reason to. The only time we were ever around each other was because, unfortunately for him, his family had become my family too. Now he was living with us, and that hadn't changed the nature of our relationship — relationship was a strong word — more like an acquaintanceship, if anything, it had made it worse.

I sat up in my bed, closing my laptop. "Come in." I replied.

The door flung open, and she walked in, flashing me a smile as she sat on the bed by my side. Her hooded eyes glanced at me, exhausted and weary. After a twelve-hour shift, I was surprised she hadn't crashed as soon as she got home.

She dropped her head on my shoulder and my chest tightened. She had only been away for a few hours, but the lack of her company was prominent.

When we graduated college, we decided that living together would be fun. We had been inseparable since high school until we were separated for four years at different colleges in different cities. She wanted to study at NYC, and I wanted to be closer to my dad, so I stayed in San Francisco.

We were still connected. Whenever she came back for holidays, birthdays, or whenever she visited her family, I was there too. So, when we graduated and Zaria moved back, moving in together was a no-brainer.

Our apartment was nice, not as luxurious as we would have liked, but at twenty-two, we couldn't afford much since we had just left college. But it wasn't all bad, it was small, and it only had one bathroom, but it had a huge kitchen island with an open living space, and three bedrooms. Plus, the price fit our budget.

"So, how did it go?" Zaria asked, tilting her head up to gauge my response.

I groaned, letting my eyes shut. I wanted to avoid this, I wanted to avoid anything that involved Gabriel.

"That bad huh?" She chuckled. "I see that you're both still alive so it couldn't have been *that* awful."

I scoffed. "Yeah, not bad at all, we just got into a huge fight where he held the remote hostage until he got his way." I kept the part where he picked me up over his shoulder to myself, afraid that I would blush when telling her and she would notice.

She bit her lip to stifle a laugh and I narrowed my eyes at her. She held her hands up. "I'm sorry." She laughed, shaking her head. "Why does he do that?"

I let out a heavy breath. "I honestly don't know Z. Why don't you ask him why he's such a jackass to me and what the hell I did to deserve it." I stuck out my bottom lip in a pout.

She smiled at my attempt of pleading her. "Don't give me the puppy dog face, I've asked him before, he just shrugged and said it's fun arguing with you." Ugh, he *was* a sadist. That was such a dumb excuse.

"Really?" I scoffed. "That's his excuse for making my life miserable?" I groaned, wiping a hand down my face. "Can we please move on from Gabriel, what's been going on with you? How was work?" I asked her, begging to change the subject.

She closed her eyes. "Goood." She mumbled.

I laughed, hearing her sleepy voice slur as she let herself drift. "Good? That's it?"

She nodded her head and finally opened her eyes, sighing as she blinked at me. "Yeah, it's been good. I'm tired but what else is new?"

"And the doctor?" I asked. Zaria had been fascinated with one of the doctors she worked with but didn't want to make a move as they worked together.

She smirked. "He's been good too."

I chuckled. "So, you made a move huh?"

She shrugged. "I think I lasted long enough. I deserved a reward." Her eyes glistened as she smiled, making the term 'reward' clearer than ever.

I shook my head, Zaria was an avid oversharer, especially when it came to her sex life, she wasn't ashamed, she had no reason to be. She was comfortable in her own skin and comfortable trusting people with her body, I envied that about her.

"And it hasn't affected your relationship as colleagues?" That was Zaria's biggest issue with getting involved with the guy, I wondered how she just let that go.

She laughed. "If anything, it makes the breaks more interesting, that's for sure."

I groaned. "Okay, let's change subject before you start revealing every position you guys do it in."

She laughed again, making no effort to deny that she was going to do exactly that.

Her smile drifted and she sighed. "Kyle texted me."

I frowned. Kyle was Zaria's ex-boyfriend, they were always on and off throughout their relationship. I wasn't the biggest fan of Kyle, especially because on one occasion, he hit on me, which resulted in her confronting him, where he eventually admitted to it and admitted to cheating on her multiple times. That caused them to break up for good four months ago.

"What did he want?" I asked. As far as I knew this was the first time Zaria had communicated with him since the breakup, why was he reaching out to her four months later?

"To apologize." She rolled her eyes. "I thought I blocked his number, but he must have used a different phone to contact me or something. God, every time I think about him, I feel pathetic." She closed her eyes, shaking her head.

I furrowed my brows. "You can't blame yourself for that jerk." She had no reason to feel pathetic over something he did.

She opened her eyes, looking at me and then avoiding my gaze, looking to the side. "You warned me. You told me you didn't like him, and I didn't listen." She laughed, dryly. "I do blame myself for that."

I couldn't exactly fault her. She was infatuated with him and didn't see what I did. I could see he was toxic for her. She came home most nights either in tears or quiet, which for anyone who knew Zaria, her being quiet was concerning.

Most times he'd want her to stay home with him on the weekends, whereas Zaria preferred to be at a club, and if he didn't get his way, he would start a fight with her. I heard many of their fights, and they didn't spend a lot of time at the apartment, so I could only imagine how bad it really was.

It wasn't my relationship, and I knew I shouldn't have said anything about it, but Zaria was my best friend and I had to make sure she was okay.

And when Kyle hit on me, I debated telling Zaria. I didn't know if she would believe me or try to defend him, I was in agony over whether I should tell her or not, but I knew I had to, even if she ended up hating me, at least she would know, and I wouldn't be hiding it from her.

I reached out and squeezed her hand. "Don't blame yourself." I told her. "You didn't do anything wrong, he should feel like shit, not you."

She smiled at me. "Yeah, I know it's just…" She sighed. "What if I make the same mistake again?

"With the doctor?" I asked. "You want a relationship again?"

She shrugged. "Maybe? I don't know, we'll see." She smirked at me, and I couldn't help but smile back, Zaria was her happy self again. Even after four months, just the topic of

Kyle made Zaria lose all attributes that made her who she was.

"Maybe he has a friend." She paused. "For my friend." She raised her brows waiting for my answer.

She already knew what I would say to that. I had no interest in dating, after two measly dates throughout the years, I didn't want any more of it. It wasn't like I was dying to have a boyfriend. I didn't crave cuddles or hugs. I couldn't see myself getting close to anyone, let alone ending up in a relationship with someone.

I just sighed. It was clear she wanted me to change my mind, but that wasn't going to happen. Especially with a stranger, I knew nothing about. "I missed you today." I told her instead, reaching for her and pulling her in for a hug.

"I know M, I missed you too. We'll catch up on the episodes of California Girlz I missed when my internship ends if you don't mind rewatching them."

California Girlz was mine and Zaria's guilty pleasure. Trashy reality tv shows were our favorites, and this one had been our top contender most nights.

I scoffed and pulled away from the embrace. "I'm guessing I'll have to miss them too if Gabriel keeps hogging the remote."

Zaria laughed, shaking her head.

"Was he always this annoying when you were living together?" I asked her.

She shrugged. "Not really, we actually got along fine."

I rolled my eyes. "Great, then it's only me that he manages to irritate."

She snickered at my annoyance. "I hear hate sex is great."

What?

My eyes widened at her. Her mouth dropped open as if only now realizing what she has said. "That was a joke." She shook her head, laughing with no humor behind it. "Please don't fuck my brother."

I couldn't help but scoff. "That would never happen." I assured her. Yes, I might have had a small crush on him but that didn't change the fact that we couldn't stand each other.

She exhaled, as if relieved by my answer. "You can handle him M, I've seen your cat fights first-hand, you have claws too. It's not like you're innocent."

I gasped. "Whose side are you on? Traitor."

I knew Zaria loved us both, she always tried to be the mediator between us.

"Yours M, I'm always on your side." She winked at me and smiled.

"Good, because if I *do e*nd up killing Gabriel, I'm going to need an alibi."

"Don't worry, I'll definitely help you cover up my brother's murder." She joked. I loved that I could talk to Zaria about whatever was bothering me, and she would listen. Even if it was to bitch about her brother.

"I'm going to bed." She yawned, getting up from my bed. "I need to wake up at six tomorrow." She pretended to cry, burying her head in her hands. "Night, M." she called out as she walked to the door.

"Night Z." I replied.

The door closed behind her as I laid in bed, staring up at the ceiling, wondering how I could manage to spend a month with Gabriel without wanting to strangle him in his sleep, slow and painfully.

I sighed to myself, rolling over to my side. If I kept thinking about this, I would never be able to fall asleep.

CHAPTER FIVE

"What's up with you today?" Allie asked.

Other than Zaria, Allie was the only good friend I had. I met Allie on my first day working at Dorset Hills middle school and she quickly became the only one here who I got along with.

She was fun. An art teacher had to be. Being creative and artistic, an enthusiastic personality normally went along with that. And Allie was nothing but a big ball of sunshine and good energy.

Being a teacher had been one of the only things in my life I was sure about. I still remembered the teachers that had made an impact in my life, made me feel worthy, and like I had something more to offer than being invisible or shy.

I wanted to create that same impact on a kids' life, to be someone thy could count on and to make sure they knew that they mattered.

But being a teacher for those reasons, hadn't prepared me for the hierarchy of the staff. The other teachers were either older, and therefore acted like they ruled the halls, or they were huge gossips, which frankly wasn't for me.

I didn't like drama and tried to avoid it as much as possible, there was nothing worse than being around people like that. The kind of people that were fake and nice to your face but also felt comfortable enough to drag someone's personal business through the mud.

"What's wrong Melissa?" She sat back, with narrowed eyes as she sipped her coffee, waiting for my response. She wouldn't let this go, she knew me well enough to know when something was bothering me, and I couldn't hide the frustration on my face.

"Gabriel's in town," I said with a sigh. Allie was the only person I had talked about Gabriel with. About my former crush on him when we were teenagers, and how, of course, he hated me. Plus, she was a few years older than me so I hoped she would have given me some advice. Because when it came to Gabriel, I didn't have a clue on how to handle it.

Zaria was my best friend, but I could never have told her I had a crush on her brother when I met him, or else when anytime I came over, it would have been awkward.

I was glad I never did. Seeing her reaction to the joke she let slip about me sleeping with her brother, she would probably feel betrayed if she ever found out. What if she thought I was using my friendship with her to get closer to him, what if she felt like she couldn't trust me after that?

Zaria was the only good thing I had in my life at that point, and I would have done anything to protect my friendship with her.

I didn't even want to think about Gabriel finding out. He would never stop teasing me about it for sure. Never mind that he already did everything in his power to make fun of me and annoy the shit out of me, I couldn't even fathom if he found out I used to be interested in him. My body squirmed at the thought of that.

Allie's eyebrows shot up as she looked at me with shocked eyes. "Wow, how long has it been since you saw him?" Her glassy blue eyes stayed focused on me as she sipped her coffee.

"Since Christmas." I told her. It had been nine months since I last saw or spoke to Gabriel. I let out a deep breath and continued. "We had an argument and I left."

I sighed as my face reddened at the memory.

After my father died, I spent every holiday with the Andersons. They became my family over the years, except for Gabriel. Gabriel and I tried to avoid each other as much as possible whenever we were around each other, but it always ended in us arguing.

I spent the morning at my father's grave, as I usually did on holidays or birthdays. Hours had passed since and I only noticed how long I had been there, when Zaria texted, me asking where I was.

I didn't tell her, I didn't tell anyone where I went every holiday, I didn't want to see the look of pity on their faces when I walked in, so I always kept this secret between my dad and me.

I texted her, telling her I was stuck in traffic, and made my way back. When I finally arrived at the Anderson's house, I greeted Naomi — Mrs. Anderson — and Zaria, they were in the kitchen cooking, and that was never my area of expertise so I left them in the kitchen, knowing my help would be more of a crutch than help.

I walked over to the living room, seeing Gabriel and Terry — Mr. Anderson — sat on the couch watching the football game, I greeted Mr. Anderson, not even glancing at Gabriel and left for their backyard.

I needed some fresh air, holidays were always hard for me, especially Christmas. I still remembered my dad waking me up with hot chocolate with only pink marshmallows —

my favorite — and dressing as Santa to open presents with me. Even when I was eighteen, and he was a shell of the man I used to know, he kept those traditions.

It was draining, having to spend the happiest of holidays acting like nothing was wrong, and then coming here and seeing Gabriel wasn't helping. I wanted to be here, to be around the Andersons, but along with that came Gabriel. I tried to ignore him, but he was unavoidable.

I sat on one of the lounge chairs by the pool, clutching my coat to my body. I was freezing but it was better than the alternative. I was tired, tired of arguing, tired of pretending I was ok when I wasn't, tired from the lack of sleep. This was better than being near Gabriel. I was already imposing on their holidays, on their family, and I didn't want to make matters worse by arguing with their son.

It didn't take long for Gabriel to find me, I glanced back seeing him stand by the door staring down at me. I rolled my eyes, letting out a heavy breath, the heat from my mouth visible in the crisp air, and turned my head away from him.

"Why are you out here?" He asked.

"Because you're not." I replied.

He snorted, approaching closer to me. "Don't quit your day job, you're not exactly a comedian."

I grew aggravated by him. I came out here to avoid him and he still managed to find me and annoy me anyway. "What do you want? Come to scare the birds away?"

"Came to check on a stubborn girl who sits out by the pool in December." I couldn't help but scoff. He had never been worried about me before, I'm sure he wasn't now. This was just an excuse to start a fight, to get under my skin, like he always did.

"Well, she's fine." I told him, glancing up, seeing him stand by my side. I stood up, motioning to the house. "You can go back inside now."

But he didn't. Instead, he stepped closer, until he clutched me by the hips. I stood still, wondering what he was doing, why he wasn't going back inside. He tilted my body back until I was hanging above the pool.

I gasped, clutching onto him. "Gabriel don't." I begged him. My chest tightened as the ache built up. I wanted to scream, and push him off, but I couldn't.

It was the middle of December, the water would without a doubt be freezing cold. If he dropped me in the pool, I would drag him inside with me.

He pulled me back until we were away from the pool, I exhaled, relieved whilst his laughter permeated my ears. "I forgot how fun annoying you is."

Fun? He thought this was fun? Nothing about what happened was remotely amusing. I glared at him before racing back inside the house. I couldn't stay there. Not after that, I couldn't be around Gabriel when all he did was make me irritated.

"You just left?" Allie asked.

I nodded. "I apologized to the Andersons and Zaria, but I couldn't stay there. I went back to my apartment and stayed there for the rest of the holidays."

It wasn't ideal to spend new year's alone, but it was too much, Gabriel was too much, and I couldn't take the risk of seeing him again.

"Melissa, you can't get yourself so worked up over Gabriel." She sighed. "You already know I think he's flirting with you, I mean, why else would he be teasing you?" she snickered.

I'd heard her theory before, and it was bullshit. She had never met him, so she didn't know how much we argued.

"No." I laughed at the ridiculous accusation. "You don't know him, Allie, he hates me. He has done since we met, besides he makes fun of me all the time, he's not attracted to me."

I wasn't blind, I knew I was attractive. I had my father's tanned skin and green eyes, full lip,s and a body that my nonna once described as 'perfect for childbearing'. But it was clear that Gabriel had no interest in me. as a friend or anything else. If not for the way he would make fun of my style of clothes, when I was younger, then for the way he always made it his mission to find a way to irritate me. To drive me into insanity.

Allie scoffed. "Please, that is denial if I've ever heard it." She shook her head. "You're gorgeous, there's no way he's not attracted to you."

I sighed. There was no way of convincing her otherwise.

"Okay, fine." She conceded. "Tell me about Gabriel, why is he in town?"

I let out a deep breath and leaned back in my chair. "He's living with us." I told her.

"What?" She cried out, her eyes widened in shock. I couldn't help but laugh at her reaction.

I nodded. "He broke up with his girlfriend and is living with us until he can find an apartment to move into."

Allie cocked her head back as she laughed. I couldn't blame her, I thought it was a joke at first too. "I'm sorry." She managed to spit out between laughs. "You... and Gabriel living together." She breathed out. "Oh my god. How is that ever going to happen?" She asked, wiping her tears.

"Ha, ha, ha," I said sarcastically. "My life is so funny, seriously Allie, what the hell am I going to do?" I groaned. "How am I going to manage to live in the same apartment as him, it's been one day and he's already irritating me."

"Wait, he's moved in already?"

I nodded. "He hid the remote from me yesterday and wouldn't let me watch tv."

"Wow." She gasped. "He really is evil, hiding the remote, that's unbelievable." She shook her head. "Did you call the police?" She asked, smirking at me.

I narrowed my eyes at her. "I'm serious. He's only been there one day and he's already annoying the shit out of me."

She waved a hand in the air. "Stop being dramatic, he's just teasing you." She shrugged. "Sounds like flirting to me."

My mouth dropped open in disbelief, how did no one else see what an asshole Gabriel was.

"He picked me up over his shoulder and wouldn't let me down until I started acting like a 'good girl' and let him watch his game." I retorted, hoping she would sympathize with me.

"Sounds kinky." She said, throwing me a wink.

I rolled my eyes. "How the hell am I going to spend a month with him?" I replied, ignoring her previous comment.

"A month?" Her eyes widened as she took in the information.

"Yeah, I forgot that detail. Gabriel told Zaria it would be about a month." I shook my head. "And I promised her I would try to get along with him."

And somehow, in the space of a single day, I had already broken that promise. I didn't even try to get along with Gabriel. I attacked him the first chance I got. After ten years of arguing with him, it was going to be hard to just forget all of that and act friendly all of a sudden.

"Good luck with that." She snickered. "Guess you'll have to kiss and make up... emphasis on the *kiss*."

I narrowed my eyes. "Hilarious."

"You'll have to act like a good girl for Mr. Anderson." She smirked at me.

I scrunched my nose with disgust. "Mr. Anderson is what I call his dad, please don't call him that."

"Fine, you'll have to be a very good girl for chef Gabriel then." She grinned.

"Nope. Stop saying that, it wasn't dirty, it was annoying."

"Uh-huh." She said back, with a suspicious grin on her face.

CHAPTER SIX

My hands hesitated as I clutched my keys in my fist.

I checked my phone, seeing it was just after four pm, and Gabriel only left work at five, so I had about an hour before he came home and managed to find a way to piss me off again.

I rolled my shoulders back, before opening the door. I pushed it open, and my shoulders immediately tensed.

What. The Fuck.

There were clothes everywhere. Boxes out all over the apartment, blocking the entire place. My brows scrunched in confusion as I looked around the place.

I had completely forgotten that Gabriel took the day off to move the rest of his stuff out of his ex's place and into the apartment. But I didn't expect Armageddon when I walked in. How many clothes did this man have?

I could swear all he wore was jeans and t-shirts.

"Gabriel!" I called out, slamming the door behind me. He had all day to put his stuff away and instead he decorated the apartment in boxes.

I stepped into the living room, tripping over the clothes that were scattered all over the apartment, boxes on the floor, kitchen island, counters, couch.

Everywhere.

"Gabriel" I called out, again. He had to be here somewhere.

He stepped out of his room into the living room, shirtless and wearing grey sweats, so low on his hips that I could see the outline of his boxers.

I had seen Gabriel shirtless many times. I stayed over at the Anderson's house so often, it was inevitable. The last time I had seen him shirtless was two years ago at Christmas, when I stayed over, as Zaria and I usually did on Christmas eve.

I could swear that Gabriel had grown more muscles since then, his chest was glistening from sweat, probably from bringing all the boxes up to the apartment. My lips parted at the sight of him, my eyes shifted down his body.

I quickly realized what I was doing, forcing my eyes to lift, meeting his face. Gabriel was standing with his hands on his hips and a grin on his cocky face, that I wanted to slap off.

"You checking me out trevi? He asked. Chuckling over the fact that he just caught me ogling him.

My face reddened at the accusation, and I quickly turned my head. "Don't change the subject. What the hell is all this?" I asked him, gesturing around the apartment.

"My stuff." He said flatly. Like that was an explanation as to why it was all over the living room and kitchen.

"Thank you for that observation, Sherlock." I wiped a hand down my face and groaned. "I came home, wanting to relax and all your shit is spread across the apartment. Clean it up, you slob."

"I'm not a slob, trevi." He walked away, picking up one of the boxes. "I just didn't have time to put it all away." He dropped the box in his room and turned around, facing me. "You're welcome to help if you want."

I scoffed. "The last thing I would ever do is help you." Help him? After he treated me like shit for ten years, yeah right.

"Thank you for the sentiment." He said, placing his hand over his chest. "Honestly, your generosity means so much to me." He grinned, like what I had said amused him.

"Jackass." I muttered, turning on my heels and walking towards my room.

"I heard that."

"You were supposed to." I yelled back at him.

God, he was frustrating. I couldn't deal with this anymore. I reached my bedroom, slamming the door like a spoiled child. I was normally so level-headed but something about Gabriel made me act out. Like I couldn't stand that the only attention that I got from him was the fact that he hated me. He did everything in his power to make my life miserable, to argue with me and I was sick of it. Having to deal with this every day was exhausting.

I couldn't talk to Zaria about this, Gabriel was her brother, she loved him, I didn't want to make her feel guilty for not being able to deal with Gabriel being here.

I let myself fall back onto the bed, letting out a sigh as I reached for my phone.

Me: Help!!!

I dropped my phone onto the bed as I closed my eyes, allowing my breathing to even out and slow down. Why did Gabriel get under my skin like that? What was it about him that made me this angry?

The sound of a notification on my phone brought me out of thought. I reached for my phone, unlocking it to see the message.

Allie: Trouble in paradise?

I rolled my eyes.

Me: More like trouble in hell.

Three dots popped up and I waited for her to answer.

Allie: What happened?

Me: Gabriel. What else. He's driving me insane.

It was the truth. However, what I didn't tell her was that he didn't particularly do anything this time, just having him around drove me crazy. I wasn't sure how much longer I could do this. Live with him, argue with him, all whilst trying desperately to ignore the attraction I felt towards him.

Having to remind myself any chance I got that no matter how attractive he was, he was still a jerk who annoyed me and teased me the whole time we had known each other.

My phone buzzed again, and I glanced at the screen as it lit up in my hand.

Allie: Maybe you should try to stay away from him.

Easier said than done.

I quickly typed back.

Me: I don't see how that's possible. We live together.

I waited for her to reply. I begged that Allie had a solution, whatever it may be, a way that I could deal with him and this situation.

Allie: Do you want to come over?

I groaned, closing my eyes. If only it was that easy. I couldn't escape him forever. It wasn't like every day after work I could invade Allie's life by coming over to her house and pester her with my problems. She had a life, a wife, and she needed time to herself.

Not to mention, I was tired. I had a long day at work, and I just wanted to relax, not that it was an easy thing to do at home anymore, since Gabriel moved in.

Me: No, I'm tired. I'll try to figure something out.
Allie: Ok, babe. Remember, don't let him affect you.
I sighed, as I typed my reply.
Me: I'll try.

I fisted my shirt before pulling it over my head. Putting on my pajamas instead. It was so damn hard not to let his actions or his words affect me, even his presence seemed to encompass me in some way.

Watching him out there, shirtless, and sweaty, made me a drooling mess, and he noticed. Making me heat up from the way he was looking at me, amused that he caught me checking him out. He didn't even do anything terrible, and I still let it affect my mood.

Maybe I was overreacting? Letting him win once again, letting him inside of my head. Gabriel had a hold on my emotions, and he didn't even know it, or maybe he did and that was why he tried his hardest to get to me. If that was his plan, unluckily for me, it was working.

I bit the inside of my cheek, scanning my room. Should I just spend the rest of the night in here? At least I would stay away from Gabriel, even if I did have to shut myself out just for the possibility to not interact with him.

I groaned, letting my head hit the mattress as I buried my head in my hands. I missed Zaria. I missed spending the night with her, catching up on whatever was going on in her life —

which, unlike mine, was eventful — and I missed talking to her, whilst we ordered takeout and watched our favorite reality shows. I missed having the apartment free of a guy who tormented me and made every emotion inside of me tenfold. I missed my life before I ever met Gabriel.

A knock hit my bedroom door and I sat up, my eyebrows pinched. What the hell did he want now?

"Yes?" I asked, warily.

"I've put my stuff away. You can come out now."

I rolled my eyes. "About time." I snapped back. "And maybe I don't want to come out."

A minute passed, no reply from him. I started to wonder if he had just left, but then he spoke up.

"Suit yourself."

I scowled as I stared at the white wooden door. If I stayed in here, he would win. But if I went out there, he would find a way to get under my skin.

I let out an exhale as I made my way to the door, my hand gripping the handle for a few seconds before I rolled my shoulders back and opened the door.

I stepped out, watching Gabriel turn to face me when he heard the door open. He was sat on the couch, his arms cast over the edge of the couch as his brows pinched, looking at me as I walked towards the couch, and him.

"I thought you said you didn't want to come out here." He said.

Christ, wasn't he the one to tell me to come out here in the first place? And now it's like he's annoyed at the fact I decided to.

I narrowed my eyes at him. "Yeah, well, I changed my mind." I bit out before sitting on the couch, crossing my legs, trying to sit as far away from him as possible. Maybe this was a bad idea. I could have easily stayed in my room for the rest of the night.

His feet were propped up onto the coffee table, as his eyes stayed focused on the game. His lips were pressed tight as he concentrated on the tv.

I couldn't stop staring at him, the game didn't interest me, but he did. His face, those lips. Why was he so infuriating, and most importantly, why did I still find him attractive?

"Why are you staring at me?" His deep voice grumbled, making me snap out of my thoughts. But he wasn't looking at me, he was still staring at the tv. My nose wrinkled in embarrassment as I got caught looking at him, again. *Get it together.*

His head finally turned to face me when I didn't reply. His eyebrows shot up as if he was waiting for my excuse and I narrowed my eyes at him. God, he was so smug, I hated that.

"Trying to imagine you with a personality." I sneered.

He smiled back, his smile instantly making my cheeks warm. "As opposed to your charming one?" He asked, cocking his head.

"I am charming," I told him. "Just not to you."

And why should I be? He was kind to everyone except to me. for some reason, he had a problem with me, and he never told me why.

"Wow, I must be special."

I scoffed. "You're definitely not. Just someone who pisses me off any chance they get."

"Right back at you." He said, before turning back to face the tv.

I rolled my eyes. "You're such an asshole."

"And you're such a brat. If you've got a problem with me, then leave. No one's stopping you."

I willed the tears threatening to pool, back down. He didn't want me here, just like always. Just like when I was fourteen and he wanted me away from him. Nothing had changed and nothing would ever change.

"This is my apartment." I pointed out.

He shrugged. "I was here first, you were the one that followed me out here."

"Because you infested the apartment full of your disease-ridden belongings like you were marking your territory, so I had to go to my room."

He laughed, shaking his head, looking at me once again. "Disease ridden?"

I nodded. "Who knows what kind of diseases you have from sleeping with a new girl every night."

He frowned, shaking his head. "None, Melissa. I'm clean." His lips turned in a small smirk. "Why are you asking? You want a ride?"

I scrunched my nose. "Never in a million years."

He shrugged, licking his bottom lip. "Your loss."

I couldn't help but roll my eyes. "Yeah, my loss of having bed sex with someone who probably can't even make a woman finish."

He grinned, leaning closer to me. "Is that a challenge?" He whispered.

LOVE ME OR HATE ME

This conversation was too much for me. I didn't talk about this, ever. Not even to Zaria, so why was I now talking freely about sex with Gabriel?

And what the hell is his deal? The flirting, the suggestive language. He had never done that before, not that we had ever been in the same room long enough to have a full conversation, but, why now? Was he trying to embarrass me by making me think he's even slightly interested just to turn around and laugh in my face?

I didn't know what he was playing at, but I wasn't going to fall for it.

I scooted over to the edge, picking myself off the couch. I closed my eyes for a second, trying to get my thoughts in order before clearing my throat. "I'm not interested in having this conversation with you," I said, turning away from him as he smirked at me, his body sprawled on the couch as his arms spread out on the back of the couch. God damn it, how was he this attractive. "I'm leaving."

I made my way back to my bedroom, without even glancing back at Gabriel. I knew he was gloating about this, no doubt. He had won. Again. I was too uncomfortable being here with him, especially where the conversation was headed, I couldn't do it.

I knew it wasn't normal for a twenty-four-year-old to shy away from talking about sex to anyone, especially their best friends, but for me, sex wasn't a topic I was comfortable with, and I didn't think I'd ever feel comfortable with.

CHAPTER SEVEN

"So, I've been thinking." I took a deep breath in.

He wiped a hand down his face. Standing with his hand on his hip whilst the other reached up to wide a beat of sweat from his forehead. I gulped. The sight of him made my pulse race, partly because of how much he angered me, but partly because of how attractive he was. There was no use denying it, no matter how mad he made me, he also made me... hot.

And I couldn't concentrate. Not when I'd intercepted him as soon as he came back from the gym and he was still sweaty from his workout, his t-shirt clung to his body like a glove, making his muscles prominent under the thin material.

My eyes snapped away from his body. *Focus*. I wanted Gabriel to hear me and hear me good. If I wanted him to go along with this, I needed to approach him in a way that he wouldn't say no.

"I have a proposition." I cleared my throat and looked down at my notebook. *Just tell him the plan, he has nothing to lose from it anyway*. "We set a schedule." I blurted out.

He squinted and tilted his head. "A schedule." He repeated.

I nodded my head. "Yes." I stepped forward before elaborating. "We set a schedule for the apartment. Each of us take turns in the common areas of the apartment, that way we can avoid each other as much as possible and hopefully, this way we won't drive each other crazy."

He narrowed his eyes and shook his head. "What's this about?"

"What do you mean?" I asked. I thought I had explained it pretty clearly.

I had time to think about it, Allie's comment coming back to me. I needed to stay away from him, but that was impossible since we lived together. The only solution would be if we didn't have to cross paths, therefore the schedule. It was a foolproof plan. One I was hoping Gabriel would agree to.

His eyebrows scrunched, frowning at me. "Is this about the boxes yesterday? I told you I didn't —"

"No," I cut him off. I had never seen Gabriel look like this, he looked almost, nervous. "It's not about the boxes. I mean it is, but it's also about us." Those words felt like venom on my tongue. 'us' was never a word I would use to describe Gabriel and me. "The arguing. The fighting. This way, we don't have to see each other until you leave."

His hand dropped from his hip and his face tensed. He clenched his jaw and his nose flared. "No." he said. flatly, before walking towards his bedroom.

"Just list—"

My words were cut off by the sound of Gabriel's bedroom door slamming closed, leaving me out here with my jaw dropped and my hands still clutching the notebook.

He didn't even give me time to explain. He just walked away and closed the door on me. I knew he would give me a hard time about this, but I thought he would at least listen to the explanation. We couldn't stand each other. This would benefit him too.

I walked over to his bedroom door and knocked.

No answer.

I knocked again, louder this time.

No answer.

He was ignoring me now. Great. I knew he wouldn't agree to anything I'd suggest but I assumed he'd at least be willing to hear me out.

"Gabriel, open the door," I called out. But he didn't answer. I wanted to explain it to him, to show him that this way we wouldn't have to see each other and hopefully that way we could stay out of each other's way.

My shoulders slumped as I walked over to the couch, sitting on it with my knees tucked under my chin. I needed him to listen. This was the only way this living arrangement could work.

Less than a minute later, Gabriel opened his door and walked over to me. I stood up and looked up at him. His jaw was still clenched, and he wasn't looking at me, his face was turned to the side. "Okay, show me."

"What?" My eyes widened, I didn't expect him to say that. He actually agreed to see the schedule.

"That dumb-ass schedule, show me." He spat out, his tone was angry.

I flipped open the notebook and handed it to him, his eyes scanned the paper and his eyebrows wrinkled. "This doesn't even make sense."

"What doesn't?" I asked, I moved around the couch to see the notebook, standing next to him. His scent radiating of musk and sweat. Even when he was sweaty, he smelled so good.

"The timing."

I looked up at him waiting for him to explain, but he didn't, his eyes never met mine, they were still staring at the notebook. "Can you elaborate?"

"For starters, the time you set for me to spend out here, overlaps dinner. What are you going to do? Lay in bed, hungry until it's your turn?" he said, spitefully.

My chest tightened, and a weird feeling pooled in my stomach. He was worried about when I was going to eat. In the middle of me trying to kick him out of my life. Even in the middle of all of this, he was concerned about me? Why? It wasn't like Gabriel was ever concerned about me before. Why would he be now?

"Well, I could eat early, plus I don't cook. I could just order take out and bring it to my room."

He wiped a hand down his face and shook his head. He stared down at the notebook for another minute before opening his mouth, ready to speak again. "And the weekends. Do you expect me to shut myself in my room all day?"

I had set the mornings on the weekend for Gabriel, he could make breakfast, hang out a bit, but then I assumed he wouldn't stay home, I assumed he would be going out with his friends or whoever else. "Well, no. I expected you to leave the apartment. It's the weekend, you could go out with your friends, or with a date." Saying those last words gave me a weird feeling in the pit of my stomach. Of course, I would be jealous of whoever ended up with Gabriel, but he was single now and I knew he would end up dating eventually.

"Sometimes I like staying in too." He grumbled.

I blinked at him. I didn't expect that. I guess he had every right of staying in if he wanted. "Okay, fine, figure out a schedule that works for you then, I'll go along with whatever time you choose. I just think this is the best way for us to stay out of each other's way, otherwise, we'll end up killing each other." I said, handing him a pen.

Zaria would be around too, so it wasn't like I would have too much alone time with Gabriel but this way, any fights would be avoided, and I wouldn't have to pull out any white hairs from the stress he was causing me.

"This is stupid." He snarled.

"Well, at least I'm trying. Do you have any better ideas?" I asked him.

His eyes narrowed at me. "How about we act like adults and try to get along."

I laughed. Was he kidding? "Because that's worked so well."

He looked at my hand, holding the pen and then back at my face. He threw the notebook on the couch and his hands dropped at his side. "Do you really hate me that much that you'd rather shut yourself in your room than spend a few hours with me?"

I stepped back, not knowing how to respond. Did I hate him? I barely tolerated him, couldn't stand to be around him without arguing. Yes, he made me angry, and we fought with each other all the time, but I don't think I hated him, I don't think I could ever hate him, no matter how much I wanted to.

But that didn't change the facts. We had spent four days together and gotten into arguments every time. I definitely didn't want this to be a regular thing between us.

There was no way he would be okay with that either, he had to see that this was a perfect plan, which meant we didn't have to see each other until he moved out.

I laughed, humorlessly. "We argue all of the time Gabriel. I can't do it anymore. This is the only way. If we stay out of each other's way, we'll never see each other, and we won't argue."

His eyes burned into mine, his jaw clenched, his arms balled into fists at his side, he looked at the floor for a fleeting second and then back at me. He stayed silent for a minute, alternating his gaze from me to the floor, to the notebook. I didn't know if he would go along with it. I hoped so, if we had to have another fight, I might lose it.

I had promised Zaria that I would try, this is the only way I could think of that would work. I would stay out of his way, and he would stay out of mine.

"Fine." He muttered.

"You accept?"

"Yeah, if you hate me that much that you make up this fucking schedule to avoid seeing me, then the least I could do is stay out of your way." He snapped.

I flinched, we had irritated each other before, many times, but I had never seen Gabriel this angry. It made me feel remorse, I wasn't sure why he was acting so angry all of a sudden.

"You hate me too. This is beneficial for both of us." I said, almost in a whisper. It was no secret that we didn't like each other but saying those words made my chest tense.

His eyes stayed focused on mine, I didn't break eye contact, I wasn't sure what he would say, if he was going to insult me or say he hated me back, not that I'd expect him to say any differently. I gulped, waiting for whatever he was about to tell me.

He shook his head and looked at the floor. "According to the schedule, it's still your designated time so after I take a shower, I'll just stay in my room until then."

He walked away from the couch towards his bedroom, stopping at the door, turning his head to face me. His gaze stayed locked on mine, he gulped and looked at the floor for a few seconds before looking up at me again. "I could never hate you." He walked into his bedroom and closed the door.

My eyes stayed locked on his bedroom door. I couldn't move. My lips were parted in disbelief. What did he just say? What did he mean by that? How could he say that he didn't hate me if he did everything in his power to make me miserable?

I didn't know what to think about Gabriel anymore. I wanted to ask him what he meant by that, but I couldn't. he had agreed to the schedule, so now all we had to do was stick to it and we could successfully stay away from each other.

CHAPTER EIGHT

My plan had worked. Kind of.

It had been two days since I set the schedule, which meant I hadn't seen Gabriel since. It was working well, we weren't seeing each other so we didn't argue. It helped that Zaria was off shift, so she was around too, she didn't know about the schedule, I wasn't sure if Gabriel had told her, but she hadn't mentioned it which made me think he didn't.

All she knew was that we were trying to stay away from each other, she had no idea that I practically tried to kick her brother out of the apartment at allocated times, I was sure she wouldn't be thrilled about it, but this was the only way I could think of to keep my promise to Zaria. I got what I wanted. The schedule was working out well in both our favors.

But I couldn't shake the feeling that consumed me after what Gabriel had said.

I could never hate you.

There were so many moments where I was tempted to knock on his door and ask him what he meant by that. Maybe he meant it in a different way, maybe it was 'I could never hate you… because I don't even care about you.'

Whatever it was, I had to make peace with it and move on, I couldn't keep thinking about those words and every possible meaning behind them. But it was no use, I couldn't help but focus on those words, no matter how much I tried to forget them.

I replayed our arguments in my head repeatedly, the things he would say, the way he didn't even look at me sometimes, it made me feel so empty, so forgettable, but then, I remembered those words.

I could never hate you.

My head spun and my stomach tumbled, I couldn't help but let those feelings engulf me. Even though I knew that Gabriel did hate me, no matter what he said.

So why couldn't I stop thinking about Gabriel? I had gotten what I wanted, what I had planned to be the perfect plan. Except it wasn't, my body shivered knowing he was so close to me, just a few feet away, sat on the couch alone, because I was too chicken shit to be in his presence.

The plan had been to avoid Gabriel. Avoid communication, avoid seeing him, avoid being around him. But it hadn't worked in my favor.

Even with the schedule, Gabriel still managed to find a way to communicate with me, by arguing of course. But I didn't even mind it, knowing he still wanted to talk to me, even if he couldn't do it face to face, made me think if those words he said, were true.

The first day, I stayed in my room, but I could still hear him out there, in the kitchen, I could hear the tv. I became obsessed with hearing him, what he was doing, imagining what he was cooking, what he was watching.

I wanted nothing more than to go out there and hang out with him, apologize for setting the schedule and give friendship a go. But I couldn't. It had been my idea, which meant I had to keep out of his way, like I promised.

Today, however, was the weekend, and unfortunately for me, I woke up early, too early. Most nights I would wake up in the middle of the night, surrounded by darkness and in distress. Apparently, it was insomnia, but I had no problem falling asleep, the problem was staying asleep. Once I woke up, I couldn't fall back asleep, my brain wouldn't shut up and would keep me up until the sun beamed through my curtains, and I needed to get up.

I stayed in bed, mundanely scrolling through the Netflix catalog settling on a murder mystery show. Maybe this wasn't the best thing to watch when I was trying to get back to sleep, but it kept me interested enough until I heard the front door close.

I opened my door, making sure the coast was clear. When I went out into the living room. It was scattered with neon pink sticky notes. I recognized those sticky notes. They were the ones I had stored in the desk I used to use before Gabriel was staying there.

I walked over to the closest note I could see which was on the kitchen counter, next to a Tupperware box filled with pasta.

Made *extra. Go crazy.*

My chest tightened at that gesture. He made food for me.

Or maybe I was being presumptuous. Maybe he cooked for Zaria and my dumb brain thought it was for me.

I walked around the apartment, looking for more notes.

Another note stuck to the tv.

I gave one of those reality shows you like so much a go.
I rest my case.
They suck.

My smile was undeniable. Okay, this one was without a doubt for me. I couldn't help but smile at the knowledge that Gabriel watched one of my reality shows, even if he said he hated it. I wished more than anything that we could have watched them together. If anything, just to see the look of disgust on his face.

Another on the dishwasher

Wash your dishes trevi, I'm not your maid.

I couldn't help but laugh at that. Even when we weren't speaking, he found a way to argue with me. This one was also for me, so I was right. Gabriel did cook for me. My smile was undeniable, and I instantly wanted to slap it off. Here Gabriel was, arguing with me about dishes and I was smiling.

I had rushed back to my room after eating the Chinese takeout I ordered so I would stick to the schedule since it was my idea. I left a fork in the sink. A single fork and he was acting like I left the whole house covered in plates.

Should I reply? Should I just ignore him? I didn't know what this meant. I basically told him that just having him around me aggravated me and he made food for me, and still found a way to talk to me.

I'd been feeling a little guilty over this arrangement ever since I proposed the idea to Gabriel. Having to isolate from each other, just because I was too sensitive, made me feel a little bad for Gabriel. He had asked his sister if he could move in for a while, obviously because he trusted her and felt comfortable with her, and then for me to make him feel unwelcome must have made him hate me even more.

I could never hate you.

I couldn't shake those words out of my head. I didn't trust them, why should I? it wasn't like Gabriel ever gave me a reason to believe he didn't hate me. Why should one time rectify that? It didn't.

I reheated the pasta, staring at the microwave, wondering how the hell I got myself in the position where I craved Gabriel's attention. Not once in my life did, I picture myself wanting someone's company, a long time ago I wanted to be seen, to have someone's interest, but I wasn't like that anymore.

I didn't want to get attached and I didn't want to be the type of person who yearned for someone. So why was I contemplating scrapping the schedule and giving his idea a go? Could we even be friends? Or was it too late for that?

The microwave pinged, snapping me out of my thoughts. The smoke rolled out and wafting my face as I desperately tried to cool the food down. Jesus, how the hell did I mess up reheating food? I was an incompetent idiot.

I wondered if my mother knew how to cook. Would she have taught me if she did? Would we have one of those mother-daughter bonding moments like a corny montage in a hallmark movie?

My father didn't cook much. The stereotype didn't apply to him I guess, because in my eighteen years of life I had never seen the man cook a meal that didn't come in a prepackaged box. Italian men were supposed to know how to cook, right?

God, I guess I wanted to torture myself by thinking of my parents right now, or *parent* more like.

I dumped the contents of the Tupperware onto a plate. He had cooked me food. Why did that small gesture mean so much to me? I wondered if I'd have to thank him. I couldn't talk to him, which meant the only other way of communication would either be through Zaria, or I could take his approach and leave a sticky note.

I didn't reply.

I don't know why I didn't. He was… acting civil for once, trying to make me see that we could get along, hell we hadn't argued since we set the schedule. But what if the reason we hadn't argued, was because we didn't have a chance to. Sure, he was still managing to communicate with me through sticky notes, but I wasn't replying.

"M? Why are you still in your pajamas?"

I turned my head, seeing Zaria walk in through the front door. Whilst Zaria looked great and like a functioning, member of society, I was in sweats and a t-shirt. It was after one in the afternoon.

"I stayed in my room." I told her.

She stepped in, taking off her shoes and rolling her eyes. "To avoid him, really?"

I turned back around. I hadn't exactly mentioned the schedule to her, and this wouldn't be the best time to bring it up

"Ok, I have something to ask you." She said, approaching closer to me.

"What's up?"

She smiled. "Before you turn me down can I just say pleaseeeee?" She begged.

I laughed. "Turn you down for what?"

She exhaled. "I want you to come out with me tonight." I opened my mouth and she held up her hand to stop me. "Again, let me just say it's been so long since we went out together and I really need to let off some steam and I know you do too, especially with Gabriel here, there's no better time." She batted her eyelashes at me, pressing her hands together in a praying motion. "Please." She said, again.

Normally I would turn her down and end up staying in for the night watching a rom-com or catching up on work. God, that sounded pathetic. Zaria was right, there was no better time to do this, especially since if Gabriel stayed home, I'd have to shut myself in my room again.

I couldn't believe I was considering this. I hated crowds, with a passion. The last time I went out with Zaria, I ended up having a panic attack in the bathroom stall, over some guy whose drink spilled on me. I hated going clubbing, which was where Zaria would most likely be going.

But what was the other option? Stay in and watch tv again like I had done for the millionth time? I couldn't believe I was actually going to do this. I was going clubbing, again.

Zaria was still batting her lashes at me, waiting for my response. Her face was curved in a slight frown, and I knew she expected me to say no like I did hundreds of times, but instead I nodded.

"Really?" She asked.

"Yeah, you're right. I need a distraction from Gabriel."

Her face transformed into a huge grin, as she wrapped her arms around me and repeated 'thank you, thank you, thank you' in my ear.

"Should I invite Allie?" I asked her. Zaria and Allie had only met twice but they'd hit it off, I never met anyone Zaria didn't connect with. She was a people person and loved talking to new people.

"Oooh yes. Tell her to invite Charlotte too."

I nodded and pulled out my phone to text Allie.

"M." Zaria called.

"Yeah?" I asked, looking up to see her with a sympathetic look on her face.

"I promise I will take care of you. If you start feeling overwhelmed and need to leave, we will, okay? I know you hate it, and it means so much you're willing to come with me."

I frowned. Why did Zaria want me to come? I was a burden on her, she would have to babysit me just so I wouldn't have a panic attack, who the hell would want that? I needed to keep in check of myself tonight, I didn't want to ruin Zaria's night by being a liability.

"I'll be fine Z."

She nodded with a huge smile plastered on her face as she walked over to the bathroom. "I'm going to take a shower. We leave at ten. And don't worry, we won't stay too late."

She walked into the bathroom leaving me out in the hallway, wondering what the hell I just agreed to.

CHAPTER NINE

"I'll have a pornstar martini." Zaria yelled over the counter to the bartender. He must have been over forty. His hair was balding, and he had a beer belly, but he still had a charming quality about him, he winked at her whilst making her drink. She smiled back at him, probably wanting him to add extra alcohol to her drink.

I glanced around the dark nightclub. The strobing lights were giving me a headache and the music was too loud, and of course ,there was the most obvious factor, the one that made me the most uncomfortable, there were too many people surrounding us. I squeezed my eyes shut. I wasn't going to ruin this, I wasn't going to freak out. It was just people, people who I'd never see again. Why was I so anxious?

We'd already had three free drinks plus some shots from some of the guys standing at the bar, which Zaria flirted for. I didn't do a single thing except stand here and wish I was currently in bed. I knew this would be a bad idea, but the look on Zaria's face earlier today nearly killed me so I would stick it out, for her.

I felt guilty taking drinks from people I had no interest in, especially when most of them were buying for Zaria. She looked stunning. Her hair was long and straight flowing down back. But her body was the real accessory, her curves clung to the fabric of her fire-colored dress and her legs stood tall, with her six-inch heels.

I hadn't worn heels in a long time, probably since the last time we went out clubbing, so I had settled on some small three-inch ones which I was clumsily walking in, hopefully, no one noticed.

"And what about you, sweetheart?" The bartender asked, turning to face me. His accent was heavily British as he smirked at me.

"Do you have anything sweet?" I asked. I wasn't a big fan of alcohol, never really was, so if I had to drink it, it would be sweet. The drinks I had earlier were Allie's suggestion, I had no idea what they were called but the taste was awful and the tequila shots we got from the guys, who were still surrounding us, made me gag.

"I have something that I think you'll like." He replied and started making my drink. Zaria sipped on hers, swaying her hips to the hip-hop music playing in the club. I'll give it this, this club had good music. There was nothing worse than going dancing to music you couldn't stand.

"Damn. You look hot." Someone muttered. I looked up to see one of the guys who had bought us drinks looking at Zaria like he wanted to eat her. Jesus, I didn't know how she did it, if someone looked at me that way, I'd run.

"Here you go, sweetheart." The bartender slid my drink toward me. The drink certainly looked sweet. It was bright red, and it had a strawberry sliced in half hanging on the rim.

"What is it?" I asked.

"Strawberry daiquiri." He said, whilst mixing another drink. "Pretty much strawberries and rum, proper sweet, don't worry." He said, smirking at me as he continued making the drinks.

I took an experimental sip of the drink. I felt the burn of the rum hit my throat, but the sweet flavor of the strawberries coated my tongue, it was delicious, not to mention it looked pretty.

"Thanks." I yelled back to the bartender, and he dipped his chin.

Zaria wrapped her arm around mine and pulled me away from the bar. "Come on." She muttered.

I was thanking the gods that Zaria was holding onto me, or I was certain in that moment I would have fallen over, especially with everyone surrounding and bumping into each other as we walked over to a booth she had reserved, where Allie and Charlotte were sat.

We sat down, the leather sticking to my thighs as my skirt rode up. I wasn't nearly as dressed up as Zaria, I kept my hair down and straight, but I was certain it was frizzy again, especially with how hot this club was. I found a black leather skirt I had bought on a whim in college, in the black of my closet, and paired it with a black corset top. Black was my safe color for tonight, I'd blend in and avoid eyes on me.

"I think I'm drunk." Zaria exhaled, as she finished off her drink.

I didn't feel anything close to drunk, maybe a little less in my head than when I first got here, but I guess the first few drinks didn't count for someone like me, they just made me a normal person instead of the anxious wreck I usually was.

"You've had two drinks." Charlotte laughed. "Lightweight."

I had only met Charlotte twice, when I had invited Allie out with Zaria and I so I thought tonight would be a perfect opportunity for us to hang out again. She was nice, and so in love with Allie, which sometimes made my stomach hurt. Seeing how she looked at Allie had me wondering if anyone would ever look at me that way. Did I even want someone to look at me like that?

For most of my life I'd been alone, retrospectively, it was kind of my fault. I shut myself off from everyone, but I think that's how I liked it. I liked being alone, and I didn't want someone coming into my life and disrupting that. Maybe that was why all my previous dates had never worked out, I had been self-sabotaging.

But looking at Allie as she cuddled up next to Charlotte and whispered in her ear, making her blush, made me rethink all of that. How horrible would it be if I opened myself up a little, maybe let someone into my life?

"We had shots before you guys got here." Zaria said, pointing between me and her, making me cringe at the taste of the tequila hitting my throat.

"I'm never drinking tequila again."

They all laughed, and Allie nodded. "I agree."

Zaria sighed. "You just didn't know how to do it right." She shook her head, turning to face the girls. "She didn't lick the salt and threw away the lime because it was 'too acidic'"

Allie and Charlotte turned to face me, with a dumbfounded expression.

"I shrugged. "What? It was."

They all laughed again, and Charlotte turned to me. "It's supposed to cut the taste of the tequila. You lick, sip, suck."

"Speaking of…" Zaria said, gesturing to the end of the bar.

The guy who bought us drinks. Jim? John? Whatever his name was, was walking over to our table, eyes focused on Zaria. Thank God. He approached the booth, smiling at us. "Hey ladies."

"Hey." We all said in unison.

He turned to Zaria. "Hey, want to come dance?" He asked her.

Zaria leaned into the booth, crossing her legs. "I don't even know your name." She flirted. She definitely did, I was pretty sure it started with a J.

He laughed. "It's Josh, Josh Turner." *I knew it.*

She leaned forward a little, letting him look at her cleavage without making it look obvious. Damn, she was good. "Well, Josh Turner. Do you remember mine?" She asked.

He smirked, leaning forward a little. "Of course, I do. Zaria." He indicated to the dance floor with a tilt of his head. "So, do you want to dance?"

She smiled and then looked at me. "You okay?" she asked.

I nodded at her. I'd be fine, I was luckily in a booth so I wouldn't have to squeeze through people just to have a space to breathe.

She stared at me, raising a brow at me, making sure I wasn't lying. I rolled my eyes. "Z, I'll be fine, you can't babysit me, go have fun."

She hesitantly stood up, smiling at Josh, telling him she'd love to dance. She turned back to me before leaving. "We'll have a dance later, okay?"

Dance? In the middle of a crowded, hot, sweaty club with guys gyrating against me? Um, no.

Maybe she would be too drunk to remember. I nodded at her and she turned to face Josh as they made their way through the hordes of people. At least I had Allie and Charlotte to keep me company.

"We're going to dance," Charlotte said, grabbing Allie's hand as she stood up from the booth. *Or maybe I'd be alone.* "Will you be okay?" She asked.

I nodded, focusing on my drink. Wondering how many more I would have to ingest to finally be carefree for a night.

They walked out of the booth, holding hands to not get lost in the crowd.

I set the straw aside, finishing off the drink. My head buzzed a little, I was tipsy for sure. Maybe another drink and I'd be a regular functioning human being.

"Damn. Tough night?" I lifted my eyes, seeing a tall man standing by the booth. His hands were stuffed in his pockets. His brown hair was perfectly styled, and one arm was covered in tattoos whilst the other was bare, tanned skin. His muscles visibly cutting into the white t-shirt he was wearing. White in a club. That was ballsy.

The last time I was here, I wore a pink top and ended up getting a drink spilled all over me, leaving me in a sticky unfixable mess. I had to throw that top out, I miss that top.

His eyebrows raised, waiting for me to answer him. Did I just zone out? How long was I staring at him?

"Um." Crap, why wasn't Zaria here? She would know what to say and most likely he would end up talking to her instead of me. I wouldn't blame him, I wasn't really the chatty type, more like the nervous anti-social 'let me sit in a corner alone' type.

"Um." I tried again. But nothing else came out. What the hell was wrong with me? I needed to be drunk to have a conversation, apparently.

"Rendered you speechless?" He joked.

I snorted. My eyes widened when I realized what I had done. I mean, it wasn't exactly like it was only his presence that made me a stumbling mess. "I'm sorry I didn't mean—"

"It's fine. No hard feelings. So why the heavy drinking?"

I smirked. "I wouldn't exactly call a fruity drink 'heavy drinking'."

He took that as an invitation to sit down. I didn't mind it... I think. "No," he laughed. "But you were drinking it like it was hard liquor."

I sighed. "I just wanted to feel..." *Normal.* "Free?" it came out as a question. What exactly did I mean by free? I knew what I meant in my head. I wanted to be free from the anxiety keeping me locked down every day, I wanted to be free from my own mind and the overthinking about every single thing that happened in my life. But to him, it probably sounded like I escaped from prison and was making the most out of my night as a free person.

Apparently, he understood because he nodded. "I get that."

The alcohol was probably getting to me because I started finding him very intriguing, even though we had spoken for exactly two minutes, I was enjoying myself. For once in my life, I felt good. Was this how everyone else lived? I envied them.

"Well, if you're looking to be free, I can help you with that." He said.

My brows furrowed. "How?"

He grinned. "I'll be right back." With that, he left the booth, and I was alone again. I looked out onto the dancefloor seeing Zaria and Josh dancing, his hands were holding onto her hips as she grinded on him, his mouth on her neck. Zaria seemed to be having fun, why couldn't I?

Allie and Charlotte stood at the bar, Charlotte was behind her, her arms wrapped around her waist and her head was on her shoulder. Would I ever find that one day?

My eyes snapped to the guy I was talking to, seeing him walk back holding a tray of drinks in his hand. Oh god, I didn't even know his name and I was confiding in him in my need to get drunk tonight?

"What's your name?" I blurted out as soon as he sat back down, slurring a little. Okay, the alcohol was definitely taking effect.

He smiled. "Glad you asked. I've been dying to know yours. I'm Cam. And yours?" He asked, handing me a shot glass with some kind of liquid in it.

I picked up the glass and stared at him. I blinked once, twice. "Melissa." I said, and then stared down at the drink in my hand. He was a stranger, someone who, less than ten seconds ago, I didn't even know the name of. Who knew if he spiked my drink?

"Is something wrong?" He asked.

"I don't know you." And then handed him back the glass. I probably seemed like an asshole, but I didn't know what he could be capable of.

"Oh, right. I forgot about that." He said, taking the glass from my hand and drinking the contents of it. He licked his lips and then handed me another glass. "You have nothing to worry about, I didn't spike these. If that wasn't proof, then I can buy you your own round of shots if you'd like?" He shrugged.

I took the glass from his hands and stared down at it. "What is it?"

"Vodka. Didn't take you for a tequila kind of girl." I wasn't. Those tequila shots I had earlier nearly made me spill my lunch all over myself.

I smiled at him and drank the shot, cringing when the burn hit my throat, but it was a much better taste than tequila.

"So how do you feel?" He asked after two more shots. The previous drinks had kicked in and I was feeling the effect of them. I was less conscious, less observant, which was probably a bad thing for my safety, but great for my head. God, I needed this.

"Free." I replied, smiling at him.

He stood up from the booth and reached out for my hand. "Want to dance?" He asked.

Did I want to dance? Not particularly. I wasn't the best dancer, and I barely knew this guy, but now was not the time for overthinking and reasoning. I wanted to have fun.

I stood up and took his hand as a reply. We headed through the crowd into the middle of the floor, I didn't look around, I didn't even apologize for bumping into people on the way there, I focused on Cam and kept repeating to myself 'you will have fun' because I deserved to.

I swayed my hips, imitating Zaria's previous moves and he settled in behind me. His hands held onto my hips as I swayed to the music, he didn't touch anywhere else, just my hips.

He flipped me around and wrapped his arms around my waist, so I followed suit and wrapped mine around his neck. We were slow dancing in a club. I didn't mind it though, this was nice, I wasn't thinking about what I looked like to everyone watching or if his hands were drifting closer towards my butt— Oh crap.

I was.

His hands drifted lower and lower until they were just above my butt. I didn't know what to do. The alcohol was meant to subdue me and my brain, but it wasn't working, because all I thought was: what the hell is he doing?

His hands grabbed my butt and pressed me into him. I could feel his bulge press into my stomach, and it was wrong. The whole thing was wrong, and I hated him, and I hated this, and I hated that I couldn't act like everyone else.

Zaria was dancing with a stranger, and she loved it, so why couldn't I? Why was I feeling violated by him dancing with me? This was normal, I should be into this, into him, but I wasn't.

I stepped back, putting some much-needed space between me and his sweaty body. I hated how it felt pressed against me.

"What's wrong?" He whispered in my ear.

"I... I don't want to do this." I stepped away from him, seeing his lip curl as he took a step closer to me.

"But we were having fun." He said. "You had no problem taking drinks from me, for free, but now you don't want to dance?"

My eyes widened and I stilled. What the hell? Why did men think that if they bought you drinks it was a green light into your pants?

I turned to rush back to the booth, but his hand circled around my wrist, stopping me. "No, don't leave now." He pulled me closer by the wrist until his mouth hovered over my ear. "We still have unfinished business." He whispered. His hot breath hitting my ear making me shiver.

I pushed his chest, causing some people to turn and look at us, I didn't even care in the moment. I would probably lay awake for days to come, overthinking how I could have handled it better and without calling attention to myself, but in that moment, I didn't give a shit. I needed him away from me.

"I don't owe you shit." I sneered at him. I turned, stumbling my way back to the booth. My vision was a little blurry from the alcohol, but I widened my eyes, trying not to fall as I pushed through the crowd.

"Fucking cock tease." He muttered from behind me. Right, of course I was. Every girl was a cock tease when they said no. I had some shots with him and apparently to him, that meant I wanted to sleep with him.

A pair of hands grabbed my shoulders, and I squeezed my eyes shut and gasped. Cam found me. What was he going to do?

"Are you okay?"

My eyes snapped open. I knew that voice.

"Gabriel?"

His face came into focus, barely, as I tried to adjust my eyes to see him. There were two Gabriels, and I didn't know where to look.

His eyes scanned my face as his grip on my shoulders tightened. "Did that asshole hurt you?"

Cam?

"You saw that?" How long has he been here?

He nodded. "Zaria told me you were going clubbing, and I came to check on you two."

Oh. He was here. He saw Cam. He saw me drink with him and dance with him. Oh god, Gabriel saw me grinding on a complete stranger. I didn't know why that unnerved me so much, but it did.

"Why are you here? You hate this type of place." He asked.

I wasn't sure how he knew that, probably because he would never have thought I was the type of person to have fun, he had said it himself. But that's why I wanted to come, to prove to myself I could, and instead it backfired.

I sighed. "I was trying to stay away from you."

"Is that why you didn't reply?" He said. I knew he was talking about the notes from earlier. I wasn't even sure why I didn't write him back. He was trying to call a truce, and I could have made it easy on him.

But I didn't know what it would mean. If we communicated, would we go back to arguing again? The whole point of the schedule was to avoid fighting.

I ignored his question. "I don't know where Zaria is. She was dancing with some guy earlier." I told him.

His grip on my shoulders loosened and he nodded. "Yeah, I saw her earlier grinding on a guy." He cringed. "Not exactly what a big brother wants to see."

I laughed and then stilled. I was laughing with Gabriel. I was talking to Gabriel without yelling at him. Was this the alcohol or were we actually capable of having a conversation?

"Why were you drinking shots with a stranger? And then dancing with that same stranger?" He asked, his brows furrowing.

"He's not a stranger, his name is Cam." I slurred back at him. My vision was a little blurry, but his scowl deepened.

"You're defending him?" He shook his head. "I saw what he did Melissa. He had his hands all over you."

I let my head hang. Why was I defending some guy I barely knew who groped me? I sighed and shook my head. "I just wanted to be normal." I whispered.

I wanted one night where I could act like someone who had fun, someone who went with the flow and didn't have to overthink everything. My voice was so low, and the music was too loud, I was sure he didn't hear me. Until he replied.

"You are normal." I lifted my eyes seeing his brows still furrowed. He looked confused as to why I would think I wasn't normal. But he wouldn't understand, he didn't have that thing I had in my head that sometimes made me want to scream. I couldn't just act like him, and Zaria did. I didn't work that way.

Zaria showed up by my side. "Hey bro" She smiled at Gabriel. She was still drunk and happy, but the alcohol had slipped out of my system the minute Cam touched me, sobering me up, mostly. "What are you doing here?" She asked him.

"I came to pick you guys up. Ready to go?" Gabriel asked his sister.

"Yeah, I need food." She exhaled.

"Where's Allie?" I asked. I hadn't seen her or Charlotte since I saw them at the bar.

"Oh, they left. Charlotte saw me coming out of the bathroom and she said Allie and her wanted some 'rest.'" She laughed. "That's code for they're horny."

We laughed as Gabriel greeted some guy that he recognized, embracing that 'cool guy' pound hug that guys do.

Zaria turned and looked at me. "Did you have fun?" She asked, smiling. God, she was so happy, and she wanted me to be happy too. This was what it was about, wasn't it? She thought a night of drinking and dancing would make me happy like it made her, but we didn't work the same.

I couldn't deny her of that. I smiled at her and nodded. Gabriel shook his head in my peripheral, but I widened my eyes at him begging him not to say anything. She didn't need to know that I almost had another panic attack and some creep groped me.

He rolled his eyes and gestured with his hands for us to go. Zaria walked gracefully towards the exit, and I followed, trying not to twist my ankle.

Gabriel laughed, behind me. "Let's go trevi."

CHAPTER TEN

I'm never drinking again.

Those are the words of every single person with a hangover. But I was serious. I hated alcohol anyway, the taste was as bad as it made me feel the morning after.

I always kept my curtains open. I loved waking up with the heat of the sun shining on my face, but today was not that day. I groaned, covering my head with my sheets, letting the darkness surround me.

Was it socially acceptable to sleep in all day? And maybe even stay home from work for a week? The thought of having to get up early tomorrow and teach a bunch of kids made me want to throw up all over their small heads.

I grabbed my phone from the nightstand, seeing it was nearly one pm. Christ, I couldn't remember the last time I had slept this late. I needed to get up.

With a valiant effort of my sore feet and tired arms, I managed to get out of bed, somehow managing to stay upright long enough to make the room stop spinning. I took small steps to my bedroom door, needing some kind of liquid down my dry throat.

My door opened and Gabriel was stood in the kitchen. Shit, I forgot about the schedule. I could cry. All I wanted was a glass of water. It was so irrational of me to create that schedule, thinking I could keep him away.

His eyes found mine and stared back at me as I debated whether I should just say fuck it and go out there anyway or if I'd chicken out and stay in my room. Instead, I did none of those, and stood still at my bedroom door and stared at Gabriel.

He smirked, shaking his head. "You can come out here, trevi. I'm not going to kick you out."

I snickered at myself and decided to take him up on his offer. He was a bigger person than I was, because if it were me, that was exactly what I would do.

"How are you feeling?" He asked.

I narrowed my eyes at him. "Should we be talking?"

His face dropped. "Cut the shit, Melissa."

I sighed, sitting at the kitchen island. "Fine, I feel like shit, happy?"

He laughed, making my head hurt even more. "A little, yeah."

I groaned, letting my head hit the kitchen island. "Glad to know you're enjoying this." I mumbled into the cold surface.

"Here." His deep voice grumbled, still way too loud.

I hesitantly lifted my head, seeing him stand by the island, holding a glass of water. God, I could kiss him right now.

Huh? Wait, no I didn't mean that, I just meant that I really needed water and he was here with water, that was all, right?

I gulped, looking at his face. I hadn't seen him since we set the schedule, with the exception of yesterday, but that didn't really count, I was drunk, and I could barely make him out in the dark.

Once we got home, I went straight to bed, not even bothering to talk to Gabriel more than I had, back at the club. We hadn't really communicated since I set the schedule, the only form of communication being the notes, but for some reason, I didn't acknowledge that it was still Gabriel, almost as if the notes felt more impersonal than talking to him face to face.

What if my fears about fighting again once we finally saw each other were real? He was right here in front of me, and I didn't know what to do. I wasn't sure whether I should ignore him or go back to my room? Should I talk to him? what would I say? My mind was so confused, and my heart was pounding against my chest at the mere sight of him.

"Thanks." I mumbled, and he dipped his chin.

I threw back the glass, drinking it like I hadn't had water in over a week. The cold liquid coating my dry throat, made me gasp as I inhaled the water.

I set the empty glass on the kitchen island, wishing I had about ten more. I looked up, seeing Gabriel look at me with his arms crossed over his chest. Did he stare at me the whole time I was drinking?

"Why are you looking at me?" I asked.

The edge of his lips turned in a small smirk. "Trying to see if you're going to throw up or not. You hungry?" He asked, raising his brows at me.

My face contorted in disgust. I couldn't even think of food right now. I didn't feel like I was going to throw up but if I ate, then I definitely would.

He laughed, seeing my expression. "Got it."

The sound of a door opening made both of us snap our heads in the direction of Zaria's bedroom. She stumbled out of the room, still in her dress from last night and her hair messy and wild. Shit, I was so consumed with what had happened that I forgot to check in on Zaria. Whenever she went out, I helped her take off her clothes and get her into bed, I helped her get hydrated before she fell asleep. I helped her, except yesterday I didn't.

"Shit, Zaria I'm sorry." I stood up, walking way too fast until the room started spinning again. I stilled, waiting until I could walk towards her again.

She blinked at me. "For what?"

I gulped. I didn't know why I felt like she expected me to do those things for her, I just did, and she clearly didn't seem upset by it, but I felt guiltier than ever. Just because I was feeling overwhelmed last night didn't excuse me helping my best friend, she was still drunk and I had been mostly sober, I could have taken care of her.

I grabbed her hand, sitting us down on the couch, she sighed as she let her head hit the back of the couch and closed her eyes. I smoothed the hair out of her face. "I should have taken care of you last night." I whispered.

Her eyes opened a crack. "You did. You came out with me, I had fun, thank you M." She said, closing her eyes once again.

I couldn't help but smile. All she wanted was a night out with me, to make me happy and forget everything for just a second, and it sort of worked.

I heard heavy footsteps across the wooden floor, looking up and seeing Gabriel lean on the back of the couch, looking down at us. "You do that often? Take care of her I mean."

I nodded. "Whenever she comes home drunk, I always help her get into bed feeling at least slightly comfortable." I gulped, looking away. "But yesterday I was so caught up in everything, I forgot."

I felt a hand on my shoulder and turned to see Gabriel's hand there. "Don't do that. You were drunk too."

"Barely." I sighed. "If I hadn't been thinking about you, none of this would happen." I blurted out and my eyes widened. "I mean, thinking about not talking to you, because of the schedule." I explained.

He smirked. "We're talking right now, trevi."

He was right, we were talking and somehow managing not to fight. Could we really get along like he'd suggested? I looked down into my lap and fidgeted with my hands.

I sighed and said the only thing I was certain about. "I made a mistake." I admitted. I looked up at him, scrunching my nose.

I was embarrassed of letting him know that the whole schedule idea was dumb, and I that I was sorry, but it was the only thing I knew I had to tell him.

"How so?" He asked. Was he really going to make me spell it out for him?

"About the schedule, I made a mistake."

He smirked. The motherfucker smirked. He knew what I was talking about, he just wanted me to admit it. Of course, he would. He chuckled and stroked his beard, smugly. I narrowed my eyes at him. I was embarrassed about admitting it and he was taking pleasure in my demise.

"Shut up." I told him, facing away from him.

"So, you miss me." He said, rather than asked. He was so smug.

I scoffed. "No."

"Uh huh, then why do you think you made a mistake?"

I sighed. Why did I think that? Because he was being nice for a change, because he was acting less like an asshole, because I missed his face.

"Because I miss being out here, that's it." I had already admitted that I made a mistake, I wasn't going to admit to him that I missed having him around. No chance in hell. He already had a big head, I couldn't imagine him how he would react if I told him the real reason, I wanted to scrap the whole schedule idea.

He shook his head. "I don't believe that for a second. You seemed too eager to shut yourself in your room just so that you wouldn't have to see me, or be around me, so what is the real reason?"

I couldn't face him, he would see right through me and know, he would know I was lying. And if I said the real reason, his head would get so big that it would explode. I fidgeted with my fingers, trying to find something to say that would get him off my back, but I sat there in silence for way too long.

"So, you miss me." He repeated when I didn't reply, taking my silence as an answer.

"Shut up."

He laughed. "I missed you too trevi, you're the only one who calls me dipshit, where else would I be greeted with such kindness?"

I wasn't sure if I should bring up the schedule and whether he wanted to scrap it, like I did. Somehow, I was wrong, here we were, in each other's presence and having a conversation like those ten years of bickering didn't happen.

It was clear we were going to have to work at this, being friends wasn't exactly going to be easy or natural for us, but I think we could do it.

Zaria's eyes fluttered open, as she got accustomed to the light coming in from the windows. She turned to face me and then looked up, seeing her brother. "So, you're not avoiding each other anymore?" She asked.

I bit my lip, looking up at Gabriel. I didn't know what the answer was. If I said, no, then did that mean we were going to scrap the schedule? I waited for Gabriel to answer, his eyes met mine and he smirked. "No, we're not avoiding each other anymore." He said.

"Good. Figure this shit out, it's annoying having to hear you pick on my best friend." She told Gabriel. I looked up to see Gabriel smiling down at me. My stomach flipped and I averted my eyes.

Zaria picked herself off the couch and groaned. "I need to take a shower." She announced before walking over to the bathroom and stepping inside.

Once the door closed, I turned to face Gabriel. "Did you mean that?"

"What?"

"About not avoiding each other anymore."

He blinked at me, then nodded. "Yeah, we can forget about the schedule, if you want." He ran a hand through his hair. "Are we good?"

I nodded, biting my lip to stifle a smile. "Yeah, we're good, I was a dick for doing that."

He laughed as he nodded, agreeing to me being a dick. I couldn't get angry at that, I was a dick. What I had done was irrational.

"Does this mean we have to be friends now?" I asked him.

He chuckled. "Let's not go that far, I think for now we agree to not fight so much and see where it goes from there." He extended his arm out to me. "Deal?" He asked, flashing a grin.

"Oh good." I said. "Another one of your 'deals'"

He rolled his eyes. "Just shake my hand trevi, damn."

"Fine, deal." I said, reaching out and shaking his hand. My hand instantly burned from his touch. I didn't want my body to react to him like that. I gasped and retreated my hand. I couldn't tell if he noticed my reaction, if he did, he didn't say anything. I quickly averted my gaze, to avoid him seeing my face, which I was sure was red and flushed by now.

CHAPTER ELEVEN

I admit. I was wrong about Gabriel.

Maybe he wasn't that bad after all.

It had been two days since we ran into each other in the kitchen and yesterday hadn't been completely soul crushing like I thought it would be. I was worried it would be awkward or we would revert to fighting like a couple of two-year-olds, but that didn't happen.

We managed to act like semi-normal roommates. We weren't exactly friends, but we were friendly. After ten years it would take a while to adjust to the idea of not hating the other. The insults hadn't completely disappeared, but it had eased a little.

It was surprisingly easy to be around Gabriel. Even after everything. But it still would be hard to act like those ten years of animosity between us never happened, like we didn't drive each other crazy for years, like we didn't loathe the other and everything they said.

But I knew that hating Gabriel wasn't an option anymore. I was sick of it, sick of arguing with him, and staying away from him hadn't helped. Acting friendly with each other was the only way, and if Gabriel was willing to try and make it work, then so was I.

"Hey trevi what's up?"

I looked back, seeing Gabriel walking in the door with a small smile on his face. It was weird, knowing he would smile when he saw me now, as opposed to before, when he would scowl at the mere sight of me.

How did a few days change so much?

I had been sat on the couch grading papers, ever since I got home, and I was starting to get brain fog. I placed the papers on the sofa and groaned, letting my head hit the back of the couch cushions.

"Grading papers." I replied.

"Sounds like you need a distraction. How about we watch California Girlz?"

I turned to face him, squinting with a huge grin on my face. "Hmm, look who's obsessed with my 'stupid' reality shows now."

He scoffed. "Don't get it twisted, this is for your entertainment not mine."

I chuckled. "Uh huh, so how do you feel about Jasmine winning?"

His mouth dropped open, and he furrowed his brows. "Jasmine is winning? Last time I watched it Christy was in the lead."

I smiled at him, not saying anything else. He just took my bait.

He realized what I just did, and his expression dropped. "Shut up." He muttered.

I laughed. It was adorable how much he was invested in the show, even more than me at this point. I checked his watch history, seeing he was ahead of me by two episodes.

He made his way over to the couch and leaned over the top of it. "Jasmine would never win. She has the personality of a thumbtack."

"Kind of like you." I supplied back with a smile, letting him know I was teasing.

He narrowed his eyes at me. "Don't push it trevi."

He stood up, walking around the couch, and sat on it. He reached for the remote, turning the tv on. "So, what do you want to watch?" He asked, scrolling through the movie catacatalog.

My brain was pure mush after teaching all day and then grading papers. Tv was exactly what I needed, I didn't have to think or put in any effort, just watch the images on the screen. "Ooh that one." I said, pointing at a film I hadn't seen yet, it looked cute, it had a dog on the screen.

"Of course, you'd pick a film with a dog."

"I like dogs." I said, crossing my legs on the couch as I leaned back.

"I remember. You used to go crazy over Ollie." He smirked.

The mention of Ollie made my eyes water. He was the Anderson's dog. A cute little border collie, he was so energetic and would spend hours rolling on the ground. He was old when I met Zaria and died shortly after.

"God, I miss that dog." He sighed.

We sat in silence watching the movie when a notification from my phone averted my attention from the tv. I reached for my phone that was on the coffee table and saw it was a text from Zaria.

Zaria: Hey M I'm on break, how's it going?

I smiled, knowing she was checking up on whether we had killed each other yet. She knew that we weren't avoiding each other anymore, but she didn't know we had agreed to get along.

Me: Don't worry, I'm still alive.

Zaria: HA. I'm more worried about you killing Gabriel.
She wouldn't be wrong. Most likely I'd be the one to end up killing Gabriel for driving me crazy. Gabriel was always more irritated than angry when we argued.

Me: Well, he's fine too. We've actually been getting along.

Zaria: No. Way.

Me: Yes. Way.

Zaria: This is unbelievable, I'm tempted to leave the hospital to come and see for myself.

Me: Don't be so dramatic.

Zaria: Hard not to be. How do I know you're not lying to me, and his head is cut off as we speak?

I let a laugh escape. Zaria was so dramatic, I loved it.

"Take a picture with me." I told Gabriel.

He blinked, looking at me. "For what?"

I showed him my conversation with Zaria, and he laughed. "Okay, you can't blame her, we don't exactly have the best track record." He ran a hand through his beard. "Why do you need a picture?"

"Well, your sister clearly thinks you're in danger in my presence, so I need to show her proof that you're alive."

"Okay, got it." He nodded and chuckled.

I lifted my phone to take a picture of me and Gabriel, who, of course, held up his middle finger behind my head, flipping me off whilst I flashed a smile, showing Zaria I was no threat. I sent the picture to Zaria and instantly got a response.

Zaria: OMG, it is true.

I laughed, shaking my head.

Me: Happy?

Zaria: Relieved, yes. Got to go back inside, bye M
Me, Bye Z.
We went back to watching the movie in silence. I was expecting a happy film about the dog and the family, maybe some cute dog scenes that made me laugh. I wasn't expecting another version of Marley & Me.

To my side, I heard a sniffle and turned to see Gabriel wipe his eyes.

"Are you crying?" I asked him, barely being able to see him through my hazy eyes that were filling up with wetness.

"No." He said, clearing his throat and trying to wipe his eyes without making it obvious. "Watch the movie."

I smiled. Maybe it was psychotic to smile at the sight of someone crying, but I couldn't help but revel in this moment. Gabriel and I were watching a movie together, amicably and he felt comfortable enough to cry in front of me, even though he was trying to deny it. That made his attractiveness skyrocket.

I let a laugh escape. I was happy, damn it, but he turned to face me with a scowl on his face. "No need to laugh. The dog reminds me of Ollie."

The dog looked nothing like Ollie, but I didn't mention that to him, I just nodded, and a tear escaped whilst the smile stayed on my face.

I turned my head to watch the movie when my stomach interrupted it by gurgling loudly. I slowly looked at Gabriel, who I knew, heard it too.

He laughed. "Hungry?"

I nodded. "Starving." I reached for my phone again. "I'm going to order take out, do you want some?"

He shook his head, looking at me with pity and a little disgust. I couldn't help but laugh, seeing his reaction to my eating habits. "You eat takeout every night."

"That's not true."

"Oh, it's not?" He asked, his eyebrows wrinkled.

I shook my head. "Nope, don't forget about those leftovers." I smiled at him, and his lips curved slightly "Thank you, by the way."

He shrugged. "No worries, I normally make extra anyway."

My smile faded and I looked away from him, trying not to make it obvious that comment affected me. He was obviously talking about his ex-girlfriend, Lucy, and how he would cook for her when they lived together.

A pang of jealousy hit deep in my stomach, and I adjusted myself on the couch, trying to act normal. Why was I jealous?

Wanting to change the conversation I chuckled. "Yeah, well it's not like I can cook anything anyway except for cereal or grilled cheese sandwiches." I shrugged "Take out is my best option."

He tilted his head and dipped his chin. "I'll cook dinner."

I held up my hand in front of him. "You don't have to do that."

He nodded and got up from the couch. "I know, I want to. I can't let you live off grilled cheese sandwiches." He shot me a smile and my breath quickened. He was still looking at me and I couldn't escape it. His eyes were so beautiful, I could easily get lost in them.

I pressed my lips in a tight smile and turned to face the tv. I couldn't look at him any longer. Why was Gabriel affecting me like this? Yes, I had a minor crush on him when we were teenagers, but now my stomach was flipping any time he looked at me.

After what seemed like forever, Gabriel finally called out to let me know the food was ready. I made my way to the kitchen island where there were two steaming plates of restaurant-quality food waiting for me.

The small gesture of Gabriel offering to cook for me made my cheeks warm and a smile pulled on my lips. My expression quickly dropped when I realized that he did this for his ex-girlfriend, I wasn't special, he was a chef, that's just what he did.

"Smells good." I stated. It really did. I took a seat on the island. I glanced to my side, seeing Gabriel bring a wine bottle and two glasses towards me, setting them on the island.

"Is that for me?" I asked.

A smile tugged on his lips, and he tilted his head at me. "No, it's for my other roommate, you might know her, horns, and a red tail?"

"Funny." I smiled at him with nothing but sarcasm.

He popped the cork off the wine bottle and poured it into two glasses in such a classy way I couldn't look away. How was it that Gabriel could make pouring wine attractive?

"White wine goes well with salmon." He explained, handing me the glass.

He took a seat on the stool next to mine and I took a bite of the food. I'd had Gabriel's food before, of course, including those leftovers he made but something about this made it even better.

Maybe because it was piping hot and didn't need to be reheated, maybe it was because he was sitting right next to me or maybe it was because I could finally let myself appreciate it fully without needing to insult Gabriel. Whatever it was, it made my tongue dance with flavors, and I couldn't help the small moan that escaped my lips.

My eyes shot open with the realization of what I just did and turned to face Gabriel, knowing he must have heard that too. My assumption was proven right when I was met with a huge grin on his face. I closed my eyes ashamed of what just happened and when I opened them, he was staring at me, smiling, his tongue poking the inside of his cheek.

My brain had stopped working. That was the only explanation for why I was just staring at him back, not saying a word, I blinked at him, not knowing what to say. Luckily, he broke the awkward silence.

"If you moan like that just at my food, I can only imagine what you'd sound like if I had anything to do with it."

I narrowed my eyes at him. "Keep imagining dipshit, if you had anything to do with it, I'd be screaming." I turned to take another bite of my food but was caught off guard when I heard Gabriel laughing. I looked at him, confused about why he was laughing.

He looked me up and down and licked his lips. "Screamer huh?"

I smacked my face with my hand when I realized what I had said and what that implied.

"I'd be screaming for help." I explained.

"Uh-huh." His face still had a smile on it, and I wanted to slap it off. I couldn't deny it to myself, the way he looked at me had my stomach churning and my mind running wild with the fantasy of Gabriel.

We ate the rest of the meal in silence, I was too embarrassed by what had transpired to even dare talk in case I said something else as absurd as what I had just said.

"That was delicious, thank you again."

Gabriel shrugged, picking up the dishes and placing them into the sink. "It's no problem trevi."

I rolled my eyes at that nickname.

He saw my expression and smiled, shaking his head. "Pretending you hate that nickname must be tiring."

"I *do* hate that nickname." I told him.

He didn't respond, instead, he reached inside the freezer and pulled out a tub of ice cream. I hadn't bought any, which meant he had. When he lifted off the lid, I could see it was strawberry ice cream, my favorite, and my mouth instantly started to water.

"You feel like dessert?"

I nodded my head, eagerly. I was stuffed, but I guess there was always room for dessert.

He took out one bowl and scooped some ice cream into it, I opened the drawers to grab a spoon and handed one to Gabriel. He shook his head and my eyebrows wrinkled in confusion. "You're not having any?"

He shook his head again. "No, strawberry ice cream isn't exactly my favorite."

Okay, now I was even more confused. "Then why did you buy it?"

He ran a hand through his beard. "I know it's your favorite and I thought I should do something nice for you since I clearly crossed a line that ultimately made you want to kick me out."

My eyes widened. He bought this ice cream just for me? "No, it was my fault. I just couldn't argue anymore, and I got sick of it"

He dipped his chin in understanding. "I'm sorry anyway."

I chuckled. "I would have never thought Gabriel Anderson would be apologizing to me."

His eyes narrowed and that made me smile even wider. "Don't get used to it, you have a lot more to apologize for than me." With that, my smile was wiped off clean.

My eyebrows furrowed. "What do you mean?" and then my expression fell. The schedule. He was still pissed at me for it. "Oh."

"Yeah, oh." He laughed, but he was not amused, he was pissed. "Seriously Melissa, I get it, you were sick of fighting, but did you really think that keeping me out of the apartment at specific times would stop that?"

I looked down at my hands, fidgeting with my fingers. I knew I had fucked up. It was ludicrous and immature, but I had enough of arguing with him day and night. "I'm sorry." I said, almost in a whisper. "It worked though, didn't it?" I looked back at him, and his face was different, hurt almost. Did I really hurt him that much? I assumed it would be best for both of us, that way we wouldn't have to see each other until he moved out.

He scoffed. "Only because you felt guilty and called it off. Otherwise, you would be shut in your bedroom right now and the only way we'd communicate was through sticky notes."

I smiled, remembering the notes. Even after shutting him out, Gabriel still went out of his way to cook for me and talk to me in a way that wouldn't be face to face.

"Okay." I breathed out. "Sorry. I was wrong, I should have never created that schedule. Are you happy?"

He scanned over my face for a while before dipping his chin. I finally brought a spoonful of ice cream to my mouth and smiled. This gesture was really sweet, and now I felt even guiltier. But this ice cream was helping a little. Ice cream fixed everything.

"Good?" He asked.

I nodded. "Delicious." Gabriel was leaning over the kitchen island watching me eat the ice cream. His eyes were intense as he watched the spoon enter my mouth. I gulped. "Want some?" I asked.

He shook his head. "Nah, I don't like it."

I narrowed my eyes at him. "Have you ever tried it before?"

He looked at the bowl and then his eyebrows raised a little. "No, actually, I haven't."

I scooped some up on my spoon and handed it over to him. He brought

the spoon up to his mouth and tasted the ice cream, his eyes never leaving mine. I didn't want to break eye contact, I couldn't stop my mind from thinking about his lips, keeping eye contact was the only thing stopping me from staring at them, leaning closer and kissing them.

I saw his eyes flutter for a second. "You're right." He said, licking his lips as he looked at me intensely, I could hardly breathe. The way he was looking at me was intoxicating, I had never seen that look from him before. I squeezed my legs together to ease the ache. "Best thing I've tasted." He placed the spoon back into the bowl and made his way over to the dishes in the sink.

CHAPTER TWELVE

My mind was drifting where I didn't want it to go.

Allie was talking about her weekend away with Charlotte. Something about going to a gallery in Los Angeles. Normally I'd be listening, wanting to live vicariously through her, but currently my brain was affecting all logical thinking and letting my thoughts drift into stupidity like hope.

Last night had been a step forward in mine and Gabriel's... friendship? And what did I do? Overthink everything he said and did. What could this mean? What did he mean when he said that? What was that look that lingered on my eyes a second too long? I couldn't let myself get distracted by foolish thoughts. He was being nice instead of being his usual asshole self, and my mind was twisting that into possibly meaning more.

I couldn't do that. I wouldn't do that.

For my own sanity, I had to let this go.

"And then she spilled wine all over herself." Allie said, her voice snapping me out of my thoughts.

I shook my head, blinking at her, trying to remember what she had just been talking about. I forced a smile on my face and nodded at her, trying to make it seem like I hadn't just drifted off into thought and practically ignored everything she had just said.

Allie narrowed her eyes at me. "You didn't hear a single word of what I just said, did you?" Her eyes held my gaze until I snapped my eyes closed. Busted.

"I'm sorry." I sighed. "I just...got lost in my thoughts."

She took a sip of her coffee and nodded, sympathetically. "Mhmm, Gabriel still giving you a hard time?" She asked, as she sat back in her chair.

I winced. I hated how she knew how much Gabriel affected me, she always knew whenever I looked off or bothered, it had something to do with Gabriel. Everything else in my life was pretty great but this one guy, got under my skin like nobody else.

"Not exactly." I said, hiding my guilty face with my mug, drinking my tea.

Her eyes shot up and she leaned forward, with an eager grin. "Interesting, so there's been some development with Chef Anderson. Details, please."

I rolled my eyes at her and stifled a smile. "Nothing like that, we're just in a better place, we're actually getting friendly that's all."

"Uh huh, friendly as in fuck buddies or…"

I swatted her hand. "Allie, stop." I couldn't help but laugh. Allie was someone who looked sweet as a cherry when you looked at her, but as soon as she comfortable with someone, she had a dirty mouth and would make innuendos whenever the chance arose. I guess growing up with three brothers, she had learned it from them.

"I told you it's not like that." I continued. "He doesn't like me at all, trust me. His girlfriend was the polar opposite of me." Which was true. Lucy was blonde, tall, and carried a chest that made even me drool.

I had only met her once when Zaria and I ran into Lucy at one of our shopping dates. Zaria had met Lucy before but seeing as Gabriel and I hated each other at the time —

especially after the argument at Christmas — I had no reason to be introduced to his girlfriend.

Lucy was an influencer and quite successful too with over 500k followers, she and Gabriel made a gorgeous pair. I hated to admit that, but it was true.

"Plus, a few weeks ago we couldn't stand to be in the same room as each other, we're just making the best out of the situation, being friendly with each other so that we can live together without committing homicide."

Allie smiled, knowingly, but luckily, she didn't continue. She just nodded. "Ok, I won't pry."

"Plus, he's still annoying." Gabriel still managed to get on my nerves, even with the progress we had been making, sometimes he would drop a little dig here and there, but it was nothing like it was before.

"Who's annoying?"

Crap.

Creepy Chad was hovering over our table and approaching the empty seat beside me. I shifted my eyes to Allie and widened them. We both couldn't stand him. He was the biggest flirt I had ever met, but it was never reciprocated. Chad was in his early thirties, standing a few inches taller than me, and had dirty blonde hair.

He was a gym teacher, so he kept in pretty good shape, he wasn't ugly, per se, but I wasn't interested. That didn't matter to Chad, he was creepy, given the nickname Allie and I would address him by — whenever he wasn't near of course — and would find ways to touch women any way he could.

He would put his hand on my hips when he was trying to get past me, even if there was plenty of space. He would hit on me and most of the other teachers very obviously and didn't take no for an answer. No matter how many times I had turned him down, that didn't stop him from coming over and flirting or asking me out.

"No one." Allie and I had said in unison.

"Hmm, ok. Gossiping, I won't ask any more questions."

I inwardly rolled my eyes.

"So, Melissa." I pressed my lips into a tight smile, not turning my head to look at him. "Are you going to the school dance on Friday."

How did I want to answer this question? Did I want to be honest and say yes or lie and then get caught red handed in my bullshit if he was there. I looked up at Allie and she shrugged, slightly. Truth it was.

"Um, yeah." I said, still facing forward, my eyes locked on Allie's. "Allie and I are chaperones." Allie glared at me, cursing me for calling her out and I scrunched my nose at her. *Sorry*.

Allie had also been on the receiving side of Chad's unwanted advances — even being married and gay — and I didn't want to push her under the bus. The thought hadn't occurred to me, and I just hoped Chad would leave us alone.

"That's great." He grinned, spreading his arms across the chair. "Would you like to be my date to the dance?"

I let my eyes close for a second. A date? I mean, this was work, technically. We were there to chaperone the kids at the dance, not to bring dates.

"Oh." I shifted, uncomfortably. "I didn't know you were going."

He snorted and I could see his body turn to face me. "Yeah, most of the teachers are going, Newman insisted that she wanted as many of us as possible to be there, apparently some of us aren't pulling our weight when it comes to helping out with extracurriculars." He rolled his eyes like that was ridiculous.

I scoffed. Yeah, most of the time Allie and I were the only volunteers.

"So would you like to be my date?" He repeated.

I looked up at Allie and swallowed. She had her hand over her mouth, assessing the situation. It wasn't like she could save me from this. I sighed and turned my head to look at Chad. He had a shit-eating grin, and I squinted my eyes. "I'm just going there to chaperone the kids, so-"

"Yeah." He scoffed, again. "Me too, I just figured we could go together, and hopefully we could get to know each other better."

I breathed out. He couldn't take a hint, it didn't matter how direct I was with him, he wouldn't accept that I didn't want to go on a date with him, now or in the future. "No, thank you." I didn't like being confrontational, especially with someone like him who's demeanor made me uncomfortable.

He clasped his hands together, setting them on the table and shrugged. "I don't see why not, we're two colleagues, and there are no anti-fraternization policies"

I sighed. I knew he wouldn't let this go. I faltered and looked down at my lap. I was annoyed and just wanted him away from me.

"She has a boyfriend."

I lifted my head and stared at Allie, who had blurted that out. My eyebrows shot up, widening my eyes and my mouth dropped open.

What?

Why did she blurt that out? I didn't have a boyfriend.

"Huh. Is this true?" Chad asked, frowning at me. He seemed like he was disappointed, maybe he would stay away if he thought I wasn't available. I kept my gaze on Allie as she signaled with her eyes to go along with it.

"Yes." I lied. "I have a boyfriend, so I can't be your date." I bit away the 'sorry' that was on the tip of my tongue. I had nothing to be sorry for, even if he thought I was single, a simple 'no' should have sufficed.

"Well." He leaned back into his chair, clearly finding this amusing. Maybe I was wrong, and he wouldn't falter, he could possibly think this was just a tactic to make him jealous, or he could think this was competition. I swallowed and turned to face him. His face was painted with a smug tilt of his lips as he looked from Allie to me. "You should bring him."

Huh?

"You should bring your boyfriend to the dance on Friday." He explained.

Was he serious?

"Oh, um…" I stuttered. "I'm sure he's busy." I said, thinking of an excuse as to why I couldn't bring my boyfriend to the dance. I couldn't possible enter holding air, cause my 'boyfriend', didn't exist.

"Oh, c'mon. It's on Friday night at seven, I'm sure he can swing by."

I resisted the urge to groan. He just didn't know how to let it go. God damn it. How was I supposed to get out of this now?

"Um, sure, I'll ask him." I didn't know what I would do to get out of this.

He stood up and rubbed his hands together. "I can't wait to see the lucky bastard who shares a bed with Melissa Trevisano." I wrinkled my nose in disgust. I didn't want him thinking about my bed, or me for that matter.

Chad turned his back and made his way out of the teachers' lounge. I relaxed, knowing he was gone, and instantly groaned at what the hell just happened here. A boyfriend? How was I ever going to pull that off?

I turned to look at Allie and groaned, leaning forward, letting my head hit the table.

"I know, I'm sorry babe."

I lifted my head to look at her and my eyes softened at her apologetic expression. I sighed. "It's fine, I mean it worked, right?" I laughed.

How was I supposed to make this work though? A fake boyfriend? Where would I find one of those? I couldn't just not show up, I had already committed to it. If I came without anyone, Chad would get suspicious and know I was lying, and his advances wouldn't stop. I closed my eyes and sat up straight. "How am I supposed to find a fake boyfriend in two days?"

Allie reached over and caressed my hand, I was screwed. There was no way out of this. Allie gasped and I narrowed my eyes at her.

"You could try tinder." She said. I scoffed, really? Tinder? The only guys on tinder were looking for hook-ups and easy sex. There was no way I would find someone willing to help me. "I mean, they'd probably want something in exchange for it." She grinned gesturing to my body with her hands.

I looked down at my tits and back up at her, narrowing my eyes at her. "I'm not sleeping with a stranger so he can help me with a favor."

She shrugged and went back to considering ideas, I mean, this was her fault after all.

"Wait," I told her. "You have three brothers, surely one of them could be my fake date."

She shook her head. "Sorry, they're all married or in relationships."

I squinted my eyes at her. "Emphasis on the fake. I'm not looking for a match-up, I just need someone to keep up pretenses so that Chad doesn't get suspicious."

She laughed. "I know Melissa, but do you want to explain to their wives that a hot single girl wants to take them out on a 'fake date' to scare off a guy at work?" She held her hands up, shaking her head. "I'm not trying to get my eyes clawed out by my sisters in law." She squinted, pointing at me. "And neither do you."

"You're right." I breathed. I couldn't very well expect their wives to be ok escorting someone they've never met. No matter how good their relationship was, it was a risk most women didn't want to take, not that I'd ever steal anyone's husband, but they didn't know me or had any reason to trust me.

"I really am sorry I got you into this mess."

I sighed. "I know, I'll figure it out." Whatever that meant. I had no idea how I was ever going to come up with a solution. Either ask someone to be my fake boyfriend or find a real date and beg him to pretend we were madly in love.

CHAPTER THIRTEEN

Online dating was the worst.

Picture after picture of guys either holding up a fish or flexing at the gym. I rolled my eyes at myself. The bio's didn't help at all, most of them listing their height or how much they could bench press.

Some, portraying a list of desirable attributes they were looking for in a woman, and if you didn't match their checklist, don't even bother swiping right. The most common being a joke about their dicks or bragging about sex.

Swipe left.

My eyes started to glaze over with boredom. I had spent over an hour sat on the couch, trying to find somebody decent enough that I could take as my fake boyfriend to the school dance on Friday. So far, no contenders.

This plan was so incredibly stupid, I didn't know why I was going along with it. It wasn't like I had any more options though, so tinder it was. Somehow, I had managed to find a few profiles that didn't completely disgust me, and swiped right, only to be disappointed when the messages rolled in.

Hey sexy, need a seat? My face is available.

You horny?

The human body has 206 bones, want me to give you another one?

Endless messages that made my body cringe and solidified the reasoning by my lack of a dating life. This was hopeless. There was no way I was going to find somebody who would help me with a favor for nothing in return. I threw my phone aside and lay down on the couch, facing the ceiling. What was I going to do? I could just show up at the dance alone, but then creepy Chad would know I was lying. I doubted a boyfriend would stop him from hitting on me any chance he could get, but it was worth a try.

♡

My eyes fluttered open as my surrounding came into focus. I blinked the sleepiness away from my eyes and opened them.

I glanced around and realized I was lying on the couch covered in a blanket, with my feet propped up on Gabriel's legs whilst he was watching tv.

This was way too close for comfort. We had just started being... whatever the hell we were. Friends, acquaintances, normal roommates.

I scooted away from his lap and sat up straight, putting some distance between us on the couch. This seemed too intimate for someone who was already having a hard time controlling my breathing around him.

"Hi." I croaked when he made eye contact with me, noticing I was awake.

He chuckled. "Hi back. Sleep well?"

I nodded. "Yeah, I haven't had a nap in ages. I didn't even realize I had fallen asleep." I scrunched my nose, from embarrassment, cheeks burning, and looked up, back at him. "Thank you, by the way."

"For what?"

My head tilted at him. "For the blanket. I know I didn't have one before I drifted off, *hence*, it must've been you who covered me with one." I said rubbing my arm, it was definitely starting to get cold, and I hadn't thought about the fact I was wearing a tank top and sleep shorts and hadn't bothered to get myself covered, or into bed. "And for laying me down. I would have gotten a kink in my neck if I woke up with my head hanging on my shoulder."

His gaze stayed locked on mine, for a few seconds he was silent and then he waved a hand. "It was no big deal, trevi, you were occupying my sacred tv watching space *hence* I had to move you." His lips turned up slightly, in a smile.

I laughed. "You know, it's my sacred tv watching space too."

He shook his head. "You were asleep, you weren't watching tv."

I reached for my phone and saw that it was after eight pm. That meant I had been asleep for three hours, which didn't qualify as a nap. I sat back and glanced over at Gabriel. "So, what are we watching?" I asked.

He shrugged. "I don't know, any requests?"

"Anything but horror." I informed him. I cannot and will not watch horror films, no matter how much Zaria, the horror movie enthusiast, tried to persuade me into watching them.

"What? Horror movies are the best." Gabriel called out. Of course, he and Zaria would both be horror fanatics. Oh god, I was living with psychopaths.

I turned to face him and glowered at him. "Don't even think about it. I'm not watching a horror film. End of discussion."

"Nah, you're going to sit here and watch this with me. C'mon trevi, I've been putting myself through torture enduring those annoying reality shows you demand to watch. It's my turn now." Asshole. I knew he wouldn't let this go.

"You didn't seem to mind the reality shows the other day." I grinned. "Give it up Gabriel, we know you love them."

He smirked. "So where did we settle on the horror movie?" He asked, smiling like he had just won the lottery.

"Nope. I'm not watching it. I'm leaving then, you can watch it by yourself, I'm not joking Gabriel." I shifted to get up from the couch, I guess I could get out of the house and go for a walk or just stay in my room. I felt a hand wrap around my wrist, and I looked over to see Gabriel holding me down. My skin was on fire, his touch burning into my memory. I gulped.

"Stay." His insistent stare burned into my eyes. "I'll put something else on."

"It's fine, you can watch the film I'll just leave."

He shook his head. "No, I don't want to watch it alone, I want you here with me."

I sucked in a deep breath and freed myself from his hold. I wanted to be here with him too. So badly. "Fine." I said, sitting back down. I felt a hand around my waist as Gabriel pulled me closer to him. My head laid against his hard pecks.

What was happening? My heart was pounding against my chest. He pressed a light kiss against my hair, and I closed my eyes and inhaled deeply.

"I can hold you like this if you want, I don't want you getting scared." He whispered, I could feel his breath on the top of my head, and I closed my eyes.

My heart was beating so fast, could he feel it? I hoped not, this was embarrassing. I couldn't stay here, as much as I wanted to, it felt too weird. Too... good? I lifted myself up and shifted away from him. "No, it's fine. Just choose another film." I scrunched up my nose and looked at him embarrassed. I could feel my cheeks burning up, hopefully, it wasn't noticeable.

I could see his jaw clench and then unclench as he licked his bottom lip. He nodded, silently and turned back to tv going through the movie catalog again. I couldn't take my eyes off him, I could still feel his hand wrapped around my wrist, his arms wrapped around my waist, his hard chest underneath my head, his lips pressed softly against my hair. I wanted to know what he tasted like, what he kissed like. What his chest felt like pressed up against mine.

Gabriel continued scrolling through the movies until he landed on an action movie. He glanced over at me, waiting for my approval and I looked at him with disgust. "Really? An action movie?"

He laughed. "What, not a fan?"

I shook my head, sighing. "They're not exactly my favorites. I'm more of a chick flick kind of girl."

"Tough." He said, turning back to the tv. "You said it was my choice."

I let out a dramatic sigh and leaned back into the couch. "It's fine, we can watch this," I turned my head, a doe-eyed expression on my face. "If you want."

He chuckled. "You're such a brat." He faced the tv and continued watching the movie, not taking the bait. I frowned in defeat, I guess we were watching an action movie... yay.

D*ing*
Ding
Ding

I looked up at Gabriel, wondering where that noise was coming from, he looked at me and tilted his head down, gesturing to my phone that sat on the coffee table.

Ding

Before I could sit up and reach for my phone, Gabriel beat me to it, grabbing my phone and reading the notifications on the screen. His jaw dropped and his eyebrows shot up. He threw his head back, laughing at whatever he saw. That caught my attention.

I sat up, hastily and tried to retrieve my phone from him, but he swatted my hand away. "What is it?" I asked. I didn't know who could be messaging me, maybe Zaria, but why would that elicit a reaction from Gabriel?

Gabriel's eyes were scanning my phone whilst his shoulders bounced from the laughter. What the hell was on my phone?

"Gabriel." I called out, waiting for an explanation.

"Josh says 'hey hot stuff, I'll help you with your favor… if you help me with mine. My penis.'" Gabriel started doubling over, erupting in laughter and I was too stunned to speak. Oh my god, not only did I receive a gross message from a random creep online, but I also now had Gabriel reading it out loud.

I tried to snatch my phone back, but he turned his body, using his back as a shield. "Give me my phone."

He ignored me completely and continued reading the messages off my phone "Landon says 'Hey, teach. I'm a naughty boy and you look like the kind of girl I need to teach me a lesson.'" He snorted. "Smooth, dude."

This was too humiliating, I should have never joined an online dating app. "Gabriel, give me fucking phone now!" I yelled out. "It's not funny, just give it to me."

He shook his head and held me back, pinning his back to my front. "No way, this is too good."

"Dipshit!" I shouted, "This is an invasion of privacy, give me my phone back now."

He turned around, his face still painted with a grin as he placed the phone into my hands. I sighed, relieved but Gabriel's laughter didn't stop.

"Why are you on tinder?" He asked, still laughing at the messages he read.

"None of your business." I spat back.

"What favor did you need help doing?" He said, arching his eyebrow.

"Oh, shut up, it's nothing like that." Of course, Gabriel would automatically think of something dirty.

"Then what is it?"

I bit the inside of my cheek and put my phone on silent. I didn't want any more embarrassing messages coming through. "I needed help with something for Friday." I told him.

"Need help with what? Maybe I could help."

I scoffed and laughed at him. "No, you can't help."

There was no way I was about to announce to Gabriel that I was too pathetic, that I had to find a fake date for an event to scare off a creepy gym teacher.

"And why not? What is this favor?"

"Doesn't matter. Let's watch the movie." I picked up the remote and turned the volume on higher.

Gabriel didn't let me avoid the subject. He snatched the remote from me and muted the tv. He turned to me, his eyes burning into mine, I had never seen him look so intense before.

"Melissa." He sighed. "Talk to me, what do you need help with? Is it... is it serious?" He asked. His jaw clenched as his eyes drifted to my stomach, and I flinched back.

"I'm not pregnant." I spat.

He sat back and sighed in relief. "Fucking hell woman, tell me what it is, I'm thinking of all the worst possible scenarios right now."

I sighed and rolled my eyes, fine. "I need a date... more like a fake boyfriend for a school dance on Friday."

His brows furrowed and he tilted his head. "Why, exactly?"

I let out a deep breath and closed my eyes for a second before opening them again. "Because there's this creepy gym teacher who works at the school and won't stop hitting on me, even after I reject him time and time again." I ran my hand through my hair and continued. "He asked me to go with him to the school dance as his date, we're both chaperoning, as well as a bunch of other teachers. I rejected him, but he wouldn't take no for an answer and Allie blurted out that I had a boyfriend, and now he wants to meet said boyfriend."

Gabriel's eyes turned black, and his jaw clenched. "Do you need me to teach him a lesson?"

"Calm down rocky." I chuckled. "I just need to find someone that can pretend to be my boyfriend on Friday, that's all. That's why I was on tinder, but that was a mistake, as you can see." I huffed out a laugh.

"I'll go with you."

What? I must have not heard that right. Gabriel Anderson volunteering to help me with no ulterior motive? There was no way.

I laughed at him. "You can't be serious?"

"Why not?" He retorted.

I snorted. "Because why the hell would you help me?"

He shook his head. "Got any other options?" He asked.

No.

But I wouldn't be that desperate that I would bring my best friend's brother, who just a week ago couldn't stand me, to be my fake boyfriend in front of all my colleagues.

When I didn't reply, he continued. "Maybe Josh can be your date to the dance. I'm sure he'd be more than happy to help you as long as you stick your hands down his pants." He scoffed and then continued "Or maybe Landon, he might just let you spank him if he ends up being a bad date." He glowered at me. "Or maybe-"

"Okay." I interrupted him. "I get your point. But this doesn't change anything, I can find someone else to go with me, you don't have to go."

He leaned back into the couch and closed his eyes, letting out a heavy sigh. "You are the most stubborn woman I've ever met." His eyes opened and his head turned, to face me. "I offered to help you trevi, why not accept it?"

I shrugged. "I don't want to be your charity case and then have to owe you for it."

That was a lie.

I couldn't handle being around Gabriel pretending we were dating, touching, being close to each other. It was too dangerous, I needed to keep distance between me and Gabriel.

He laughed, but there was no humor in his voice. "What?"

I shrugged at him.

"Charity case? I'm helping you out Melissa, you don't owe me anything." He closed his eyes and rubbed a hand down his face. "Christ. How horrible must I have been to you to make you question me? To make you think I'd take advantage of you needing help just to hold it over your head for my own personal gain."

I knew he wouldn't do something like that, it wasn't Gabriel. He was an asshole and made jokes, but he wouldn't do that, it was a shitty thing to say. "I didn't mean that, I just meant... shit, that was fucked up, I know you wouldn't do something like that."

His eyes softened and he dipped his chin. "So, let me help you. It's not like you have any other options as we've established."

I sighed. "Fine, you're right."

He laughed. "Pigs must be flying right now. I never thought I'd hear those words from Melissa Trevisano." He placed his hand on his chest, dramatically. "I'm shocked."

I narrowed my eyes and shot him a tight smile. "Stop being a jackass. I said you're right, I need your help."

He smirked and locked his hands behind his head, stretching out his legs onto the coffee table. He was smug about this, and I hated it. "Of course, you do, trevi. This is going to be fun." He turned his head to look at me and flashed a toothy smile.

Arrogant asshole. I couldn't believe I just agreed to this, this was going to be anything *but* fun.

CHAPTER FOURTEEN

I was going to kill Gabriel.

"Get off your phone." I barked.

He barely lifted his head. "Hm?"

I shook my head, cursing under my breath. I knew this was a mistake, asking Gabriel for help, well, technically I didn't ask. But trusting him with this, was stupid. I should have known he wouldn't take this seriously, if he thought he could just walk into the school on Friday and wing it, he was wrong. We needed to be prepared.

Unfortunately for me, he was staring down at his phone, not paying attention, and it was up to me to make sure he knew exactly what to say and do.

"Gabriel. did you hear what I said?"

"Yeah, sure I got that."

The bastard wasn't even listening. I needed to get his attention. I picked up a pillow from the couch and lunged it at his head. He flinched and his eyes, finally, met mine.

"Hey." He called. "Stop being aggressive."

I hid my grin and sighed, walking over to the kitchen, where he stood, having his afternoon coffee. "Can you please pay attention? This was your idea, I told you I didn't want you to do this, and you insisted."

He groaned, clearly annoyed, and put his phone away. "Fine, what do you need?"

"I need someone who isn't completely incompetent but unfortunately for me, that isn't happening anytime today."

He laughed. "Got it, you're pissed."

"It's more than." I exhaled. "The dance is tomorrow, and we need to get our stories straight, so no one suspects it's fake."

His eyes squinted. "I thought this was just to scare away one person." He said, taking a sip of his coffee.

I nodded. "It is. But the other teachers will be there too, and they'll want an introduction, especially the older teachers. They'll be too mesmerized by all that." I said, gesturing to his body. My eyes lingered on his muscles, still visible under the white t-shirt he was wearing.

He cleared his throat and my eyes snapped back to his face. I could feel the heat rising to my face the longer I went without saying anything.

The asshole smirked. "Seems like you're mesmerized too trevi."

Too embarrassed to say anything I walked closer to the kitchen island and scoffed. "You wish." *Liar*.

I ignored his quiet laughing and made my way to the kitchen island, sitting on the stool.

"You know, you shouldn't drink coffee," I said. "It stunts your growth."

"Where did you hear that?" He snickered.

"Clueless."

He laughed, shaking his head. "That's a myth."

My mouth dropped open. "It is?" I asked, in disbelief.

He brought his mug to the kitchen island, where he stood. He took a sip, antagonizing slow, licked his bottom lip, and smiled. "I don't seem to have that problem."

"Maybe you do somewhere else." I teased.

He placed his mug on the table and took a step closer. He looked down at his crotch, forcing my eyes to land on that part of him too. His eyes lifted to mine, and he smirked. "Is that a challenge?"

I narrowed my eyes at him. "I'd have to put my glasses on for that."

He approached the kitchen island, "I don't think that would be necessary."

I rolled my eyes. "Maybe your big ego is compensating for something." He took a step closer, and I stood up, backing away from him.

Gabriel took another step, closing the gap between us and I gulped. This was not what I was expecting. I was playing with fire. "Are you backing down, trevi?"

Yes.

"No." I gulped again. "I'm just done with this conversation."

His eyes met mine and he nodded, taking a step back. "Okay, Melissa. I'll let you off the hook." He turned, walking over to the sink. I sat back down at the island, my eyes still on Gabriel. He reached the sink and his head turned back around, his eyes locked on mine "For now."

I exhaled, relieved to be free of this conversation. I didn't know what I was thinking. I never spoke like that, I didn't tease or flirt. Wait, was I flirting with Gabriel? I shook my head, placing my notebook on the island and opened it. I wasn't going to think about it anymore, we needed to get through this.

"Oh great." He mumbled, sitting at the island next to me. "My favorite notebook."

Gabriel was still upset about the schedule situation, and I still felt guilty. I cleared my throat and opened to a page that had the talking points listed.

"What's all that?" He asked. gesturing to the page.

"Things we need to know about each other. People talk and ask questions, we can't go in unprepared and wing it, what if there's incoherence's and Chad catches on?"

"Chad." He chuckled. "You said he was a gym teacher? I can already picture what he looks like from the name alone."

I smirked. "Ok humor me. What does he look like?"

"He's got that surfer look from California, his hair is always styled in a messy look but secretly took him longer than it takes you to do your hair." He said, pulling on a strand of my hair. "He's a blond, of course, but more of a dirty blond and he probably has muscles in his biceps but neglects his skinny legs."

My jaw dropped open. Unbelievable. "How did you know that?" I asked.

He grinned. "I looked him up after you said he was giving you a hard time."

I swatted him on the arm. Of course, he did. "You didn't say anything to him, did you?"

If Gabriel messaged him this wouldn't be good. I mean, Chad deserved someone telling him to back the fuck off, but it would look like I went to my 'boyfriend' and complained about my co-worker. I would hate for someone to think I couldn't handle my own problems.

Chad hadn't said anything, but he also had barely spoken to me since I turned him down, just a quick hello in the halls. Which was definitely what I wanted.

He shook his head. "No, I'm not stupid. Don't worry, I'll make sure he gets the fact that you're unavailable and he should back off.

"Except it's not a fact. It's very much fiction." I reminded him.

He focused on my face for a little too long before shrugging. "Regardless, I'll make sure he leaves you alone, and if he doesn't," He clenched his jaw. "I'll be breaking his skinny legs."

I laughed and shook my head, turning back to the notebook. "Okay, number one. Let's start with the basics. What's your favorite color?"

He laughed, shaking his head. "Favorite color? Who's going to ask that?"

I shrugged. "You never know." These questions might have a little more to do with the fact I wanted to know more about Gabriel and not so much about the rest of the people there, but he didn't have to know that.

"Hmm... blue."

I scoffed. "That's such a typical boy answer."

He snorted. "And your favorite color is pink, that's a typical girl answer."

I put my hand up to stop him "No, actually, misogyny has made women hate pink because it's associated with being girly and therefore being weak and fragile. Pink is a powerful color, and I won't be ridiculed for liking it."

He chuckled and placed his hand on his chest. "You're hurting my ego trevi. I was joking. Do you really think I'm that shallow? You're right it's a badass color."

I smiled. "Thank you. So, why blue then?"

"Blue's my favorite color because it reminds me of the ocean. I go to the beach a lot. Sometimes I just go out there and sit, looking out at the sea for hours."

I stayed quiet for a moment, appreciating his explanation. "Wow, that's actually…deep." I sneered and shook my head. "Didn't think it was possible with you." I teased.

"Yeah, well. We already know you don't know me, there's more to me than just a hot bod." He flashed a huge grin.

"And modesty is, for sure, one of them." I answered, dryly.

"Exactly, now you're getting it." He remarked, completely ignoring my sarcasm. "Okay, what else?"

I scanned over the list. "Umm… what's your favorite food? I know you're a chef, so you probably have lots of favorites, but if you only had to choose one thing to eat for the rest of your life, what would it be?"

He laughed. "Yeah, I guess I do have a lot of favorites." He scratched his beard. "But if I was to choose one, that I would choose to eat forever, it would be my mom's cooking. Her Piri-Piri chicken, and jollof rice."

I gasped. "Oh my god, yes. Every time she would make that, my mouth would water for days afterwards." I closed my eyes reminiscing on the days I would eat over at their house. I was so fond of the days I spent with the Andersons. Mrs. Anderson was a great cook and any time I would stay over at their house, she would be more than happy to feed me.

I always felt like I over stepped a boundary and felt like a burden. More often than not, I went back home, earlier than

I wanted to, not wanting to overstay my welcome, but Mrs. Anderson never made me feel like I was unwanted in her house and my heart warmed anytime she would be around.

Mr. and Mrs. Anderson became my second parents after I met Zaria, especially after my dad died, I was alone, completely alone. I knew I had cousins, but they were all in Italy and I had never met them or the rest of my family. All I was aware of was, my dad had an argument with his family and moved to America, and never spoke to them again.

The only other member of my dad's family I had met, was my nonna. She only visited a handful of times, and I didn't even know her name, my dad just told me she was nonna. She was kind and quiet, and whilst she was here, she told me stories about my dad's childhood in Italy. She met my mother once,

I was around nine and it was the first time she visited.

My mom left us two weeks after my eleventh birthday, I hardly remember her. Sometimes I have dreams of old memories, but none that I visibly remember when I'm awake. Maybe it was my way of not letting myself think of her, so I wouldn't miss her.

After that, it was just me and my dad, he was a great dad, so I didn't have any complaints in that area. But once he got sick, I knew I would be alone. His disease was too advanced, and he was withering away too quickly. He became a shell of the man I used to know, and it broke my heart.

"I miss Naomi's cooking." I added.

He looked at me with a serious expression, that I couldn't really figure out. "You didn't get to enjoy it last Christmas." He said, with a hint of sadness in his voice.

I bit the inside of my cheek and faced away from him. "I apologized to her. I just couldn't spend the day arguing with you anymore." He didn't know I had spent the morning at my father's grave, and that I was already on edge that day.

He sighed. "I'm sorry Melissa, it was a stupid prank, I didn't know you would take it so hard." He put his hand on my shoulder and gave it a shake, forcing me to look at him. I turned my head and faced him, his eyes searching mine, apologetically. "Really, Mel, I'm sorry."

Mel. My breath caught in my lungs. I could hear my heartbeat accelerate in the silence, I needed to snap out of this, this was too much for me. Too emotional. I couldn't do emotional, not with Gabriel, we were barely even friends.

I shook my shoulder out of his reach and laughed. "It's fine, really, I just got... annoyed that's all."

I could see his eyebrows pulled down, confused about my sudden change of demeanor, and then his face relaxed, and he tipped his chin, in a small nod of understanding. "Okay. Got it. So, do you want to move on?"

I raked a hand through my hair and forced a smile. "Sure, what else should I know?" I glanced at the list and picked another one of the topics we should discuss. "What's your favorite film?" I continued, moving on from the sore subject.

He looked down and a small smile was pulled on his lips. I looked at him, confused as to why he was embarrassed to tell me his favorite film. "What is it? Why are you embarrassed right now?"

"I'm not embarrassed, I just don't want you to give me shit for it."

"Why would I do that?" My eyes glistened with eagerness. "Tell me, I'm intrigued now." I gasped and my eyes widened. "Is it something girly that you're too macho to admit to, like legally blonde? Are you secretly an Elle Woods fan?" I asked him, a grin plastered on my face.

He laughed and shook his head. "No. it's not legally blonde, although, that film is iconic."

I dipped my chin in agreement. "Glad to know you have taste. So, what is it then?"

He sighed and looked at me. "It's Ratatouille."

I smiled at him. "That's not bad at all, why would you be embarrassed by that?" My eyes widened in realization. "Is that why you became a chef? Because of Remi the rat?"

"No. Maybe. Yes."

I laughed. "Oh my god, that is adorable. I can imagine thirteen-year-old Gabriel wanting a rat to pull on his hair to teach him how to cook."

"Okay see, this is why I didn't want to tell you, it *is* embarrassing. It's not the only reason though, yes, that started my dream of wanting to be a chef but after that, I would shadow my mom in the kitchen and watch her cook, she taught me and over the years it became my passion."

"That's sweet, the only thing I know how to cook is grilled cheese." I scoffed.

"Yeah, I know, this doesn't mean I'm your personal chef now, though, trevi. I'm very expensive."

"Sounds like you're a hooker." I sneered.

He looked at me and smiled provocatively. "Might as well be, from the sounds you make from my food."

I pulled my lips into a tight smile. "So humble, you never fail to amaze me."

"Thanks, I know, I'm pretty amazing."

I sighed. "Okay, let's end this here before your head gets too big and falls off your shoulders."

"Wait, where did we meet?"

"What do you mean? I met you when I went to Zaria's house for the first time, I was—"

"No." He cut me out with a laugh. "I mean, if people ask, what are we going to say? Where did we meet?" He explained.

"Oh, um… let's just say we met at the grocery store."

His nose wrinkled in disgust. "You watch chick flicks and that's the best you can come up with? Have you never heard of meet-cutes? That's bullshit. Let me think." He rubbed his beard and stared behind me, lost in thought. After a few minutes of agonizing silence his eyes lit up and he cleared his throat. "Okay, got it. We were at a bakery and we both reach for the last donut, it was a caramel donut with chocolate sprinkles, both our favorite flavor." He smiled. "Huh, how is that?"

"I hate caramel." I said flatly.

"Really, Mel. That's what you're focused on? Okay, what do you suggest?"

"Maybe, I was out, getting ice cream and it dropped to the ground and you came over and offered to buy me a new one, we locked eyes and instantly felt an attraction. You asked me out on a date, and we've been dating ever since."

He laughed. "What's your obsession with ice cream?"

I shrugged. "It was the first thing that came to mind."

He smiled, shaking his head. "Okay, that's not bad, we can go with that."

I let out a relieved sigh. "Thank God. You need to know things about me now. Just in case anyone asks."

He looked at me, for way too long, it must have been for about five seconds, but those five seconds stretched into eternity, having his dark brown eyes burn into mine. I felt my breath stuck in between my lungs, struggling to let it escape. He blinked, like he hadn't just stared into my soul, and shrugged. "I know you enough."

That snapped me out of whatever just happened, and I snorted. "Bullshit. You know nothing about me."

"I know you, Mel, I've known you for ten years." He argued.

I scoffed at him and clasped my hands together in front of me. "Okay, I'll bite. What exactly do you know about me?"

He looked into my eyes, once again and blinked a few times before he answered. "Well, we've established that your favorite color is pink, your favorite movie is home alone, and you watch it even when it's not Christmas, your favorite ice cream flavor is strawberry, and you hate caramel." He winked. "You get angry when people interrupt you, but you hate confrontation more than anything, so you don't speak up for yourself. You scrunch your nose when you get embarrassed about something, and you cry at proposal videos."

My heart stopped.

How did Gabriel know these things about me? Not even Zaria knew some of those things.

I blinked at him, too stunned to speak, my lips parted in shock. I stared at him, not knowing what to say, how to break the silence.

His lips curved in a small smile, and I shook my head. "How...what...huh?"

He laughed and then licked his lips, a smile sprouting his lips. "I pay attention." He said, matter of factly, like he hadn't just admitted to knowing every detail about me I thought nobody knew.

A breathy laugh escaped my lips, my eyes still stuck on his, my mouth was open, ready to say...something, anything. "How do you know any of that stuff?"

He shrugged and ran a hand through his beard before running it through his hair, too short to grab anything, he sighed and shook his head. "Mel, c'mon, I've known you since you were fourteen, you spent days, nights, weekends over at my house, of course I know you.

"Wow." Apparently, I had nothing to say, but that. My mind had gone blank.

"Melissa Trevisano... speechless. Never thought I'd see the day." He snickered.

My admiration defused and I narrowed my eyes at him. "You just ruined that." I laughed.

"Are we done? Now that we've established, I'm an expert in everything Melissa Trevisano." He grinned.

"Yes." I replied. "I think we're good,"

He stood up from the stool and looked down at me. "We'll make every teacher at that school drool from jealousy at the sight of us."

A weird feeling escaped my stomach and made its way down into my core. Hearing the word, *us* come out of Gabriel's mouth, made my mind wander where it shouldn't. The idea of us was so far out of reach, there was no point of me thinking about it. I smiled at him and nodded. I didn't trust myself enough to say anything else.

CHAPTER FIFTEEN

"Okay, let's do this," I muttered to the mirror, trying to get myself prepared for the night that lay ahead of me.

A night of lying to my co-workers, pretending to be dating Gabriel Anderson. Not that I hadn't thought of it.

I had.

A lot.

But it was never something I thought would be happening. My enemy, the player of Crestview High had willingly, offered to help me with this ploy, I was apparently going through with.

"This better work." I spoke to my reflection. I smoothed my hair, that I had straightened and applied my lip gloss.

I sighed and looked at myself in the mirror, fixing my dress, that I had chosen for tonight. A long sleeve black dress, ending at mid-thigh, with a square neckline. I bought this dress over a year ago, in case I had any dates to go to, but this dress remained, unworn in my closet. I shrugged at my reflection and a small smile escaped my lips. I didn't really get the chance to make up and dress up, it was nice.

"Hello? Are you done in there?" Gabriel asked, knocking on the bathroom door. I glanced at my phone and saw that we still had ten minutes until we had to be there, why was he in a rush?

"Almost." I called out.

"What could possibly be taking so long?" He asked, frustrated.

I rolled my eyes, annoyed at his lack of patience, and sighed at myself, fixing my makeup, responding with silence.

Knock

"Hello?"

I looked back at the door and ignored him, once again.

Knock

"Trevi. Answer me."

I let out a groan of frustration and opened the door. "What?" I asked.

He searched my face and then his eyes made their way down the length of my dress and back up to my face, his jaw clenched as his eyes were wide open.

"Yes?" I snapped my fingers in front of his face. "What did you want?" I asked him, placing my hand on my hip.

He shook his head as he looked down my body, once again.

"Is something wrong?" I asked him. His expression looked…weird? Maybe he thought it was a little much for a school dance, but I wanted to look nice, at least for a night.

His eyes made their way back to mine, and he licked his lips. My breath quickened at the sight of him, in a white button-down shirt, black jeans, and a black blazer. He looked so professional, so…good.

Unwillingly, I looked down at his body, appreciating how his clothes fit his figure, not loose, not too tight, fitting him perfectly in all the right places. His peck muscles were still visible through the light thickness of the shirt. I gulped and my eyes made their way back to his face, to find him staring at me with a mischievous smile.

"Like what you see?" He asked.

My eyes widened and I stepped back. "What... no." I replied, stunned.

He let out a laugh and his tongue hit the inside of his cheek. "Sure looks like it, the way you're devouring me in your head."

"Ew, no. I was just shocked seeing you without your clown costume for once, dipshit." I pushed him on his chest and automatically regretted it. I could feel his muscles underneath my touch and now my hands felt like they were on fire.

I put my hands behind my back and turned around, facing the mirror. I picked up my powder and lightly add some more, maybe I wouldn't need blush, the way my cheeks were red right now. I picked up my lip-gloss and put it in my bag, I looked up into the mirror and I could see Gabriel standing behind me looking at my reflection in the mirror. I could feel my face burning up again and looked down. He really did look good.

I sighed and turned around, giving Gabriel a tight smile, and then walked out of the bathroom, hitting his shoulder with mine on the way out.

"Oops." I said, biting my lip to mask my smile.

I tried to take a step, to make my way to the front door but I was stuck. I looked behind and saw Gabriel's hand wrapped around my wrist.

"What are you-"

He pulled me closer to him and leaned down until his mouth was next to my ear "Don't play with me, Melissa." Gabriel said, his voice deep and husky.

"I don't know what you're talking about." I replied. What did he mean by playing with him?

"You know exactly what you're doing, wearing that dress."

I looked up at him, eyebrows furrowed. I was so confused. I shook my wrist out of his hold and stepped back. "What do you mean by that? Are you saying I look bad?"

His eyebrows wrinkled in anger. Confusion? I wasn't sure. He shook his head slightly but then his face relaxed and he raked a hand through his hair, letting out a slight groan. "No. I just- don't worry about it."

What just happened? He sounded frustrated. Why was he angry? If he didn't want to go through with this plan, he shouldn't have offered. I just prayed to God that he wouldn't back down at the last minute.

"Do you not want to do it anymore? I could have found someone else, probably, if it makes you uncomfortable." I said, my voice slightly cracking.

"What? No. I didn't mean it like th— never mind, I don't want to quit this, I said I would help, and I will."

I looked up at him and narrowed my eyes, slightly, I couldn't see any hint that he was lying. I nodded my head. "Okay. Should we get going?"

He lifted his jacket sleeve and glanced at his watch. "Yeah, we have about five minutes before we need to be there." He gestured his head to the door. "Let's go."

I started walking towards the door, not very well. I was still getting used to wearing heels. I walked slowly, stumbling as I made my way. I was sure that with a little practice I could get the hang of it again. It would be fine.

"Is that what you're wearing?" Gabriel said, I turned my head seeing him behind me, his eyes widened at my clumsy form.

I glanced down at my shoes and back up at him, I shrugged. "Yeah. Why?"

He shook his head. "Nothing, be right back." He strolled into Zaria's room and confusion flooded my face. Why was he going into Zaria's room? I blinked and turned my head, making my way to the front door. I leaned into it, waiting for Gabriel to come back.

"Okay, let's go." He said, appearing by my side. He opened the door and pointed to the hallway with his hand, gesturing for me to go first.

I stepped out into the hallway and waited for him to close the door. It was time to go to this dance. Pretending wasn't really my strong suit, I just hoped I managed to do it well and that creepy Chad didn't catch on, and hopefully, this made him back off.

CHAPTER SIXTEEN

"Close the windows."

We had spent ten minutes in the car, mostly arguing.

"I like having the windows open." Gabriel said, opening them even more.

"And I would like to show up to this, not looking like I was in a fight with a deer." I opened the sun visor, sliding open the mirror inside. My eyes widened. My hair was a mess. I attempted to smooth it down as best as I could.

"You look fine." Gabriel muttered.

"Fine isn't exactly what I was going for." I rolled my eyes, looking back at the mirror.

He rolled up the window, leaving a little bit open. At least he compromised. "Is there someone you're trying to impress?" He asked. I glanced over to him, seeing his hands clutching the steering wheel and his jaw clenched.

"Only you." I scoffed, only slightly kidding.

Did I want Gabriel to look at me differently? Maybe.

He had always seen me as his little sisters' annoying best friend, who he hated, and I just wanted his attention. Especially when I was younger and had a crush on him. But this wasn't the same. I didn't have a crush on Gabriel. Yes, I found him attractive but there were no feelings involved... right?

He stayed silent, staring out at the road. I sighed, turning up the volume on the radio, which Gabriel turned back down.

"Why did you just do that?" I asked.

"I can't concentrate when the music is loud." He told me.

I groaned, letting my head fall back into the seat. The car was quiet, the music softly playing whilst the wind blew through the little crack, he had left open.

By the time we got to the school, I was ready for this night to be over. My mind worked overtime thinking of everything I needed to say and do to make this believable.

"Stop." My eyes snapped to his, seeing him look over at me. "Get out of your head, it's going to be fine." He said, as the car slowed down.

I bit the inside of my cheek. I hated how he knew what I was thinking. Was I that obvious?

I stepped out, shutting the car door behind me. "Let's just get this over with."

"Jeez, trevi, bring the excitement down a notch." He said, sarcastically.

I rolled my eyes at him and glanced into the car window, at my reflection. I took a deep breath in and exhaled, repeating this until I felt calm enough.

"Okay, we have some pretending to do." I forced a smile on my lips and walked towards him.

He extended his hand, and I took it, he linked his fingers with mine, making my stomach drop. I was holding Gabriel's hand. This felt too intimate, and I didn't want to do that, not with Gabriel, not when it wasn't real, but we had a show to put on.

"Oh, look. You're almost the same height as me." He remarked, grinning down at me. Gabriel was a tall man, standing at 6'5", he towered over me, but I wasn't short either, I had long legs that aided in my 5'8" stance. These heels added an extra three inches and Gabriel still stood taller than me. I'd have to go on my tip toes to kiss him. Wait, no thinking about kissing him.

I looked up at Gabriel who was staring down at me, his lips pulled up slightly in a smirk. I blinked at him, not being able to pull my eyes away from him. The moonlight made his face even more beautiful. I broke eye contact first, clearing my throat. "Let's go."

He pulled us forward and I was relieved I was holding onto Gabriel, because at this moment, I was leaning my whole weight on him, barely being able to walk in these heels.

We made our way to the doors and looked at each other, briefly, before opening them and walking inside. I lead the way into the gym and let out a deep breath before walking in.

"Hey." Gabriel whispered, so low, only I could hear. "It's going to be okay. We've got this."

I nodded and we walked in. The place was already set up and most of the students were already here, dancing in the middle of the gym. I smiled at the sight of them, this was why I volunteered most of the time, this was why I was a teacher.

My smile disappeared when I saw Chad walking towards me and Gabriel, waving a hand in the air to catch my attention. I quickly looked up at Gabriel and my eyes widened, trying to communicate with my face that the ruse was on. This was it. He looked back at me, squeezed my hand, and dipped his chin in acknowledgment.

I looked back at Chad and forced a smile on my lips, he made his way to us and looked back and forth between Gabriel and me.

"Hey, Melissa, glad you could make it." Chad called out, looking up and down my body, his eyes widening. That made my nose crinkle. I felt shivers travel down my body and now I wished I never wore this dress. "You look great, wow." His eyes remained glued to my chest.

I forced a humorless laugh, clearly uncomfortable and looked up at Gabriel.

"This is my boyfriend, Gabriel. Gabriel, this is Chad, the school's gym teacher." I introduced the two and hoped Chad bought it. Why wouldn't he? I mean, it wasn't like I would bring a fake date to avoid his unwanted advances, except that was exactly what I had done. Chad didn't know that though, so I shouldn't be this worried about him being suspicious about us.

Chad's eyes finally left me and moved to Gabriel. His posture straightening, like he was afraid of him. He extended a hand and Gabriel took it, the two shaking each other's hands.

"Nice to meet you, Chad." Gabriel said, in a voice an octave deeper than normal, maybe was playing the overprotective boyfriend card to scare Chad off, and honestly, I was completely okay with it. Hopefully Chad took the bait and got scared into never looking at me again.

"Nice to meet you too. So, you're Melissa's boyfriend... interesting."

To my side, Gabriel's eyebrows furrowed and so did mine, what did that mean?

"What does that mean?" I guess Gabriel could read my mind now.

Chad's eyes widened as he stepped back, clearly, he was intimated by Gabriel and realized what he had said. "Oh, nothing." He said, with a nervous laugh.

Gabriel and I looked at each other for a second, both of us confused and glanced back at Chad, waiting for him to explain.

"I just meant, you know, she's very closed off." He said, pointing at me. "I was just interested to see who could finally crack her open." I winced at that comment, knowing he meant it more than a metaphor.

I refrained from gagging in front of him, wanting to scream in his face that I wasn't closed off, I was just not interested in him, but I didn't.

"Oh... okay." Came from Gabriel. He clearly wasn't interested in keeping up conversation with Chad and I could relate. "Nice to meet you... um Chaz." He said, tugging my hand and walking away from him.

"It's Chad." Chad called out, behind us.

"Yeah, whatever." Gabriel muttered, still walking away.

I let out a small laugh and looked up at him. "That wasn't exactly the plan, the plan was to pretend we were dating, not to act like an ass."

He scoffed. "*He* was an ass, the way he was looking at you like you were his next meal made me want to punch him."

I chuckled. "Possessive, are we?"

He looked down at me and his eyes squinted. "Nah, I just wanted him to understand you were off limits."

"Hmm, okay." I said.

We made our way to the snack table, and I groaned at the lack of food. The dance had barely started, how was everything nearly gone? I picked up a slice of Pizza and Gabriel did the same.

I could see from the corner of my eye, some of the older teachers, huddled up and whispering, glancing over at us. I rolled my eyes and looked over at Gabriel, seeing him look back at where I was looking. "What's their deal?" He asked, without taking his eyes off them.

"Those are some of the older teachers. They gossip and talk about everything and anything. Obviously, tonight's conversation starter is us."

His eyes looked away from them and back to mine. "Then, let's give them something to talk about." He put his slice of pizza down and moved his hands to my waist.

I pushed him off, trying not to call attention to us and whisper hissed. "What are you doing?"

He furrowed his brows, and his eyes were looking at mine. "I was going to kiss you, I thought that's what you wanted, for me to pretend to be your boyfriend."

We should have talked about the rules before, I hadn't thought about that. I didn't want to kiss Gabriel. I mean, I wanted to kiss him, badly, but I didn't want it to be fake. I didn't want Gabriel to pity kiss me because I needed a favor. I wanted him to kiss me because he couldn't help himself, I wanted him to want me, but that was never going to happen.

I shook my head and looked down. "No. I don't want you to kiss me, I didn't think about it before, or I would have brought it up." I looked back at his eyes and sighed. "I just wanted you to pretend to be my boyfriend to make Chad back off, I don't want you to kiss me because of this." I gestured around the room.

He looked at me for what seemed like an eternity. His jaw clenched and his eyes turned black. Was he mad? He turned his head to the side and when he turned back, his expression was flat. "Fine." He spat out.

I was taken back by that response, not understanding why he seemed annoyed. I thought he would be happy about this, it meant he didn't have to do something he didn't want to.

"Hey babe." I turned my head and saw Allie approaching us, my smile immediately returned. She knew this was fake, so I didn't have to pretend with her. I rolled my shoulders back, relieved and opened my arms to embrace her with a hug.

"Hey, Allie." We embraced and when we came apart, her eyes travelled to Gabriel.

"And this is?" She asked. I had forgotten that she had never actually met Gabriel. I had talked her ear off about him but never actually showed her a picture of him before.

"Um, this is Gabriel." I said, nervously. I didn't know how she would react to me bringing Gabriel as my fake boyfriend. What if she blurted out my secret crush on him? I widened my eyes at her, trying to send secret signals for her to stay quiet about everything I had told her about him.

Her eyes widened and a smile spread across her face, she looked back at me, and her eyes were lit with mischief. "Gabriel, huh." My face remained expressionless as I hoped to God, she wouldn't say anything.

"Yeah, nice to meet you…?" Gabriel said, holding out his hand, ready to greet her.

"Allie." She finished, for him, greeting him with a handshake. Her eyes travelled down the length of Gabriel's body and made their way back to his eyes, she shook her head and chuckled. "Wow, Melissa's told me so much about you."

"Aww, honeybun, you been telling people about me?" He teased, failing at his ridiculous attempt to convince Allie he was my boyfriend.

Allie and I looked at each other for a second before we doubled over laughing.

"What? What's so funny?" Gabriel asked.

I turned to him, grinning. "Allie knows that this is fake. It was her idea."

"Yeah, honeybun." Allie said to Gabriel.

He looked at me and then looked at Allie. "Oh." Is all he said. He was quiet for a moment before he shook his head and chuckled. "Sorry, I just wanted to make it convincing."

"Oh, it was convincing all right." Allie called out, with a humorous tone in her voice.

I squinted my eyes at her because I knew what she was implying. In return she looked at me with the biggest smile on her face. She obviously was set on her theory that Gabriel liked me and I had to applaud him. He obviously made a good impression as my fake boyfriend if he got Allie to believe this was real. That meant that Chad believed it was real and would hopefully stay away.

"Melissa, sweetie, come over here." Deborah, one of the many teachers that were in the corner of the room, huddled together called out.

"Hmm, looks like you made quite the impression." Allie teased Gabriel.

I rolled my eyes and turned to face Gabriel. "Looks like we have some more pretending to do."

He smiled. "Yeah." He extended his hand and I looked over at Allie to see she was grinning so wide it looked like she had a hanger stuck in her mouth. She flashed me a toothy grin and I ignored her, reaching for Gabriel's hand, once again.

We made our way around the gym, introducing Gabriel to my other co-workers. He would put his arm around me and squeeze my shoulders when talking about our 'relationship' and my smile was real, so I didn't have to pretend on my end.

The practicing the night before had paid off, People had all kind of questions about Gabriel and our relationship, how we met, how long we were together and when a couple of the women pulled me off to the side asking questions about Gabriel, I had the answers ready.

This night felt like it lasted for an eternity. My feet were staring to hurt, and I was hungry, the lukewarm slice of pizza being the only food I had ingested. It had been over two hours since we had arrived, and I was more than ready to leave. There were more than enough teachers chaperoning here, which meant I didn't have to stay.

"Okay." I clapped my hands together. "The plan obviously worked, does that mean we can go now?" I asked Gabriel.

"We've been here for two hours." He pointed out.

I groaned and pulled him aside. I reached up to his ear and kept my voice low so no one would hear. "I'm tired, my feet are hurting, I'm hungry and I just want to get out of here." I told him. "We came here to show Chad that the boyfriend was in fact real, and we did that, can we *please* leave now?" I looked into his eyes, pleading him with my own.

His lips turned, ever so slightly, into a side smirk and he grabbed my hand "Sure, let's go."

I sighed, relieved. "Thank God."

He interlaced his fingers with mine, leading the way to the parking lot and my heart thumped against my chest. Having his fingers entwined with my own made it feel so tender, so intimate. There was no reason to be holding hands, there weren't any people around. I panicked and pulled my hand out of his and wrapped my arm around his. This felt more friendly than romantic, that was better than falling for hopeless expectations.

We continued our way towards his car and my feet were in so much pain I could barely make it. When we finally reached his car, I leaned into it and removed my shoes. Gabriel looked at me and chuckled, shaking his head. He opened the trunk of his car and pulled out some black flats.

My eyes widened, I recognized those shoes, they were Zaria's, that's what he got from Zaria's room?

"I knew you would need these." He admitted as he handed me the pair of shoes.

My heart thumped even louder against my chest, so loud, I was afraid he could hear it. I took in a deep breath, willing for it to stop beating so hard, but it was no use. Gabriel had been so thoughtful as to bring a pair of flats with him because he knew I would get uncomfortable in these heels.

Maybe I was wrong about Gabriel this whole time. Maybe, he wasn't as bad as I made him out to be in my head.

I bit the inside of my cheek to stifle a smile. I didn't want him to see how much that small gesture had made me smile.

"Thank you." I said, quietly, almost in a whisper.

He nodded his head and picked up my heels from the floor, he opened the car door and placed them in the back seat, and then opened the passenger side of the car, holding the door open, I took my seat and waited for him to close it.

This night wasn't so bad after all, maybe Gabriel and I could become friends. We made it through an entire night without arguing, granted, there were other people around, people that we had to convince of our relationship, but I could see us becoming actual friends.

He opened the car door for me, and I got in, letting out a breath of relief when my feet were no longer on the floor. The heels were definitely a mistake.

"So, you're hungry?" Gabriel asked, sitting in the driver seat.

I let my head hit the back of the seat and turned my head to look at him. "Starving."

He chuckled. "Ok then, let's go."

Gabriel put the car in drive, and I was more than ready to get home.

CHAPTER SEVENTEEN

"Wait, where are we going?" I asked.

I glanced around, seeing the unfamiliar surroundings, this wasn't the normal route to the apartment. Where the hell was he going?

"You said you were hungry. We're going to eat."

I groaned. "I want to go home." I was tired and done for the night. I wanted to peel this dress off my body and eat whatever I could find and climb into bed until I was buried in my sheets.

"And we will. Let's get some food in you first before you pass out."

I scoffed. "I won't pass out. Plus, you're a chef, why don't you make me food?"

He laughed, shaking his head. "I told you, I'm not your personal chef, you couldn't afford me honey."

I turned my head, looking out of the window. I didn't want him to see what that term of endearment did to my face. I was sure I was as red as a tomato and that wasn't a very flattering look.

My stomach grumbled after a few more minutes of driving and I grunted again.

"Stop complaining." He said. "We're almost there."

The car stopped a few minutes later and I glanced up seeing a diner I had never been to before. My go to was takeout so I didn't really get the chance to dine out in the city. The sign was lit up, neon red letters blinking spelling out 'Grub 'n' Stuff Diner.'

He opened the car door and I blinked at him. "I have to walk?" I asked him. My feet were on fire, even with the flats, the heels had done the damage and it was painful to walk in.

He laughed. "Just to the diner, it's less than thirty steps."

I blinked up at him. Thirty steps were too many.

"I mean… I could pick you up if you want." He grinned. "Throw you over my shoulder like I did the first night, when you were acting like a brat."

I sat up straight, facing him. "I wasn't acting like a brat. I wanted to watch tv in my apartment and you came barricading in and expecting everything to be your way like I would just submit to your every demand."

"You were being a brat." He retorted.

I sighed and opened the car door, wincing as soon as my feet hit the floor. I was tempted to take Gabriel on his offer to carry me inside. He made his way to me, letting my lean on him as we made our way to the diner, sitting in a booth near the window.

"Good evening, what can I get you?" The waitress stood above us with a notepad and pen in her hand, her eyes were focused on Gabriel.

She was beautiful, her face was youthful, most likely younger than me by a couple of years, her hair was blonde, pinned up neatly with an orange clip, matching her uniform. Her face was blushed with rosy cheeks and her eyes were blue and doe-eyed, which glistened as she smiled at Gabriel. I didn't blame her, he was handsome. Very handsome.

I bit the inside of my cheek and opened the menu in front of me. Why was I jealous? There was no reason to be jealous over someone who was nothing to me, we were barely friends. He was single now, he had every right to flirt with whoever he wanted.

"We're still looking, thanks." Gabriel said with a smile, and her cheeks flushed as she smiled back at him, making her dimple prominent.

I looked back down at the menu and scanned it, my mouth was salivating at the choices in front of me. I closed my menu settling on the pancakes and glanced up to see Gabriel smirking at me.

"What?" I asked.

He shook his head and laughed. "You were close to drooling."

I scrunched my nose. "I'm *really* hungry." I told him.

Gabriel sat back and put his hands behind his head. "I'm just saying, you don't act like that over my food, it's a little heart-breaking trevi."

I chuckled. "That's not true, do you not remember the mini orgasm I had when I was eating the salmon."

His tongue poked the inside of his cheek and he sat up straight. "I do. I remember it very well."

I looked out the window, I could feel the heat rising to my cheeks. Was he flirting with me? Was it just to make the waitress jealous or did he get a kick out of making me blush?

"Hey there again." The waitress called out. I turned back to see her back at our table, still not making eye contact with me. "Have you decided on what you would like?"

"Yes, I would like the burger with cheese and a coke, thank you." Gabriel said, handing her the menu. She took it from him and tucked a strand of her hair behind her ear, smiling at him. She clearly was infatuated with Gabriel and there wasn't a damn thing I could do about it except abide the unwanted enviousness in the pit of my stomach.

"And I'll have the pancakes with maple syrup and a strawberry milkshake, thanks." I said.

She glanced my way and her smile faded, a frown replacing it. Had she not noticed me before? I smiled at her, handing her the menu, trying to convey that I was no threat to her and in return she gave me a tight lip smile.

The waitress took our menu's away and left the table. As soon as she wasn't in listening range, Gabriel laughed.

I looked up at him, his eyes were glistening whilst his shoulders were shaking with laughter. "Why are you laughing?"

"Looks like you have some competition." He announced.

I furrowed my brows, confused. "Competition for what?"

His laughter faded and he shook his head. "The waitress looked like she wanted to skin you alive because you were sat with me."

Oh. That.

I wasn't sure if he noticed it, it seemed like he was interested in talking to her.

I scoffed. "Yeah well, I'm not competition, you should make that clear to her, so she doesn't spit in my food. Give her your number." I scrunched my nose, looking away from him. Why was I pushing him? Maybe if he asked someone out it would make it clear to me that he was off limits, more than he already was. "Even if she did think we were together, it didn't seem like that would stop her,"

"I can't blame her." He said, smirking. "A beautiful girl sitting with me, alone, at night. It does look like we're on a date."

I snickered. "Yeah, right." Beautiful? Gabriel had called me beautiful. There was no way he was serious. After making fun of me for my braces and hair styles in high school, he would never think I was beautiful.

"Melissa, can I ask you something?"

I furrowed my brows. "Sure?"

He looked at me, scanning my face before he spoke. "Why did you need me tonight?"

"What do you mean?"

He sighed and clasped his hands together in front of him. "Why did you need me to come to the dance with you?"

Was I missing something here? "Umm... I needed someone to act like my boyfriend to scare off Chad, I told you this."

He waved his hand. "Yeah, I know. I mean, why me?"

What the hell?

"Because you offered?" I laughed, "I tried to find someone else, that didn't go well."

He chuckled. "Yeah." He took a deep breath and spoke again "I mean, other than tinder. You could have met someone and asked for their help, no?"

I shrugged.

"There's no way you haven't been approached before."

I looked down, fidgeting with my hands in my lap, ignoring him. I didn't want to talk about my dating life or lack thereof, especially with Gabriel. Yes, there had been men who approached me in public before and had made conversation with me, and asked for my number, but after what happened in college, I couldn't trust anyone. The two guys I did give my number to had asked me out on a date and both had been a bust.

They were very forward and made sure I knew they liked my body but weren't interested in anything else I had to offer.

Luckily the waitress had shown up with our food and her frown was back on every time she would glance my way. I slumped my shoulders, there wasn't anything I could do about this girl being jealous. She placed my pancakes and milkshake in front of me and I hoped she didn't spit in my food, but I was too hungry to care.

"Thank you." Gabriel said to her, with a smile as she walked away, and I rolled my eyes.

"Jealous?" He asked.

I scoffed. "No." *liar.*

I took a sip of my milkshake and looked over to see Gabriel watching me intently. He smirked. "Sweet tooth?"

"Biggest." I admitted, smiling at him.

He nodded, smiling and took a bite out of his burger. We sat in silence eating our food. I wasn't one of those people who needed to fill in the silence, I was very content to sit here and eat in silence. Especially when I wanted to inhale the food after barely eating all day.

Feeling bloated and full, I let out a breath and Gabriel looked up to see my empty plate.

Gabriel took a sip of his coke and glanced up at me. "You didn't answer me."

"Huh?" I asked.

"Before, I had asked you why you felt the need to go online to find a guy decent enough to take you out on a date."

"This wasn't a date."

He chuckled. "You're right about that. If this was a date, I'd be taking you home and stripping that tight dress off your body like you were my gift to unwrap on Christmas day." I swallowed, hard. "But this would definitely be a date for whatever guy you could have asked." He continued. "And a fun one at that, spending the whole night clung to your side and being in on a secret that no one else knew." He shrugged. "I don't see who wouldn't want to do that."

I sighed. "I just don't go on dates, okay? It's not that big of a deal, so thank you for helping me tonight."

He dipped his chin. "You're welcome." He took another sip of his drink and then parted his mouth "That's not all though."

I groaned, rolling my eyes. "What now?"

He furrowed his brows. "I don't think I've ever seen you with a guy, Zaria never mentioned you dating."

"Why would Zaria tell you anything about me?"

He shrugged. "We tell each other everything, you know that." He laughed. "And Zaria is an oversharer. She would have told me news about you, especially if it had to do with you dating."

I laughed. "Believe me, I know she's an oversharer, but no, there haven't been any guys."

"Why?"

"Why do you want to know?" I countered.

He looked at me for a while before shrugging. "I was just wondering, even after high school, you never seemed to date."

I groaned. "Can we leave please?"

He chuckled. "Stop avoiding the question trevi, why did you never date?"

I stayed quiet for a while, looking out of the window. "Because no one was interested, okay?" I admitted. I ran a hand through my hair, annoyed that we were even talking about this.

"What?" Came from Gabriel. I looked away from the window to him, his brows were furrowed.

"In high school, after high school, no one was interested. Yes, there have been men who approached me before, but I could tell that they weren't interested in anything else other than sleeping with me." I sighed. "I'm not a hook-up kind of girl, so no, I never dated anyone after college with the exception of a couple of assholes."

I looked back out of the diner window, anticipating his reaction.

"Bullshit." He spat out.

I glanced back at him and furrowed my brows. "What?"

"I said, bullshit. I know for a fact that's bullshit."

I laughed. "How do you figure?"

He stroked his beard. "I know it's bullshit because even back in high school guys wouldn't stop talking about you."

His admission made my mouth drop open. "What?"

He nodded. "There was even a fight that broke out between two guys over who would ask you to homecoming."

I laughed. "Okay, you had me and now you lost me. Good story though."

Gabriel must have wanted to boost my confidence with that statement, I appreciated the effort but there was no way that was true. Guys wouldn't even look at me in high school.

"I'm being serious Mel. I remember specifically that fight breaking out in the halls after some guy saying he was planning on asking you out."

I looked over at him, his face was serious, it seemed like he was serious. But it couldn't be. I shook my head. "There's no way that happened," I told him. "I never got asked out in high school, no guys even talked to me."

He shrugged. "Maybe they were cowards."

I scoffed. I didn't believe him. He was either lying or must have misheard them. I opened my purse and stopped when I felt a hand on my hand. I looked up to see Gabriel with a scowl on his face, stilling me. "What are you doing?" I asked.

"What are *you* doing?" He countered. "Don't even think about reaching for your purse, I'm paying."

I shook my head. "No, you helped me tonight, the least I could do is pay for our meal."

He laughed and reached for his wallet. "Don't even think about it, I'm serious. You owe me nothing. I offered to help and now I'm telling you. I'm paying. End of."

I sighed, putting my purse away and smiled at him. I couldn't help but feel guilty, I knew he said I didn't owe him, but I had ruined his Friday night by asking him to accompany me to a middle school dance which was probably torture for him, and now he had paid for my dinner.

The waitress brought over the check and Gabriel paid. We made our way to the car, it was pitch black outside, and my eyes were feeling heavy.

Gabriel opened the car door for me, and I smiled at him. I still wasn't used to that. As soon as I was seated in the car, I let my head hit the back of the seat and closed my eyes, I was full and all I wanted to do now was sleep.

I heard the car door close and opened one eye, seeing Gabriel was looking at me with a smirk. "We're not going anywhere else, right?" I closed my eyes again and sighed. "I'm too tired."

He chuckled. "No trevi, let's get you home."

I glanced at him. "Thank you." I whispered.

"No worries."

"No just for that." I continued. "For tonight too, thank you for helping me. I think it worked. I don't think Chad will dare to come near me anymore." I laughed. "He was definitely scared of you."

"Yeah." He snickered. "His skinny legs were nearly buckling when he saw me towering over him." He smirked at me.

"Ok, we get it, you have a big ego." I rolled my eyes

He scoffed. "That's not the only thing that's big."

Heat traveled to my face. "I can't believe you just said that." I didn't do this. I didn't talk about this kind of stuff, especially with someone like Gabriel, someone who recently I haven't stopped thinking about, someone who made an appearance every night in my fantasy when I was alone and under the sheets.

I shook my head, laughing. "Sometimes you're scarily like Zaria." That would be exactly the type of thing she would say.

He laughed and I laughed along with him, Gabriel was right, this was a fun night. I don't remember the last time Gabriel and I laughed together, never mind enjoyed the whole night being in the same room as each other.

CHAPTER EIGHTEEN

Family is something I'll never have.

The closest thing I had to a family growing up was my dad. He tried his hardest to fulfil both roles of a parent. I loved him for it, especially around the time when I was going through puberty, and my dad had to figure out how to raise a girl as a single parent. He had to figure it all out on his own. Periods, hormones, boys.

Not that he had anything to worry about with the last one, and the other stuff I mostly learned at school, but for the first few months of 'being a woman,' he tried his damn hardest. He brought home boxes and boxes of pads and tampons along with a bag full of chocolates and when he gave it to me, I started to cry.

Of course, he was newly acquainted with the female hormones, so he was stressed out, thinking he did something wrong, when in fact I was crying because I loved him so much and he was trying. Trying to make up for the fact that my mother left, she left me and my dad and didn't care enough to be my mother.

Looking around, seeing Zaria and the Andersons having a family barbeque, laughing, and smiling, made my stomach hurt. I would never have that. This was the closest I would get to having a real family, and it wasn't even mine.

"Grab those tongs for me, baby." Terry called out to Zaria, who was sat on the pool lounge alongside me.

She stood up, grabbing a pair of tongs that sat on the dining room table. She passed them to her dad and sat back down next to me. I shouldn't be feeling like this., emotional, by seeing Zaria hang out with her dad. I had seen it many times and whilst I felt a little jealous, I never felt like balling up on the ground and crying. What was wrong with me?

"Hey pops." Gabriel walked outside, greeting his dad. Zaria and I came together, and Gabriel came separate, Zaria said he had something work-related, I wasn't sure what. Gabriel and I were just starting to get friendly, there was no reason he would confide in me.

"Well, look who finally showed up." Terry joked with his son, greeting him with a hug.

Gabriel shrugged. "I had work to do, but I'm here now. I wouldn't miss family dinner, c'mon." He glanced at Zaria. "By the way, mom asked for your help."

"For what?" Zaria asked.

"Some kind of mac and cheese emergency."

Zaria laughed, standing up and heading inside the house. I stayed right where I was. In the past I offered Naomi my help with whatever she needed, but she said I was a fire hazard and I agreed. The last time I tried to follow a recipe, that my nonna had shown me, for lasagna, I ended up burning the noodles and nearly setting my dad's house on fire.

"I'm going to grab a beer, want one?" He asked his dad.

His dad nodded, flipping over the meat on the grill. "There's some in the freezer."

"Got it." He turned to face me. "What about you trevi? Want a beer?"

I shook my head. "I'm good, thanks."

Gabriel walked inside, leaving just me and Terry out in the backyard.

"How's it been?" He asked me. "With Gabriel living with you girls. I hope he hasn't caused any problems."

The Anderson's were well aware of mine and Gabriel's feud along the years, mostly trying to understand why we didn't like each other. Beats me, I spent years trying to figure out why Gabriel hated me so much and what I ever did that made him ignore me for months.

I smiled at him. "No, it's been fine actually. We've been getting along."

He nodded. "Hmm. That's good, there's nothing worse than fights within the family."

A pressure built up in my chest, but the good kind. Hearing Mr. Anderson call me family meant more to me than he'd ever know. I think a big part of it was that he was close with my dad. Seeing as Zaria and I had become best friends, and I spent a lot of time over at her house, my dad wanted to meet her parents.

He could be strict when it came to curfews and where I was going, but most of the time I would either be at home or at Zaria's house. The one time I stayed out late, was for prom, which was a fun night.

We ended up ditching prom early and hanging out at the movies. Zaria invited a bunch of people to come along, and half of the room was filled up by high schoolers in dresses and tuxes. I can't even remember what film we were watching, because the only thing I do remember was it ended in a food fight. Popcorn was thrown everywhere, and I still found chips in my bra later that night when I was in the shower.

"Have you decided what to do with the house?" Terry asked.

I sighed. "Not yet."

My dad had left me the house in his will, which meant I was an owner of a house, and paid taxes on a property I didn't even live in. I didn't know what I wanted to do with it. it felt too weird to live in it, to live where me and my dad grew up, where we spent most years, just the two of us, where my mother left us.

But I also didn't want to sell it, it held so many memories and important moments of my life. So, like any irrational person would do, I did nothing. I didn't sell or live in it and just continued paying taxes to the government for an empty property.

If I sold it, I would feel like it would be like losing another part of him, like I was giving up on him, on what he left me in his death, on our life together.

"I know it's hard to let go." Terry continued, resting the tongs on the side of the grill, and turning to face me, with an apologetic look in his eyes I had seen a lot from him, especially. "But your dad left you that house for a reason. He wanted to help you not hurt you."

I knew what he was saying, and I agreed with him. My dad was a real estate agent, and he knew the market was rising every day, so the house wasn't supposed to be a burden on my shoulders, but an aid to help my life. I could either sell it and buy my own house or I could live in it, he gave me the choice.

Which was the hardest thing for me. I was only twenty-four and I loved living with Zaria so what was the harm in holding on to the house until I decided what to do with it?

"If you ever need anything, you know we're here for you. And the house isn't going anywhere, you still have time."

"Time for what?" Gabriel asked, walking out with two beers in hand.

"How about you mind your own business." Terry said to Gabriel with a laugh, reaching for the beer and turning his attention back to the meat.

Gabriel smiled at his dad, shaking his head as he walked over and sat on the pool lounge beside mine. He nudged me with his shoulder. "Time for what?" He asked.

I sighed. "For the house. My dad's house, I still don't know what to do with it."

He nodded, looking out at the pool, taking a swig of his beer. We both sat in silence, the only sounds filling the air were the birds and the sizzling from the grill.

After a minute, Gabriel broke the silence. "Remember when we were last here?" He said.

I scrunched my nose thinking how different things were, from the last time both of us were out by the pool. The last time I was here, we hated each other, and now… not so much.

I wanted to know if he regretted it. If he regretted any of the things he did and said to me, and why he ever did them. But before I could ask him any of that, we were being called inside by Zaria.

I grabbed the tray that Terry handed me and brought it inside, placing it on the dining table, alongside the rest of the food that Naomi had cooked inside. The table was filled with food and the sight made me drool. I was guilty of coming over for the food, seeing as back home, most of the meals were in plastic containers and reheated in the microwave.

We said grace, as we always did when we had a meal together. Another Anderson family tradition I treasured. And then we filled our plates with food.

The conversation drifted from Naomi's arch nemesis at work, to Zaria's new boy toy at the hospital. I could tell she was trying her hardest not to let any crude details slip, seeing as she was talking to her parents, but she failed, mentioning that they snuck off at breaks to have sex. There was a groan from Terry and a tut from Naomi, clearly disapproving their daughter's urge to talk freely about her sex life, and then laughter across the table.

All my life I preferred to be alone, I didn't want to impress anyone else, crave their company, or seek for validation that I was wanted or loved. Love being a huge factor into not wanting any of that, seeing as I had a crumbling foundation to go off, watching how much my mother devastated me and my dad by leaving.

Naomi and Terry though, were different. I could see how much they loved each other and their kids, and now, seeing this, I wanted that. I wanted love, marriage, kids and a family of my own.

I looked down at the plate of food in front of me, mostly full. I gulped, feeling sick just looking at it. the appetite that had been there at the beginning of the meal, had disappeared. This always happened when I was on my period. Mother nature had arrived yesterday, and it was killing me. The second day was always the worst. I couldn't even stand up without feeling like I got kicked by a soccer ball in my lower abdomen.

I should have stayed home, but I hadn't been to the Andersons since Christmas, and I missed them, missed this. What was a little pain in exchange for a fleeting moment of happiness?

I groaned when another cramp hit my stomach, making me clench my fists by my side.

"Are you okay?" Gabriel asked.

My eyes lifted, meeting his. His eyes were widened, as if he was almost… worried. Was that possible or was I seeing things? I licked my suddenly dry lips and nodded. "Yeah, I just need some water." I stood up from the table.

"Sit back down, sweetie I'll get that for you." Naomi said, standing up from the table.

I shook my head. "No, really that's okay, thank you." I walked out of the dining room, heading towards the kitchen. I grabbed a glass from the cabinet and filled it with water when another cramp hit. I grabbed the sink with one hand, doubling over as the pain increased.

I left my Advil at home, what an idiot. I knew I was going to be in pain today, I should have come prepared.

I let the pain subside for a second before lifting the cup to my mouth, and drinking the contents of it. I heard footsteps approaching closer and turned my head seeing Naomi enter the kitchen.

"Do you feel better?" She asked.

I nodded. "Just period cramps, I'll be fine."

"You barely ate."

I winced. I always finished my plate, my dad always said that not eating the food someone else prepared for you was disrespectful, it was probably an Italian culture thing, but it resonated with me.

"I don't have much of an appetite." I told her.

She nodded and then approached closer, lowering her voice. "And how have things been with Gabriel?"

I smiled. "It's been great. We finally stopped arguing."

She laughed. "I can see that."

I furrowed my brows, wondering what she meant, but she beat me to it before I had a chance to ask.

"I see how you look at him." She said, lowering her voice a little more. "You've always… admired him, but now you look at him differently."

What did that mean? Did she know I used to have a crush on him?

"Being in love is a wonderful thing, sweetie. I hope you know that." Huh? Red alarms went off in my head. Love? "Don't let it scare you, Melissa." She continued. "I can see you love him very much, and I'm sure he cares for you too."

I shook my head. "Mrs. Anderson I—"

She laughed. "How many times I've got to tell you, call me Naomi. You're not a stranger."

I bit my lip. "Naomi I… I'm not in love with Gabriel."

I might have a little teeny tiny crush on him, but we were just starting to get along with each other. I didn't love him, I couldn't love him.

She smiled, squeezing my hand. "Should we go back inside?"

I nodded, letting her lead me out of the kitchen and into the dining room. I couldn't stomach eating any more of what was left on the plate, so I just sat back down, waiting for everyone else to finish.

Zaria's brows furrowed as she read a text on her phone. She sighed, putting it back in her purse. "I'm being called in to the hospital today. I have to leave like now." She stood up from the table, putting her jacket on and grabbing her purse.

She leaned down, giving her parents a kiss goodbye, and then turned to Gabriel. "Melissa and I came here in my car. Can you give her a ride home?"

He nodded, taking a sip of his drink and my cheeks blushed, focusing on his features and his lips covering the rim of the glass. It was the hormones, that was it.

Zaria had left and I was going home with Gabriel. Alone, in his car. I needed to get a hold of my emotions or whatever the crap this was, if Naomi was sensing something, then it might be obvious to Gabriel too. I cleared my throat, and stood up, clearing the plates from the table, and taking them to the kitchen to wash the dishes.

CHAPTER NINETEEN

"Lie down." Gabriel said, as soon as we walked into the apartment.

We spent most of the car ride in silence, except for the music playing, quietly because Gabriel had this weird thing where he couldn't drive if the music was loud.

I wasn't in the mood to talk about anything. My head was pounding, and my stomach was being tortured from the inside out. His voice was smooth and deep, making me blush at the sound of it. I wondered if it had anything to do with what Naomi had said. I shook my head, wanting those words to leave my head. I wasn't in love.

"Huh?" I asked him, leaning down to take off my shoes. I wanted to strip myself as soon as I got home. I hated wearing bras and constricting clothes. I lived in pajamas or sweats most of the time.

"Lie down on the couch." He repeated.

I furrowed my brows, hands on hips and I looked up at him. "Why?"

"Are you always this stubborn?"

I rolled my eyes. "Can I at least change first?" I asked him. I wasn't quite sure why I was asking him for permission, I didn't even know what he was up to.

He nodded. "Thank you." I said sarcastically. I made my way to my room, taking off these clothes and settling into my comfy sweats. I looked down, seeing they were the same ones Gabriel had said were my 'homeless chic' look. I chuckled, remembering how we used to argue every time we saw each other, and how happy I was that was no longer the case.

I opened my bedroom door, walking over to where he was stood in the kitchen, seeing a heating pad and two Advil on the counter. He did this?

"How did you know?" I asked him, scrunching up my nose. "Did your mom tell you?"

"No." He said, handing me the pills and a glass of water.

"Then how?" I asked, before taking the pills.

He scoffed, grabbing the heating pad off the counter, holding it in his hands. "I have a sister and a mother, Mel." He grabbed my hand and pulled me towards him. "C'mon." He said, pulling towards the couch which had a pillow on the armrest. "Lie down." He told me.

He did this for me?

"I don't know what to say." I mumbled.

"A thank you would be a start." He smirked.

I shook my head, looking up at him. "Thank you." I almost but whispered.

He dipped his chin and I looked up at him and smiled, and he smiled back, gesturing to the couch with his hands.

"What about you? I asked. "I can just go and nap in my bed, I don't need to lie on the couch."

He groaned. "For fucks sake woman, stop being so stubborn and get your butt on the couch."

I snickered and sat on the couch. I didn't want to occupy this space if he wanted to watch some tv though. "Gabriel I—"

I yelped when I felt his hand cover my mouth. "If I hear you say you'll go to your room one more time, I'll pick you up and throw you on the couch myself. Lie down and rest." He lifted his hand from my mouth, and I lay down on the couch, propping my head on the pillow and laying on the armrest of the couch. He placed the heating pad on my lower stomach and covered me with a blanket.

I will pick you up and throw you on the couch.

I couldn't believe he just said that, and I wasn't sure if it was the hormones coursing through my body, but at that moment, I wished he had.

My stomach fluttered. He was taking care of me. I hadn't had anyone do anything close to this in a long time, not since I was a little girl.

I looked up at him and gulped. I wanted him here. "Stay." I whispered.

He sat on the edge of the couch and brushed the hair away from my face. "I'm not going anywhere, Mel. Rest." I closed my eyes and nestled into the pillow. I had never felt safer or warmer.

♡

My eyes fluttered open, seeing the tv turned on.

"Hey." I blinked, looking up. Gabriel was above me, I was lying on his lap. How did that happen? Last I remembered I was lying on the opposite side and my head was on the armrest. "You feeling better?" He asked.

I nodded. "How long was I asleep for?"

He rubbed his beard, reaching for his phone. "About an hour, you hungry?"

I nodded again. I had barely eaten at the Anderson's house, and the appetite was back.

He lifted my head off his lap, getting up from the couch. I sat up. "Where are you going?" I asked. I felt safe in Gabriel's arms. Well, technically, his legs. I felt safe in Gabriel's vicinity. And more importantly, I felt comfortable here. Having social anxiety, I didn't feel safe or comfortable with anyone, there were only a few people in my life that I did feel comfortable with, and Gabriel had become one of those few people.

I wasn't sure how much I should be this close to him, given that for the past ten years I had an undeniable crush on him, even when I hated him, it was because he hated me. I always wanted to be seen by Gabriel.

"I'll be right back." He walked into the kitchen, and I sighed, turning my head back to the tv, shocked to see what he was watching.

"You're watching Clueless?"

"Yep." He called back.

I laughed. "Why?"

"Because I wanted to see what crap you're getting your fake information from."

I chuckled. I would never have imagined someone like Gabriel to watch a chick flick like clueless, but I would have never imagined him to be such a reality show buff either.

"Clueless isn't crap." I retorted. "I'm surprised you're watching something like this, it's not very manly." I joked. Most men wouldn't be caught dead watching a chick flick, especially alone, they thought it somehow denounced their masculinity.

Gabriel stood behind me, placing his hands on the couch "I thought we already established I don't give a crap about that. I'm manly where it counts."

"Uh huh, and where would that be?" I teased. I knew I shouldn't be taunting him. We were forming a friendship, I didn't want to ruin that by making him uncomfortable, but it was fun to tease him.

"Don't push it trevi. We both know you don't want to go there." He handed me a plate. "Eat."

I grinned. "You made brownies?"

He shrugged. "Zaria would always inhale my chocolate when it was that time of the month, figured you'd like it."

"I do." I took a bite out of the brownie and almost groaned, the perks of having a chef as a roommate were expanding. "Thank you." I said, the words muffled by the brownie stuffed in my mouth.

He laughed. "Good?"

Words couldn't explain. I nodded, eagerly.

He smiled and dipped his chin. His eyes dropped to my mouth before he leaned in, running a thumb across my chin, cleaning up some chocolate that had fallen. I couldn't take my eyes off him.

I gulped, seeing him smile as he looked down at me.

My stomach dropped and my heart accelerated, I was tempted to press my hand to my chest feeling it quicken almost beating out of my chest. I knew this wasn't anxiety, I knew this was something else. Something I wasn't ready to accept.

Naomi's words kept crawling back to me, and now I couldn't deny it. She was right.

LOVE ME OR HATE ME

I was falling in love with Gabriel Anderson

CHAPTER TWENTY

How could this be happening? I couldn't be in love with Gabriel. He was everything I hated. Arrogant, annoying, egotistical, handsome, kind, thoughtful.

Shit.

How did I let this happen? I knew I shouldn't have gotten close to him. Every day we spent getting closer and becoming friends, I was fooling myself. I always had a crush on Gabriel, why did I think getting to know him and trust him and feel comfortable around him wouldn't complicate things.

Especially with Zaria, she was my best friend, and I had a hard time keeping the small crush I had on Gabriel a secret from her, how was I ever going to explain that I was in love with her brother? This was a nightmare.

I wasn't sure how I was supposed to act in front of Gabriel anymore, he would see through me, without a doubt. Naomi had noticed it. She knew I was in love with him before I'd even acknowledged it. Who's to say Gabriel wouldn't too? He'd notice how I acted in front of him, get uncomfortable and keep his distance from me to let me down easy.

I wasn't going to let that happen, I'd put the distance between us first. I hadn't seen him since that night when he made me brownies. I had muttered that I wasn't feeling well and went straight to my room, staying there the entire night. Yesterday I had bolted to my room after coming home, to avoid seeing him. I didn't want him to see me like this, I was too scared of how I would act if I was around him. These feelings would only get stronger, and I couldn't handle the inevitable pain of heartbreak.

I couldn't stay in my room forever, that was one of the reasons the schedule hadn't worked, how was I going to avoid him for the rest of the time that he was staying here?

"Ugh" I groaned, letting my head hit the back of my headboard, I was bored to death, but leaving my room would mean seeing Gabriel and that wasn't an option, not for a while, until I managed to contain whatever I was feeling towards him.

Hate, animosity, annoyance. That was easy to express and manage, even when Gabriel made my life living hell, it wasn't fun, but I could get over it, but love? How would I ever get over loving him? This was the first time I had ever fallen in love with someone, and just my luck, it had to be Gabriel. The boy who hated me growing up, my best friend's brother.

Allie was as smug as could be about this whole living situation with Gabriel, so I couldn't tell her about my new feelings, she would start plotting to get us together and I was certain that it wasn't going to happen.

Zaria would never accept this. For all she knew, I hated Gabriel since I was fourteen and while that was partly true, she didn't know the reason I hated him was because I had a crush on him, and he actively shared his displeasure with me.

A knock on my door startled me, I sat upright and waited. Zaria was at work today, so that meant...

Gabriel was knocking on my bedroom door. I would have to open it and lie about the reason I had been avoiding him for the past two days.

"Trevi?"

Silence.

Maybe if I didn't respond, he would think I was sleeping and wouldn't bother me anymore.

Knock

"Mel, I can hear you breathing open the door,"

"Yeah of course you can, I'm not dead."

"She speaks."

Shit.

I closed my eyes and pulled the sheets over my head, digging into the mattress. I wanted to escape. My bed, this house, being here with him, this whole situation.

I didn't reply. I opened my eyes and was met with darkness surrounding me. Darkness was nice, peaceful, quiet. I could think here. What was I going to do? Tell him? That wasn't an option. Act like I hated him still? That wouldn't make sense after we had established a friendship.

Knock.

I pulled the sheets back, getting out of my bed. I had to face him. I had to make up a lie that would explain my weird behavior these past couple of days and I didn't know what that was. I needed time to think, to form a plan of what I would say, what I would do, how I would push all these feelings down and act like they weren't eating at me.

I took a deep breath in and walked over to my bedroom door. I slowly opened it to find Gabriel facing away from the door, rubbing the back of his head. He swiftly turned his head, realizing I had opened the door. I gasped when my eyes met his. I hadn't seen him in merely two days but somehow, he had become handsomer, grown taller, or maybe my mind was playing tricks on me. But I had never been more attracted to someone than I was to this man standing in front of me.

His eyes searched my face, I wasn't sure what he was looking for, I wasn't sure if he had noticed me ogling him or if he saw something different in my face. Did your face change when you fell in love? Could other people tell? I could feel my face heat with worry that he would be able to see through my emotions and put two and two together.

I crossed my arms, waiting for him to explain why he was here. "Yes?"

His brows were scrunched up as he shook his head. "Are you okay?" He asked.

He was worried about me? I bit the inside of my cheek, trying to stifle a smile. "Yes. Why?"

He let out a breath. "I've barely seen you since Saturday and you haven't been nagging me like usual." He chuckled. "Just thought it was weird."

A smile tugged at my lips, and I hastily fixed my expression before he could notice. "Good to know you think I nag you. Goodbye." I attempted to close the door, but he pressed his palm on the door, keeping me from closing it.

"Wait, no I didn't mean it like that."

I sighed. "It's fine, Gabriel." I attempted to close the door, once again but his hand pushed on it, swinging it open.

"Are you mad at me or something?"

"What?" I scoffed. "Why would I be mad at you.?"

Other than the fact that I was acting like an asshole. Why wouldn't he think I was mad at him?

He shrugged. "I don't know Melissa, you tell me. Your face is scrunched up and you can barely even look at me."

I didn't think he would be able to tell. I had been avoiding looking at him, staring at the wall or fidgeting with my hands to try and prevent looking into his eyes. I couldn't look at him, what if he saw something in my expression and realized how I felt about him?

I had to avoid setting myself up for failure. I had to fight whatever urge I had to just look at him and be engulfed by his charm. If I didn't have to look at him, I wouldn't have to confront the fucked-up situation I was in. I was in love with my best friends' brother, who less than two weeks ago, I despised to be in the same room with.

I stared down at my hands, fidgeting with them. "I'm not mad, I'm just... not feeling well."

He didn't buy it before, I doubted he would buy it this time. I looked up and saw him staring at me, confusion painted across his face. He nodded and stepped back. "I won't bother you anymore." His back facing me as he turned around and walked away. I closed my bedroom door, staring at it for a minute.

I felt just as guilty as when I told him I couldn't stand to be around him and created the schedule. But this was different, I *did* want to be around him, all the time. It hurt to stay away from him, I wanted to see his face and be near him, I just...couldn't.

I couldn't do that to myself, to force myself to be around Gabriel knowing he would never love me like I loved him. It wasn't as if he was an ex-boyfriend, and I could just cut him out of my life. Zaria was my best friend, and Gabriel was her brother. He would always be in my life.

How was I supposed to go on acting like I felt nothing towards him, how was I supposed to watch him pack up and leave this apartment and date other girls. Girls who were social, outgoing, fun and nothing like me. Girls who were lucky enough to kiss Gabriel, sleep in the same bed as him, have him. I would never have him, he would never be mine.

♡

I had successfully managed to avoid Gabriel for another day. Zaria was off from work tomorrow, which meant I was relying on her to act as a buffer once again, and hopefully I wouldn't have to avoid or be alone with Gabriel.

I let out a sigh when my body met the hot water beneath me. I had been doused from the rain and a warm bath was exactly what I needed. Gabriel wouldn't be home for another half hour, which meant I had plenty of time to enjoy a relaxing bath before I had to scurry and hide in my room, once again.

Only one more day, tomorrow I could go back to pretending. Zaria didn't have a clue that I once had a crush on her big brother, they wouldn't find out about this either. No one had to know but me, I had to live with these feelings and find a way to not let it affect how I acted around Gabriel or Zaria.

My eyes snapped open at the sound of a door closing.

I sat upright, trying to hear for voices, what if this was a break-in?

I reached for my phone and nearly choked when I saw the time. I had somehow gotten carried away and fell asleep. It was five-thirty pm, the only explanation being, it must have been Gabriel.

I would have to escape to my bedroom without him noticing me, how was I ever going to do that?

I stepped out of the bath, looking around for my towel. Which was somehow not here. I ran a hand down my face. How could I forget to bring my towel? What was I going to do? The closest thing to me was a hand towel, there was no way that would cover anything. How the hell was I supposed to leave the bathroom and get into my room, without Gabriel seeing...without a towel.

The clothes I had on previously, were drenched from the rain, there was no way I could put them back on.

"Shit." I muttered to myself.

Zaria wouldn't be home until later tonight, and I couldn't leave here naked.

That meant...

I took a deep breath in. Here goes nothing.

"Gabriel?" I called out.

"Trevi? Is that you?"

"Can you bring me my towel?" I asked. "It's in my bedroom, I forgot to bring it with me."

"You forgot your towel?" He laughed. "Sorry, Mel but I'm so busy right now, I guess you'll have to get it yourself."

I closed my eyes and groaned. Of course, he would act like an asshole. I couldn't blame him, after I practically closed the door in his face yesterday, I wouldn't want to help me either.

I opened the bathroom door to a crack. Gabriel was leaning against the couch, facing me, with his arms crossed against his chest and a smug grin plastered on his face.

I cleared my throat. "Can you at least turn around so I can get to my bedroom?"

He chuckled and licked his lips.

"Please?" I added.

He simply shook his head, not even responding.

I closed the bathroom door, once again and sat on the edge of the bathtub burying my head in my hands. What was I going to do? I couldn't just walk out naked.

The sound of a knock at the door startled me. "Yes?"

"Open the door, Mel."

I was naked.

"I'm not... um... decent." I told him. I could feel my cheeks start to heat.

His laughter radiated on the other side of the door. "I know. Just open it."

I stood up and made my way to the bathroom door, opening it slightly. I was very aware of the fact that I was butt-ass naked, with nothing to cover myself up with. I angled my body to hide it behind the door, only letting my head peek out. "Yes?" I asked again.

He shook his head, grinning. "You're fucking hilarious trevi."

I scoffed. "And you're an asshole. Glad to know you find amusement in my torment. Is it really that difficult to do me this one favor and just bring me my towel?"

His hand appeared at the door, holding out my towel. I had just called him an asshole and he still gave me the towel. Gabriel was being nice.

I reached out for the towel, and he retracted it.

Maybe *nice was the wrong word.*

"What? I—"

"Why have you been ignoring me?"

I blinked, stunned by that question. I knew he was suspicious yesterday, but I didn't think he would confront me about it. He must have seen the surprise in my face because his lips pulled up.

"I...umm."

"You've been avoiding me." He told me. "Deny it."

I couldn't. He was right. I was avoiding him, but I wasn't about to tell him the reason why.

I looked down at the floor, what was I supposed to say?

I've been avoiding you because I realized, I'm in love with you.

Yeah, I didn't think so.

He cleared his throat and I looked up at him. I sighed. "Can you just give me my towel?" I reached out to grab it, but he stepped back, bringing it behind his back.

"I'll give you your towel when you tell me what I did to make you mad at me again."

I narrowed my eyes at him. "That's blackmail."

He shrugged. "Hardly."

I shook my head. "I told you I'm not mad at you."

His eyes narrowed at me. "Then what?" He asked. "What is it?"

I glared at him. "Maybe I just hate seeing your face every day."

Lies.

Maybe I could pretend, act like I hated him and wasn't madly in love with him, I could do that right?

He scoffed. "C'mon Mel, let's not tell lies."

I couldn't help but laugh. I had never met a man so conceited and arrogant as him. What did that say about my character that this is who I fell in love with?

I placed a hand over my face and groaned. "Gabriel, please," I begged. "Just... I'm not mad at you, just give me my towel so I can get dressed without having to flash you."

He smiled for a fleeting second and the next, his jaw was clenched. He nodded and handed me my towel. I took it from him, wrapping it around my body.

I opened the door, fully and stepped out into the hallway. "Thank you." I muttered.

He turned around, walking back over to the couch and I made my way over to my bedroom. I closed the door behind me and shut my eyes. Gabriel knew I was avoiding him, and he wanted answers. Answers I couldn't give him.

I dried myself off and got dressed. I had managed to be around and talk to Gabriel without accidentally blurting out that I loved him, maybe I could be around him.

Opening the door, I could see Gabriel in the kitchen, cooking dinner. He turned to face me. "So, you're not avoiding me anymore?"

I scrunched my nose, thinking of what to say. "I wasn't avoiding you, I just...wasn't feeling well."

He scoffed. Okay, so he didn't buy it. "Please, Mel, for once just tell me the truth." He stepped closer to me, scanning my face. "Was it something I said? Or are you still pissed at me for all those years I was a dick to you?" He rubbed the back of his head. "Look." He sighed, "I'm honestly sorry for that shit, I never wanted to hurt you, you were the only one who would dish it back and I didn't think I would actually make you this upset." He shook his head, letting out a dry laugh. "Fuck, I mean you can't even look at me, I was an asshole and I'm sorry Mel."

My breath hitched. My skin was on fire. I didn't know how to respond to that. Was I still angry about all those years he would tease me and argue with me? Maybe? But he wasn't the sole blame, he was right, I did dish it back at him. I was as much at fault as he was.

I shook my head. I wasn't resentful over that, we had found a way to get over it and overlook it. No matter how angry I had been at him in the past, I wouldn't hold it against him, and I didn't want him to think that was the case.

"No." I breathed out. "Gabriel, it's honestly fine, I've forgiven you for that, I'm not mad at you."

He narrowed his eyes at me. "Then why have you been avoiding me?"

I knew what I had to say. I couldn't let him blame himself over something that wasn't his fault — well, technically it was — but there was no way in hell that he would know about that. I let out a deep breath and took a step closer. "It has nothing to do with you." I lied. I couldn't tell him the truth, but I could ease his guilt over my sour mood. "It's just personal issues, I'm not angry at *you*." I smiled at him "And

I'm sorry too, for equally acting like a jackass all those years."

His eyes lifted, boring into mine. He smiled and dipped his chin.

I could pretend.

For as long as these feelings lasted, I could pretend.

The problem was, I wasn't sure they were ever going to go away.

CHAPTER TWENTY-ONE

I loved being a teacher. For as long as I could remember, it was my dream career path.

I knew that there was a stigma around teachers, being the last choice in a career but for me, it was my first choice. My teachers had been a big impact growing up, and I wanted to be that. To be someone's support system if they needed one.

But no matter how much I loved my job, grading papers would always be the demise of my day. I had been sat on the couch for over two hours, but the stack of papers never seemed to reach the end. I needed a break.

I heard keys jingle from the other side of the door and I stilled, expecting to see Gabriel.

Zaria walked in, her curls in a neat bun on the top of her head, still dressed in her scrubs, she looked stunning. I smiled at the sight of my best friend.

"Hey M." Zaria said, approaching the couch. Her being here before Gabriel was, made me relax a little, knowing that I wouldn't have to spend any more time with Gabriel alone, not if I could help it. No chance of blubbering about my feelings or acting like a fool in front of him.

"Hey." I called back, putting the papers on the coffee table, away from me. "You have no idea how happy I am you're here."

Her eyes narrowed. "Because of my brother?" She asked. "I thought you two were finally getting along."

She knew Gabriel and I were no longer avoiding each other, but I hadn't told her anything else, too scared to admit I had feelings for her brother.

I chuckled. "You could say that." This was going to be hard. Lying to my best friend was something I hated to do. The only thing I had ever lied to her about was Gabriel. I felt like I was betraying her in a way, betraying her trust, her friendship.

"What was that?"

"Huh?"

"You flinched like you were just thinking of something, what was it? Was it really that bad with Gabriel?" She sighed. "What did he do?"

Crap. I didn't even know I had flinched. It wasn't anything to do with Gabriel, per se. More to do with the fact that I felt like shit lying to my best friend. She had shown me nothing but love and loyalty throughout the years, and here I was shitting on our friendship.

I waved my hand, dismissively. "No no, it wasn't anything he *did*. It was… eventful." I exhaled. "He was fine, we were fine, it was just… a lot."

Zaria nodded. "I get you. He can be a lot." She stepped back and flashed a toothy grin. "But then again, so can I."

"I can never get enough of you." I smiled at her and she squeezed my hand.

"Do you want to go somewhere?"

"Yes." I breathed. I needed a break. From work, from this apartment, from Gabriel. I needed to just chat with my best friend and stop overthinking everything going on with my life.

She rushed to her bedroom. "Let me just get changed and we'll go." She disappeared inside her bedroom, her door closing behind her. I looked down, I had put on my pajama shorts and tank top the moment I stepped foot in the apartment. I needed to get dressed too.

♡

"I heard about this place from Jeremy." Zaria said, opening the door to a small café I had never been to.

It was surprisingly cute for such a small place, tucked away on the corner of the street. The overpowering smell of coffee hit my nose and I winced. I had never been much of a coffee drinker. Zaria was the opposite, she was a coffee addict and couldn't go a day without a cup of coffee, black, so that the caffeine would be as strong as possible.

"Oh, is that the doctor you were fawning over?

She rolled her eyes. "I wouldn't call it fawning... more like admiring him."

I snorted.

She exhaled. "Fine, I was."

"What can I get for you today?" The barista asked. He was tall, I crooked my head up to look at him. His golden skin shining with the light coming in from the glass door and his dark brown curls sat messily on his head. His eyes were pinned on Zaria, and I smiled, Zaria was beautiful, I had seen many guys look at her like that before, but she seemed oblivious to him.

Her eyes were on her wallet, pulling out her card. "One large coffee, black and..." She looked over at me. "What are you having?" She asked.

I looked over to the barista. "A hot chocolate please, with extra chocolate." He took my order, not once looking at me. I was used to being invisible around Zaria, it was nothing new and I didn't take it personal.

We paid and moved over to the side, waiting for our drinks, when she finally looked up at me. I nudged her on her arm. "He's cute."

She turned her head, spotting the barista that was very obviously devouring her in his head, just a minute ago. She smiled, nudging me back. "Then go ask for his number."

I rolled my eyes. How was she this oblivious? She was usually the first person to notice when someone was flirting with her. "Uh, babe, I don't think it's me he's interested in."

His brows furrowed. "Meaning?"

"Meaning, he couldn't keep his eyes off you, and you barely looked at him."

Her eyes widened as she tucked her curly hair behind her ear. "He was?"

I chuckled. "Yes. How did you not notice?"

She shrugged. "I mean, I haven't really noticed any guys recently."

My brows shot up. It sounded like Zaria really liked this doctor. "So, it's serious with Jeremy?"

She sighed, shaking her head. "I don't know. I think he was just interested in a causal relationship. I just... I don't think I want that anymore."

I gestured to the barista with my head. "So, go ask him for his number." It wasn't a first for Zaria to ask a guy out, she had done it many times, without any embarrassment, I couldn't say the same.

She nodded. "I will."

"Black coffee and Hot chocolate." The barista called out, letting us know our drinks were ready.

We approached the counter and I picked up my hot chocolate.

"Enjoy." The barista smiled as we took our drinks.

"Thanks." I replied.

Zaria was deep in conversation with the barista, so I let her be and walked over to an empty table, luckily there still was one. This café was small but was beginning to fill up pretty quickly.

I took a sip of my hot chocolate, the sweet taste coating my tongue, whilst I waited for Zaria to come back. She turned, walking over to me, with a smile on her face. That must mean things went well with the barista.

She sat on the opposite side of me, setting her coffee on the table. "So? What happened?" I asked her.

She gestured to her coffee cup, turning it around until I could see the black marker on the drink.

The barista had written his number on her coffee cup. "Smooth." I said.

"I know." She grinned at me. "I didn't even have to put in any effort."

"So, what were you talking about?" I asked. She was there for a while, if he had already written his number, what else were they talking about?

"He said he didn't want to come on too strong and he wasn't sure if I was interested. So, I told him that I was very much interested and was coming over to ask him for his number."

"Ah."

"Enough about me. We're on a date. Tell me about yourself Melissa." She joked.

I rolled my eyes at her "You know more about me than anyone else, Z." I wasn't sure if that was true anymore. Gabriel knew things about me that I was sure Zaria didn't know. He noticed things that I didn't think anyone would take note of. The thought of Gabriel made my skin heat up. I had come here to not think about him, to take my mind off of these feelings and what I couldn't control.

I shrugged. "There's not much to tell, work, home, work."

"And Gabriel."

I swallowed. My face starting to burn. "What about Gabriel?" I asked. Did she know? How did she find out? What would she say? Would she hate me?

"Gabriel was there too. That must have been interesting, especially knowing how much you hate each other. Or hated I should say." I exhaled, relieved. She didn't know, she didn't suspect anything.

"Oh, right." I cleared my throat. "Well, there's not much to say, he annoyed me some days, and then others he didn't."

She nodded, taking a sip of her coffee and I repeated, with my hot beverage. My mouth was suddenly very dry.

"He told me about Friday." The school dance. I didn't even tell Zaria about that.

"He did?"

Zaria nodded. "I was surprised I didn't hear it from you, he told me about Chad still giving you a hard time and that you needed someone to scare him off and he offered." She took another sip of her coffee. "That was…unexpected, to say the least. To have to hear from my brother that he basically took you out on a date." Her face was unreadable, I couldn't tell if she was mad or if she was unbothered by it.

"Are you mad?" I asked her. Zaria and I had never been in an argument, if we got into one because of her brother, or worse because of my feelings for her brother, I didn't think I'd be able to handle it.

She shook her head, reaching out to squeeze my hand. "Mad? Of course not." She shrugged. "I was just surprised that you didn't tell me, that's all."

My throat clamped close, and my stomach dropped. She just wanted me to be honest with her. Maybe I could tell her about Gabriel.

"I mean," She continued. "If you were to actually date him, that would be a different issue."

Maybe not.

"It would?" My voice came out high-pitched and I cleared my throat. "I mean, not that it would ever happen." I laughed.

She laughed along with me. "Yeah, when we first became friends, I was scared that you'd ditch me for my brother but then the two of you hated each other so I knew that was off the table, which made me more relieved." She waved a hand, dismissively. "Anyways, we know it will never happen, even if you guys are becoming friends, he's not really your type anyways and Gabriel... well Gabriel doesn't really have a type unless it's the kind of girl who leaves in the morning."

Ouch.

Hearing from your best friend that the guy you're in love with only liked to sleep with a girl and ditch them in the morning hurt, and Zaria knew why. I wasn't sure if she was aware of what she had just said, hurt me.

"Hi." I looked up to see a man stood by our table. Two guys asking her out on the same day? This was new, even for Zaria. "I couldn't keep my eyes off you and was wondering if you'd like to go out sometime." I glanced over at Zaria to see she was staring back at me. Why wasn't she looking at him? She gestured to the man with her head, and I looked up at him, to see he was staring back at me. He was asking me out?

"I know this is forward, but you've got to take your shot, right?" He smiled. He was tall, not taller than Gabriel— No. I wasn't going to compare him to Gabriel. I was trying to stop thinking about Gabriel, maybe going out with someone was the way to do that.

I looked at the man in front of me, he was attractive, very much so. He was wearing a suit which probably meant he worked in a high-salary job, an office job, most likely. His eyes were strikingly blue, and his hair was dark brown, perfectly styled on his head.

He was handsome and seemed nice, from the thirty-second interaction I had with him.

I glanced at him and smiled. "Yes, sure. I'll take down your number." I pulled out my phone and glanced over at Zaria to see her eyes were wide open, surprised by the fact that I was taking down his number, actually planning a date with a man I knew nothing about. I was surprised too.

The man pulled out his phone too and started to tell me his number and I told him mine. "Sorry, I didn't catch your name." He said.

I chuckled. We had just planned a date and didn't even know each other's names. "It's Melissa." I told him.

"Ah, Melissa, beautiful name for a beautiful woman. I'm Shawn." He said, pointing to his chest, before putting his phone away.

"Nice to meet you, Shawn." I smiled at him.

He flashed a grin at me. "Nice to meet you too Melissa, I'll call you." He smiled before leaving the café.

I looked over at Zaria and she was grinning, from ear to ear. "Well, all those years of watching me paid off, who would have known you would ask out a guy."

"Technically, he asked me out, I just took down his number."

I couldn't help the constricting feeling in my chest. Why did this feel like a betrayal to Gabriel? We weren't together, and we would never be, he didn't know about my feelings for him, no one did.

So why did it feel so wrong to go out with another guy? I wasn't really interested in anybody else, but the man I was in love with, I couldn't have. And God, did I want him.

"Look at you." She grinned, "You're blushing."

I reached up to touch my cheek, feeling the heat radiate through my skin. What would Zaria say if she knew it wasn't about Shawn, but about Gabriel?

"I've never seen you like this." Zaria said.

If only she had seen how I was around Gabriel. If only she knew how I felt about her big brother. Except now I knew how she would react, she didn't want me and Gabriel together, if she knew that I was in love with him, she would never forgive me.

"It could all go downhill from here." I joked. "We don't know how he is yet."

"Don't jinx it." She told me. "I have a date, you have a date. This shit just got interesting."

It was. I never went on dates. I never even gave guys the time of day when they approached me. The most recent being the guy from the club, and that didn't go well.

But I knew I needed to move on, have something else to think about other than Gabriel. If someone else occupied my thoughts, then maybe these feelings for Gabriel would disappear.

"Where are you going to go? Coffee date?"

I scrunched my nose. "I hope not, I hate coffee."

She rolled her eyes. "Right, you're an aberration of a person who orders a hot chocolate at a café."

I shrugged. "They have it on the menu for a reason." I narrowed my eyes at her "Plus, you were the one who suggested this place."

She laughed. "Fine, I'll let your twisted opinion about coffee go this time."

I wasn't sure how this date would go, I mean, he was the one who approached me, so he would probably plan it. I didn't want to think about Gabriel, what these feelings meant and how to get over them.

How the hell do you get over someone you never even had? This was going to be a good thing, getting him out of my mind would be for the best. I didn't know what I was going to do, I just knew that for the first time, in a long time, I was looking forward to something.

CHAPTER TWENTY-TWO

"But he was big."

I groaned. "Z, I did not ask about his size."

Zaria had been filling me in on her 'situationship' with the doctor she had met, Jeremy. She was an avid over sharer, and not just about her life, but about everyone's. I didn't really mind until it got to the gory details of her sex life, I could live without knowing every grimy detail.

I sometimes wondered if Zaria felt bad that she couldn't really talk about that kind of stuff with me, I mean, most girls shared intimate details about sex and who they were sleeping with, Zaria being one of them. But I never reciprocated, the number one reason being that I wasn't sexually active, not since college and another being that I wasn't the biggest fan of sex talk.

Sex was a part of life, and it wasn't that I was embarrassed about it, more so that I had no experience, the only experience I did have set my expectations really low and made me not trust anyone, especially sexually.

"You asked why I liked him so much." She shrugged. "That's one of the reasons." She plucked her keys from her purse, jutting them in the door.

I rolled my eyes. "How romantic."

Zaria chuckled. "Yeah, well didn't seem like he wanted romance, only a hot body to come in."

"Sis, please." Gabriel groaned. The door flung open, and Gabriel was shirtless on the couch, and I averted my eyes to the ground. I gulped, my throat felt dry all of a sudden. I prayed, silently that I wouldn't fuck this up. I could pretend.

You hate Gabriel.

He's not attractive.

You don't want to jump his bones.

"Hey Gabriel, I didn't know you'd be here." She winced, realizing her brother just heard the last bit of her explicit conversation.

He ran a hand down his face. "Where else would you expect me to be, I live here for the time being."

"Have you found any apartments yet?"

He shook his head. "Still looking for one close to work."

My gut dropped, he would be gone soon.

I took off my shoes, leaving them at the door and walked to the kitchen filling up a cup with water.

"Are you still planning on opening a restaurant?" Came from Zaria, who now sat on the couch, next to her brother.

"You're opening a restaurant?" I asked, walking over to the couch. This was big. Gabriel was a sous chef at one of San Francisco's biggest restaurants, but he was talented. Opening a restaurant was definitely something I could see him doing.

He shrugged. "That's the plan, but there's still some issues with the location."

"Wow, that's huge. Congrats."

He laughed. "Nothing's set in stone yet, trevi."

I smiled. That nickname sounded like a poem coming from his mouth.

"Okay, this is weird." Zaria said.

My smile immediately vanished. Did she see me looking at him? How was I ever going to hide my feelings from Gabriel and Zaria?

"What is?" Gabriel asked.

"This." She gestured between me and Gabriel. "This... friendship, I mean you're not insulting each other, you're actually *complementing* each other, it's... weird."

She hadn't really been around Gabriel and I that often, she was either at work when Gabriel and I hung out and when she was home, we weren't around each other that often. I couldn't help but laugh, wasn't this Zaria's idea in the first place? "Z, you told me to play nice with Gabriel, remember?"

She nodded. "Yes, I always wanted you two to be civil around each other and you said you were but..." She shook her head. "It's just going to take time to get accustomed to. I didn't believe it until I just saw it."

I took a sip from my glass. Zaria really didn't like me and Gabriel together, even as friends she was wary. What the hell did I get myself into?

Zaria stood from the couch, walking over to me. "I'm going to go take a shower, want to have takeout, and watch crappy reality shows later?"

I smiled at her. My heart squeezed. "Always."

Gabriel cleared his throat. "Um, sorry to break up this slumber party but I don't want to spend the night stuck in a girly fest crying over reality shows."

Zaria turned, pointing her finger at him. "You're in our apartment, bro. We're watching our reality shows, you can either leave or watch them with us."

He sighed and leaned back. "Fine."

"Don't let him fool you, he's *obsessed* with them now." I told Zaria.

She looked at me and then back at Gabriel. She shook her head, walking over to the bathroom. "Who are these people." She muttered to herself. I couldn't help but laugh. If it was hard for me to become friendly with Gabriel, I couldn't imagine how strange it would be for Zaria to come home to see that her best friend and brother suddenly didn't hate each other anymore.

I walked over to the couch, sitting next to Gabriel.

"You seem happy she's home."

I nodded. "She's a buffer between us." I said, only half joking. She was a buffer, only the reason wasn't what he thought.

Gabriel opened his mouth, about to speak when my phone started ringing, interrupting whatever he was about to say.

I glanced at my phone, seeing that it was Shawn from the coffee shop, earlier today. He was calling already? It had barely been two hours since we left. I stood up from the couch, walking towards the kitchen. "Um, hi?"

"Melissa, hey." He laughed. "I wasn't sure if you'd pick up, I know this is soon."

"Yeah." I chuckled. Didn't guys wait three days to call? Wasn't that a rule? Or was it something I had seen in movies?

"Yeah, well, I was just excited to see you again. Does tomorrow at five work? We can meet up back at the coffee shop."

"I'm not the biggest fan of coffee." I admitted.

He laughed, his laugh was bright, like he was carefree and happy all of the time. I liked that. "That's fine, you can always order a hot chocolate or a tea, do you drink tea?"

I couldn't help but smile. It was nice of him to accommodate for me, even if I had just technically declined the idea for our first date. "Yeah sure, I drink tea, but I'm more of a fan of hot chocolate."

"Ah, sweet tooth. No worries, you can have all the chocolate you want." I laughed. He was sweet. Hopefully I had a better time on this date than I had previously experienced.

"Sounds great." I said. "See you tomorrow, Shawn."

"Excited to see you, Melissa."

I hung up and turned around to see Gabriel stood behind me, arms crossed at his chest. "So, who was that?"

I furrowed my brows, wondering why he wanted to know. "Why?"

He shrugged. "Just wondering if you're replacing me already, that's all."

Confusion flooded my face. "Replacing you as what exactly?"

He took a seat at the kitchen island, spreading his arm over the back of the other stool. "As your fake boyfriend." He explained.

Oh.

"Well, I'm no longer in need of a fake boyfriend so…no."

"So, you're looking for a real boyfriend?" He inquired, leaning forward on the island.

I snorted. *Just trying to get over you.* "Something like that."

"Why now?" He ran a hand through his trimmed beard.

I shook my head. "Why do you care?" He had never been interested in my love life before, hell, he'd never been interested in anything in my life before, why now?

He scanned my face for a while, his jaw clenched and unclenched. He let out a breath before answering. "I'm not in love with you or anything, don't get your hopes up, if that's what you were thinking. I was just wondering why all of a sudden you wanted to start dating."

Ouch.

That was not what you wanted to hear about someone you just found out you loved. I bit the inside of my cheek. So, he went back to being an asshole. Was it really that easy for him to hate me?

I scoffed. "It's really none of your business." I started to walk to my bedroom, I needed to get changed, but more importantly, I needed to get away from him, if he was going to throw it in my face that he couldn't fathom the idea of us together, I wouldn't be able to stand here in front of him and take it.

At one point in my life, his insults were expected, they were basic conversation between me and Gabriel, but now? We were friends, or so I thought. All I wanted was to forget this, forget him and these stupid feelings buried in my heart, forget this ever happened, and move on.

"Wait." He called out. I turned back and he sighed. "I'm not trying to be a dick here Mel, I just…" He looked away, clenching his jaw, and turned back to face me "You don't even know who this guy is, where did you even meet him? On tinder?" He scoffed.

"No asshole." I bit out. "I met him today at the coffee shop actually."

"Today? And he already asked you out already?" He shook his head.

Was it that hard to believe that someone wanted to be with me? Did Gabriel really see me as someone who wasn't wanted, wasn't attractive or desired? The more I thought about it the more I wanted to bury myself in my sheets and stay there the whole week. I was in love with this man, his face, his body, his personality — although right now I wasn't sure why — and all he could think about me was that I was unworthy of that kind of effort and attention.

I couldn't stop the heat rising to my cheeks. "God, Gabriel why is it that impossible to believe someone wants to take me on a date, what happened? I thought we were friends." I wiped the traitor tear that slipped down my cheek away, hoping he didn't see that. I didn't want to be weak, especially not in front of Gabriel.

His jaw clenched. "Maybe I don't want to be your friend." He spat out.

I shook my head. All that talk about us getting along and finally being civil was redundant. Zaria got her wish, we would never be together, not even as friends according to Gabriel. He hated me that much, that he couldn't stand to be friends with me, and here I was, stupidly in love with him. My heart betrayed me, the first time I fell in love and my heart had to break before it bloomed. I clutched my chest and let a tear slip. I didn't care anymore. He could see how much he hurt me. I turned and bolted to my room.

As soon as the door closed, I pressed my forehead to the door, letting the tears fall freely. What happened in the space of a day for this to go the way it did? I didn't know why Gabriel was so angry, there was no explanation, no reasoning but the fact that he couldn't be around me. It was obvious since the moment we met, he hated me and always would.

Love, as I was finding out, was a funny thing. No matter what he did, it seemed like these feelings weren't going to leave any time soon, even after he shut me out of his life, I still loved him. My heart still beat for the moment he would love me back, the realization that it wasn't going to be a fact, killed me.

I got in my bed and buried myself in my sheets, closing my eyes. I let sleep drift me away, willing it to take away this pain, just for a moment.

CHAPTER TWENTY-THREE

It was the day of the date. I was going on a date.

With someone I knew nothing about, except for the quick google search I did on him. After searching for what seemed like an eternity of Shawn's, I stumbled on his page. Shawn Turner. He was a lawyer, *fancy*. He was from California and graduated from Harvard. And that was my extensive knowledge on my date for the evening. I wondered if it was enough,

I kept thinking about what Gabriel had said, it was pretty presumptuous of him to call the same day he asked for my number, what if this guy was a rapist or serial killer. How was a google search of his name going to help me figure out if he had a criminal background? I ran a hand through my hair, I was overthinking again.

"Everything is going to be fine." I muttered to my reflection.

I glanced over at my phone. Four-thirty, I had to be there in half an hour. I exhaled, glancing over at my outfit in the mirror. My experience of first dates was exactly: two. For a coffee date, that meant casual, right? I looked down at my jeans and tucked my t-shirt inside. This would probably do. I would normally ask Zaria for advice, but she was still at work and wouldn't be home until six. I just hoped this worked.

I sat on the edge of the bed and sighed, staring at the ceiling. Should I leave now or arrive late. Did I want to be the type of person who specifically delayed time until I was the right amount of late? But did I want to be the person who arrived first and eagerly waited for their date?

I fell back on my bed with a groan, burying my face in my hands. I didn't know what kind of person I wanted to be. Why was it so hard to just be yourself? Why couldn't I get there at the time I got there and for it to not mean anything, not to make a statement?

I was failing at dating, and I hadn't even gotten through this date yet. The last two dates I forced myself to agree to, were dreadful. I wasn't even attracted to the guys, I had accepted, just to make myself step out of my comfort zone and try something new, something different.

Was I doing the same thing today? I was attracted to him, so it was different, right? But not nearly as much as Gabriel. No. Ugh, stop thinking about Gabriel.

I couldn't escape him, no matter how hard I tried. Thoughts of him ran through my mind, the short moment where we became friends constantly filling my thoughts. What happened to ruin that? What was Gabriel trying to push away?

I couldn't sit here and think about this anymore. More than ever before I needed to leave. I grabbed my phone and keys and walked towards the front door. I just needed to get out of this apartment, thoughts of Gabriel flooded my mind, and staying in this apartment wouldn't help.

♡

I guess I'd be the type of person who showed up fashionably late... accidentally. I must have assumed there would be no traffic from my apartment to the café. It was usually a ten-minute drive, but I had been stuck in traffic for the last fifteen minutes. I reached for my phone and noticed it was a quarter to five, I'd probably be there in ten minutes if this traffic ever picked up, but I'd still make it on time, hopefully.

Hopefully? Was I anticipating this date? Maybe. It was an easy distraction and a chance to get to know an attractive man, I just hoped my instincts were right and that he wouldn't turn out to be a serial killer.

Ten minutes later I was outside of the café. The sign was pink with blue lettering and read 'Café Petit.' Which literally translated to 'small café.' Cute. I had missed this the last time I was here. Zaria had ushered us in, excited to show me the place where she and Jeremy would get their coffee from on her breaks.

I opened the glass door and walked in, taking in the feel of this place. It felt warm and cozy, probably because it was small and only fit eight tables, but the appeal of this café was growing on me. Tucked away and hidden but filled with character.

Today the place was surprisingly empty, I could only see three tables occupied and a couple of people at the counter waiting to order. I glanced around, hoping to see Shawn but he wasn't here yet. I bit the inside of my cheek, I hoped to God he didn't cancel last minute. I didn't know him well enough, but for someone who called the same day he got a woman's number, he didn't come across as the type who would stand that same woman up.

I pulled out my phone and noticed it was five, I hoped he was punctual. God, this sounded like an interview. Punctual?

For a date? I shook my head at myself. Technically a first date was pretty much an interview, right? You asked questions about the other person and saw if they were fit for the job, metaphorically speaking.

I should have gotten some tips from Zaria to prepare for today. Knowing her, she would give me sex tips instead of actual helpful first-date advice. Like how did you flirt without coming on too strong? What if he got bored? What if I got bored?

"Next." The barista called, a different one from yesterday. This barista was a girl, she looked young, most likely a teenager, her hair was bright red tied up in a messy bun, her green eyes poked into mine as she waited for me to approach the counter.

Should I order or wait for Shawn to show up? What if he stood me up and I looked like an idiot waiting in a café without a drink, clearly waiting on someone? The overthinking got to me again. I shook my head, I should order, that way if he didn't show up, I wouldn't look like an utter moron and if he did then I could always refresh my drink.

I approached the counter and she smiled. "Good afternoon, what can I get for you today?" She asked, chewing on her gum.

"Um, a hot chocolate please." I said, tucking my hair behind my ear.

She nodded and disappeared behind the counter, making the drinks. I reached into my purse and pulled out my wallet.

"Coffee, black."

Huh? I looked up and saw the coffee sat on the counter. "Oh, um I didn't order this,"

"That's for me."

I sucked a breath. I recognized that voice. I turned around. *Gabriel.*

"What are you doing here?" I asked. I hadn't spoken to him since yesterday, when he said he didn't want to have any kind of friendship with me. I bit my cheek to stifle my eyes from welling up. Seeing him here, up close made me lose all focus.

He reached behind me, picking up his coffee. "I'm drinking coffee." He said, nonchalantly.

"Here? Where I'm having my date?"

He shrugged. That was the only answer I was going to get? I shook my head, this was ridiculous, what the hell was he doing here?

"Gabriel, just leave."

Instead, he took a seat at the back table, closest to the counter, and leaned back "Don't worry about me." He gestured to the front door "Have fun on your date."

I rolled my eyes at him. He wasn't going to leave. How was I supposed to get through this date when Gabriel was sat less than ten feet away from me? I accepted this date to get *over* him, to forget about him, and instead he showed up.

CHAPTER TWENTY-FOUR

I glanced at the front door as it opened, seeing Shawn strolling through it.

He was still wearing a suit, maybe he came straight from work. Not that I had any objections. That suit looked good on him, not better than— Nope. I'm not going to go there, I'm not going to compare them again.

He smiled when his eyes met mine and as attractive as he was, that smile did nothing for me. It didn't make my stomach drop or make my cheeks warm, not like... someone who shall not be named.

"Hi." He said.

"Hey."

He approached the counter and looked down at the drink in my hand, he frowned. "You ordered?"

I nodded. "I got here a little early, so I thought I'd order in case, you know..."

He looked stumped. "In case?"

I sighed. "In case you didn't show up." I admitted.

He laughed. "Trust me, Melissa, I wouldn't have missed this, I ah... crap, I wanted to pay for you, I did ask *you* out on this date after all. Traffic was crazy, I came straight from work actually that's why," he gestured to his suit. "I didn't want you to think I was a snob who wore suits to drink coffee or go grocery shopping." He smiled.

A snort came from Gabriel, who at that moment became painfully obvious to me that he was sitting right next to where we were standing. I didn't dare look over at him. Shawn glanced at him and then back at me. I was expecting him to ask if I knew him, but he didn't. He gestured to the barista and ordered an espresso.

We waited for his drink to be prepared and walked over to the table closest to the front door, as far away as I could get from where Gabriel was sat. It was bad enough that I could see him, but I didn't want him eavesdropping on our conversation.

"So, Melissa I hope I didn't scare you off inviting you out today, so quickly."

I took a sip of my drink. "No, not at all."

He smiled. "I guess not, since you're here."

I nodded. "It was actually refreshing not having to wait for days or weeks."

"Well, I couldn't wait to see you again, that was for sure."

I gave him a smile. So far so good.

"So, what do you do?" I didn't want to let on that I already knew this, I had googled him after all. But would he think that was stalkerish?

"I'm a criminal lawyer, a defense attorney actually. Graduated top of my class at Harvard." He said, fixing his tie.

That sounded a bit snobby, but I couldn't judge him yet, I barely knew the guy. I took a sip of my hot chocolate to hide the expression on my face.

"That sounds... interesting, tell me more." Did that sound like an interview? *Stop overthinking.*

He laughed. "Well, I defend people charged with criminal activity."

"Even if they're guilty?"

He laughed again, this time sounding less warm but more condescending "Defendants are innocent until proven guilty, my job is to prove their innocence."

Okay, so he didn't really answer the question, he just spieled some basic textbook crap.

"Oh."

"It's okay, I know it can be hard for some people to understand."

Yikes. That was... patronizing to say the least.

"What do you do Melissa?"

"I'm a middle school teacher."

He nodded, taking a sip of his drink "Ah." I furrowed my brows. "Those who can't do, teach, right?"

"What does that mean?" I asked. Did he just call me dumb or was I reading too much into it? It had been five minutes, I needed to give him more time, maybe he was just nervous. *Or maybe he was just an arrogant jerk.* I hoped it was the former, I had enough of rich snooty guys who thought they were better than everyone else. One of my previous dates was an actual narcissist, and that was not my type.

He waved a hand. "Never mind, so what do you like to do in your free time?"

My phone dinged, making me lose focus. Please let it be Zaria with an emergency. "Sorry, I forgot to silence it." I reached into my purse and unlocked my phone.

Gabriel: That guy sounds like an asshole.

Gabriel? I looked up to see him staring at his phone screen. I didn't have his number and as far as I knew he didn't have my number, before this week we had no other reason to communicate. How the hell did I have his number saved on my phone. Before I could even think, another text popped up.

Gabriel: Ditch him, he sounds like a know-it-all snooty motherfucker.

I looked up from my phone again to see him staring back at me, smiling. What the hell was he doing? And clearly my idea of sitting as far away as possible from him so he wouldn't overhear us, hadn't worked.

"Is everything okay?" Shawn asked. I debated telling him no, that my friend had an emergency and needed me home. Shawn did sound like a know-it-all snooty motherfucker, not that I would admit that, especially with whatever game Gabriel was playing at. I felt determined to see this through.

"Yes, everything's fine." I smiled at him. "So, you were asking what I like to do in my free time?" What did I like to do in my free time? Stay at home and binge-watch tv. That sounded pathetic. "Um, I guess I enjoy reading or watching tv. Entertainment, mostly." I chuckled, taking a sip of my hot chocolate. "Reality shows are kind of my guilty pleasure." I admitted, thinking it would liven up the mood.

He grunts. "I'm not a fan of reality tv shows, I find them egotistical and senseless. But books? I like reading books too, which authors do you read? F. Scott Fitzgerald?" He leaned back, clasping his hands together.

I find you 'egotistical and senseless' I bit my tongue, willing the words to stay down and I winced. "Not exactly, mostly modern romance books. What do you like to do?" I hoped if I changed the subject, he wouldn't bring up how the modern-day world was lost to troubled youth blah blah blah.

Whatever demeaning thing would positively come out of his mouth.

My phone lit up again, I had silenced it but the brightness on the table was unmistakable. I glanced at it, seeing Gabriel's name flash on the screen again. Lord have mercy I was going to murder him.

Gabriel: Seriously? Egotistical and senseless? C'mon trevi, ditch this guy, I'll watch reality shows with you.

My heart skipped a beat at his message. He wanted to watch reality shows with me. No, I couldn't let myself fall for this again, he was hot and cold. One day he was friendly, and we would joke and the other he was saying he never wanted to be friends with me. What kind of person did that?

Shawn cleared his throat and I looked up at him "I'm sorry." I said again. But honestly, these texts Gabriel sent me were more entertaining than this guy sat in front of me.

"That's okay, I guess. Are you sure that there isn't anything wrong?"

"Nope." I locked eyes with Gabriel and gave him a tight-lipped smile. I was going to finish this date and Gabriel wouldn't stop me.

"Well, uh, as I was saying, my hobbies mostly include the golf course or the gym." I resisted the urge to roll my eyes, most guys' only hobbies were 'going to the gym and fishing'. "And I love to go fishing in the summer." Of course, he did.

It was painfully obvious that Shawn was just a pretty face, at least to me. He was snooty rich brain Mr. I know more than you and he would throw his private education in your face.

I had to stick this to the end. I wasn't going to let Gabriel win this round.

My phone flashed once again. "Oh, for crying out loud." Came from Shawn. I flinched at him raising his voice.

"I'm sorry again, really, I just… can you give me a moment, I'll just be in the bathroom?"

"Sure." He said, with little to no expression. This guy was so much different than the charming man that approached me yesterday. I should have known.

I unlocked my phone and read the message.

Gabriel: Fishing? I think you'd have better luck on tinder.

I stood up from the table and locked eyes with Gabriel. He stood up and I gestured to the hall where the bathrooms were. When he approached me, I groaned. "What the hell is wrong with you? First you spit me out like I'm a poisonous apple and then you show up here, *here*, where I'm supposed to be on a date trying to… I just… how did you even know where I'd be…why Gabriel, why are you here?"

He scanned my face and then shrugged. "I'm just trying to look out for you."

Was he kidding? He was a complete asshole to me yesterday and today he just wants to 'look out' for me? I shook my head, laughing with no humor. "I thought you said you didn't want to be my friend? Isn't that what you said? So why are you here?" I poked his chest and immediately regretted it. Touching him wasn't going to help me not think about him, his body, his… I gulped and looked up at his face which was looking back down at me.

He stared into my eyes for a minute and then shook his head, sighing. "I didn't mean that I just…" He ran a hand through his hair. "Fuck. I —" He closed his eyes. "I was just pissed at you, okay?"

"Pissed?" I hissed. "Why should *you* be pissed?"

He laughed, running a thumb across his bottom lip, my gaze following it. I swallowed. Why was that so hot? "You came out on a date with a guy you clearly don't know at all, he seems arrogant and could easily take advantage of you."

I shrugged. "He's not that bad." That was a lie. This was another shitty date to add to the record, but I couldn't let Gabriel know that.

He scoffed. "Bullshit. He isn't anything that you want."

"And how do you know what I want?"

He took a step closer and tucked a strand of hair behind my ear. My eyes fluttered closed, and I immediately forced them open. That was such an intimate thing to do. I hesitated holding his hand back at the dance because it would be too much for me, and he does this? Was this really happening? "Because... I *know* you."

I took a step back, putting some distance between us. I wasn't sure what he was doing, if he thought that he was doing a friendly gesture, he was wrong. This for me meant so much more and I couldn't, I wouldn't let that happen. I had to keep these feelings under control, I didn't want to fall deeper in love with him just to be ripped open again.

His hand dropped from my hair, and he sighed. "He could have hurt you."

I laughed. "He's harmless." *I think.* "And as you can see." I gestured down my body. "I'm fine. If anything, you made him angry with all of those texts interrupting us."

"Mmm, riveting conversations about fishing and F. Scott Fitzgerald." He rolled his eyes. "He's such a snob."

I chuckled. "He probably wants to tell me all about his family's yacht that they take to travel to their private beach house."

"That's on their own island."

"Surrounded by professionally trained sharks."

"Guarded by bodyguards."

I laughed, hard enough that tears welled up in my eyes. I wiped them away with my sleeve. Why was it so natural to laugh with Gabriel? Be in this place with him where we were friends, why was it hard for him to accept?

"So, we're friends again?" I asked.

He pulled me into his chest and sighed. "Of course, we're friends again Mel."

I could stay tucked away here forever. In the comfort of Gabriel's arms. It took me way too long to realize that we were touching. I had never hugged Gabriel. This was the closest I had been to him, ever. And I could get used to it. I resisted the urge to inhale his scent. The sweet smell of oranges and leather seeped into my nose, and I closed my eyes. I could honestly stay here forever.

"I'm going to need that in writing." I mumbled into his chest.

I could feel his body heaving as he laughed. "Cute, trevi." I smiled, the biggest I could and then a sinking feeling hit my stomach. Crap. I was still on this date with Shawn. I pulled back and bit the inside of my cheek, should I just try to get out of it?

"What's wrong?" Gabriel asked.

"Shawn." I blurted out.

His jaw clenched as he peeked out into the café. "He's still out there, the bastard is persistent, I'll give him that. Do you want me to help you get out of here?"

I shook my head. "No, I'll just go back out there."

"What?" He exclaimed. "You're going to go back out there?" He shook his head. "Why?"

I shrugged. "He's honestly not that bad, plus he asked me on a date, it's only fair."

"Mel, you don't have to go."

"I know, I want to. I haven't been out in a date in so long." I shrugged. "Might as well finish this one."

His face turned unreadable, he nodded and stepped back so I could step back out to the café.

Shawn turned and exhaled when his eyes met mine. I sat back at the table. "I apologize for… all of this, it won't happen again." I tucked my phone back into my purse and tried to at least finish this date.

"I held out hope you'd be back. I thought you escaped through the back exit."

I laughed. "But you still waited?"

He nodded. "Of course. A guy like me only had one chance with a girl like you. I must say I feel like tonight didn't go as I planned, I feel as though I came off a bit… intimidating and I apologize for that." He ran a hand through his hair, messing it up a little. "I can promise I'm not as snobby as it seemed, I was just trying to impress you and well…" He laughed. "That didn't seem to work out."

What happened in the short time I stepped out? It seemed like he completely changed. "That's understandable." I said.

"It was partially my fault, I feel as if I wasn't in it fully with the distractions and…" *Gabriel.*

He smiled, nodding as if he understood. I could bet money he didn't have a clue what was going on inside my head right now.

He reached out and squeezed my hand. It was an intimate and comforting gesture and hopefully I was wrong, and first impressions didn't count, because this man sat in front of me was much more my type than the one I had before. Maybe this was his twin and they switched when I went to the bathroom? If so, I preferred this twin.

"Let's start this over?" He suggested.

"You mean… a second date?"

"I would really like to get to know you better and we can both agree this first date wasn't a good first impression on either of us."

A second date with Shawn? I had barely gotten through this one. Granted that was partially Gabriel's fault and maybe Shawn was just trying to impress me by thinking I wanted a snooty rich boy. It was obvious nothing would progress between Gabriel and I and these feelings still hadn't diminished. If things went well with Shawn, maybe they would.

I nodded. "Okay, let's do it."

"Great." He grinned. "I'll call you."

We stood up from the table and I gathered my things. He opened the café door and gestured for me to leave first. Once we were both outside, we separated with a quick goodbye. I hadn't seen Gabriel since I came from the bathroom hall, and I didn't see him in the café again.

CHAPTER TWENTY-FIVE

"So did you escape?" I looked up to see Gabriel leaning against my car door.

"How did *you* escape? I didn't see you." I asked.

He shrugged. "I took the back exit, I thought you wanted some privacy with your *boyfriend* since I seemed to ruin your date."

I laughed. Did he seem jealous or was that my imagination? "It was fine, we're actually going out on another date." I said, plucking out my keys from my purse. I walked over to the driver's seat, but Gabriel stopped me.

"You're what?"

I stepped back. He was mad? There was no reason for him to be upset. He didn't even know Shawn. Granted I didn't know him that well either but that was the purpose of going on another date, right? To get to know him better.

"Okay, calm down." I breathed. "He's not that bad, you don't even know him."

He scoffed. "Neither do you, and from where I was standing, he seemed like an asshole."

"You were sitting actually."

The corner of his lips pulled up, but he quickly realized and dropped them, and he narrowed his eyes at me. "Don't be such a smartass."

I shook my head. "I thought we were friends again. I knew I would need that in writing."

He closed his eyes, running his hands down his face. "We are friends. And as your friend I'm telling you not to go on this date."

I snorted. "You can't be serious. You can't tell me who I can or can't go on a date with Gabriel." I cocked my head to the side "Are you jealous?" I blurted out. I bit my tongue as soon as I had said that. Why did I say that? This was why I couldn't be around him, one day of being near him, talking to him, laughing with him and my brain accumulated that with him being into me?

His eyes scanned my face. "Jealous?" He laughed, "Why would I be jealous?"

Stupid, stupid girl.

Of course, he wasn't jealous. He laughed, He actually laughed, like just the idea that he would be jealous of another man on a date with me was laughable. Like merely the idea of him wanting to be with me was hilarious.

My chest hurt and I pressed at it willing it to calm down. Don't have a panic attack in the parking lot in front of Gabriel. It's fine. You knew this already, he doesn't like you, he will never like you. *Calm down.*

I felt my heart beat slower and took a deep breath in. I needed to get away. He could be my 'friend' all he wanted, but that hurt. I took a step closer, gesturing to my car. Gabriel stepped to the side. I opened my car door, noticing he was still standing behind me. How did he get here anyway? I looked around, not seeing his car, "I don't see your car, how did you even get here?"

"I parked on the other side, so you wouldn't see me."

What was his game? Purposefully hiding so I wouldn't know he would try to observe my date. "So, you stalked me?" I teased. Only half joking.

He ruffled my hair. "Sure I did." He joked.

The look in Gabriel's eyes was too much for me. He looked at me like I was a kid, a stupid kid with a crush that he would never reciprocate. I gulped and stepped inside my car, closing the door.

He stepped back allowing me to drive off. How did he manage to make me feel like this, even when this day had nothing to do with him? I was supposed to be getting over him, but instead, I wanted to be seen by him, I wanted him to care, to want me, to need me like I did him.

♡

I needed to stop overthinking this.

I didn't want to think about Gabriel at all, he basically just rejected me, hard, and I was still thinking about what it meant for him to show up at the coffee shop, he wanted to protect me, he wanted to make sure I was okay. Why? None of it made sense and none of it was relevant. I couldn't be sure about Gabriel's intentions today, not when he did one thing and said the complete opposite with his mouth. That beautiful mouth that was so close to my ear— nope, don't think about his mouth.

I shook my head, taking out my keys from my purse, opening the door to my apartment. The door flung open, and my heart dropped. Gabriel was standing in the middle of the room with his arms crossed against his chest. What the— How the hell did he get here so quick? I drove off first.

"How are you here already?"

"I know a shortcut."

I snorted. Figures.

Why was he standing in the middle of the apartment like that? Was he waiting for me? If he tried to get me to decline that date again, I would scream. He had no right to tell me what to do with my life, not when he showed no interest before. Why the sudden care for my wellbeing? Was it just an obligation out of loyalty to his sister? If so, I didn't want or need that. I didn't want any pity from anyone, I had been taking care of myself all these years. I could do it just fine.

I had learned from early on, that no one else was going to be my savior or my hero that took care of me and my problems. My mother taught me that. By her abandoning me, Ilearnedt quickly that I was the sole proprietor of my life and choices. I was the only one that had to worry about and take care of myself, no one else.

Gabriel had unknowingly done that for me, he took care of me when he didn't have to, he filled a space that was empty for a long time. Feeling like someone cared about me enough to take time out of their day specifically for my needs made me feel… special, wanted, loved. And stupidly enough, I let my feelings take over and I fell head over heels for him.

I willed myself to be strong and fight it. Be a stone-cold bitch who didn't need anyone, be the antagonizing pain in the ass I had always been to Gabriel, make him hate me, make myself hate him, but none of it had worked, not even the distance I forced between us, had killed these feelings.

I stepped into the apartment, ignoring Gabriel. I took my shoes off and threw the keys onto the kitchen island. I started to move towards my bedroom, but Gabriel had other ideas, he stepped in front of me, blocking my path.

"Move, please."

He just shook his head.

I gave up, sighing. "What now?"

"What's with you?" He asked.

My mouth dropped open. "What's with me? What's with you? You stalked me to the café, intimidated my date, which thankfully didn't work and then you try to get me to cancel on him. Why?"

He looked me over, clenching his jaw.

Say it.

Say anything. You want me. You were jealous. This was just some dumb overprotective big brother crap. Give me something.

His eyes closed as he ran a hand through his hair. They opened and he looked at me for a second before moving to the side, allowing me to pass through him.

He was a coward. He couldn't even tell me the real reason he was trying so hard to get me to cancel this date. I wasn't sure if I was just getting my hopes up, but there was a slim chance Gabriel was jealous. Could that be the reason? Did he feel what I felt?

No. He had made that abundantly clear. He wasn't interested, he had said that himself time and time again. So why was he so interested in my life now? One thing was for sure, Gabriel might not be interested in me, but there were people who were.

I closed my bedroom door and stripped off my clothes. I didn't even bother with pajamas, I needed to feel the cold hit my skin. I opened the windows as far as they would go and stood at the window, breathing in the crisp air. I couldn't breathe when I was around Gabriel, all I felt was heat coursing through my body, making it nearly impossible to be around him, it felt like every time he came near me, my body would set on fire, it was like I was pulled to him.

CHAPTER TWENTY-SIX

"Wow M, I know you hate dresses, but you look good enough to eat."

Shawn had called two days ago and planned a date at Prime Vista, one of the more upscale restaurants in San Francisco, he must make triple my salary because I could never afford to dine out at a place like that. I hoped he wasn't trying to impress me again with his money. Even though I was impressed, being rich didn't equal being someone I wanted to spend time with. Money only got you so far.

I wanted the charming guy I met at the café, the guy who called the same day because he wanted to see me again. The guy who waited even though our first date was a disaster, and I was in the hallway with another guy.

"It's not that I hate them, I just never get to wear them." I wore mostly jeans or fitted skirts when teaching, dresses weren't really part of my work wardrobe, and since I rarely went out, I never felt the need to own any.

I glanced at the mirror, taking in the dress. I had bought this specific dress over a year ago, on one of the times Zaria had made me promise her to go out clubbing with her. I never wore red, and I wasn't sure why, I had to admit I looked hot. The dress was satin and ended mid-thigh. My legs were already long, and the cut of the dress made them look longer, not to mention I was wearing heels.

Gabriel wouldn't be there this time, which made me reconsider the stilettos I had previously planned to wear and replaced them with a smaller heel.

"This isn't too much cleavage?" I panned the phone to the mirror, showing Zaria the neckline of the dress.

She laughed. "No such thing."

"There definitely is." I retorted. "I don't want my boobs to scream 'look at me.'" There was a difference between seductive and subtle and looking like I was trying too hard.

"Melissa, you do that even without showing your boobs." I rolled my eyes. She was such a hype girl, always making me feel like a million bucks, even when I didn't believe it.

I sighed. "I'm nervous."

"Don't be." She told me. "If he starts acting weird again just call me, I'll come and get you."

I told Zaria about the date, and she wasn't exactly thrilled that I had agreed to go on a second date with Shawn. But if she knew the reason was because I was trying my hardest to get over her brother, she might have been more approving.

"I'm driving there, I can just leave if I need to."

She laughed, again. "We both know you wouldn't do that, you're too nice M, seriously just call me I'll come and help you. Or Gabriel. He's home, I'm sure he wouldn't mind coming to your rescue."

I'm sure he wouldn't either, the question was, why? Gabriel would be the last person I would call, especially when it came to Shawn. If Gabriel knew I was wrong about Shawn and he did end up being a jackass who thought he was better than everyone, I would never hear the end of it, Gabriel would gloat and tell me 'I told you so.'

No. I needed to do this on my own. I was a grown ass woman, I could take care of myself, like I always had. If I really didn't like this date, I would find a way to get myself out of it, no need to get anyone else involved.

"Did you forget you're out? On a date?" Zaria cut it off with Jeremy and called the barista from the café and was out on a date with him. "Speaking of which, how are you on the phone right now? Where is he?"

She flipped the phone screen, giving me a view of her date, Trey, walking towards her with shots. Of course, Zaria's first date was at a bar.

"Looks like you're busy."

"I'm never busy for you." I smiled at that. I knew she would be there for me in a heartbeat if I called her. But she was happy, I couldn't do that to her.

"Have fun Z." I blew a kiss at my phone screen, and she blew one back.

"Don't forget call me or my bro if you need to."

"I will." I lied, hanging up.

I exhaled, looking at my reflection in the mirror. I picked up my mascara and applied another coat. I needed to breathe. This was just a date, I already met him, and he seemed nice enough, there was no reason to panic or to overthink, it would all be fine.

I took a deep breath in and closed my eyes, my mind immediately went to the one memory that I could never forget.

The Andersons pool in the summer. I was sixteen and Zaria and I had been friends for a while. Gabriel walked out of the house wearing blue swim shorts and nothing else. He was eighteen and already had his first tattoo across his forearm, his dark skin glowing under the summer sun. Zaria lay on a floatie besides me telling me about the party she had been to last weekend, which I hadn't been invited to. Zaria tried to stay with me, but I forced her to go, just because I hadn't been invited didn't mean I wanted her to sit and wallow with me at home, she liked parties and socializing, I didn't.

Gabriel was walking towards us and sat on the edge of the pool, dipping his feet in the water. I couldn't look away, this was someone who for some reason hated me but all I wanted was his attention. I jumped from the pool floatie into the pool dipping my head underwater. I popped up from the water to see Gabriel staring at me. Finally, he was looking at me.

"You look like a drowned rat."

I blinked. It was nothing but insults with him, he couldn't speak to me without arguing.

"It's a shame you didn't drown yet." I retorted.

He laughed. "Why don't you surprise me and say something smart."

I groaned. "I envy people who don't know you."

"No one else has a problem with me trevi, it's only you." I hated that nickname. He thought he was so clever for coming up with it and he knew how much I hated it. I bit the inside of my cheek. Why did he hate me? I never understood why he had such a problem with me.

"I'd agree with you, but we'd both be wrong."

"Ugh, please stop arguing," Zaria said, still on the floatie.

I approached where he was sat, dragging him into the pool. The water splashed around us as he fell into the water.

I laughed seeing him trying to swim back up. I moved away from him as he broke the surface and came up.

He shook the water from his face, as he walked towards me. He was tall, so the water only hit his chest, raising higher and higher as he walked towards me. I gulped. Why was he approaching me?

He was standing so close I could smell his cologne, even through the chlorine. My eyes fluttered for a second and the next I was underwater. I snapped my eyes open and saw Gabriel underwater beside me, holding me down by the waist. I pushed at him, until he let me go. I swam up, gasping for air when I broke the surface of the water. "Asshole." I yelled.

Gabriel smirked, staring at me. He scanned my face down to my neck then to my chest. I felt so exposed having him look at me like that. His eyes met mine and I sucked a breath, maintaining eye contact. We just breathed deeply staring back at each other.

I snapped my eyes open meeting my reflection. My cheeks were flushed, and my chest was rising with my accelerated heartbeat. Even when he hated me all I wanted was him, having him look at me that day like he had never done before made me feel seen. Being at that pool with Zaria and Gabriel — even though he hated me — was the closest I felt being at home, as part of a real family.

I exhaled. "Stop thinking about him." I muttered to the mirror.

Opening the door, I walked out of my bedroom into the hallway. I needed to leave soon.

My head jerked when Gabriel's door snapped open. He stepped out of his bedroom, and I let my eyes wander down his body. Down the white t-shirt that clung to his chest and biceps, covered in tattoos, down to the black jeans that looked so good on him. How did he look this good in a t-shirt and jeans?

I looked up to meet his eyes, which were nothing like I had seen before. He looked down my body like I had his, his eyes darkened as he looked at my dress, down my legs and then back at me. His jaw clenched but he maintained the eye contact. I couldn't. I ripped my gaze away from his. "Um... I, uh, I have to go." I picked up my purse and dropped my keys and phone inside.

I looked up to see Gabriel standing in front of the door. He was going to try and stop me again?

I exhaled. "Gabriel, please I don't have time for this, just let me go."

"No."

I blinked. "No? What do you mean no?"

He took a step closer, still guarding the front door. "I mean, no you're not going."

He wasn't serious. There was no way Gabriel was going to try and stop me from going to this date. I didn't need to listen to him, he didn't own me, he didn't get to tell me what to do or who I could see. He was no one to me, barely a friend and definitely not someone who should be acting like this. I debated asking if he was jealous, recalling how he had responded the last time I asked him that.

I shook my head, this wasn't happening. I finally got the courage to move past the first date with a guy and Gabriel was the one to interject.

"Why?" I laughed, dryly. "You don't even know him, what could possibly be your issue with him?"

His eyes darkened, burying into mine. "Melissa, I don't give a fuck if he's secretly a prince, you're not fucking going."

"I'm not going?" I repeated.

"That's right."

I had never seen Gabriel this angry. I never would have imagined it would be over something that had nothing to do with him. "You can't tell me what to do." I spat.

He took a step closer, and I eyed the door, maybe I could make it.

"Don't even think about it." He warned me.

I laughed. "So what? You're going to kidnap me and keep me hostage."

"If that's what it takes."

I couldn't help but groan, this was ridiculous. "Step aside and let me go, you're not my father, you're not my brother and you're definitely not my fucking boyfriend so why do you care?"

He didn't answer me, his jaw clenched once again as he scanned my face and then closed his eyes running a hand through his hair.

I took that as my chance and moved past him towards the door. I reached for the door handle when Gabriel's hand went flying around my wrist. He twisted me around so my back hit the door. I sucked in a breath.

"Don't try to be clever, you're not leaving."

I tried to pull my arm away from him, but it was no use. I was trapped. "What are you doing?" I hissed.

"I told you, I'd keep you here if I needed to."

I narrowed my eyes at him. "The things I do don't concern you."

He pinned both of my wrists to the door above my head, leaning in closer, close enough that I could lean in, and my lips would touch his. "Everything you do, concerns me." He whispered.

I swallowed, he was close, he was so close. "Why do you care?" I asked him again.

He groaned. "Don't tempt me." He warned.

"Or what?" I whispered.

His eyes scanned my face, landing on my mouth and on impulse my lips parted. His face turned to the side, away from me. "You better shut that pretty mouth, or I'll do it for you."

I was breathing heavy. His eyes were so intense, and I couldn't take it anymore. "Make me."

His eyes turned to face me again, looking into my eyes, they dipped to my mouth and then back again. I swallowed.

"Fuck it." He leaned in, his lips crashing on mine. I couldn't help the yelp that left my lips, Gabriel kissed me. He was kissing me. A moan grumbled at the back of my throat, and he groaned into my mouth. But then he stepped back.

My eyes snapped open at the loss of his lips on mine and his eyes were wide as he scanned my face. His chest rose and fell as he breathed hard. "Fuck, Mel I'm sorry I didn't…" He closed his eyes, wiping a hand down his face.

I wasn't sorry, I wasn't sorry at all. I wanted this, I wanted more.

"Kiss me." I whispered.

His eyes opened as he slowly looked back at me. "What?" He asked, his voice so low I could barely hear.

"Kiss me." I told him, louder this time.

He didn't hesitate this time, his lips fell on mine and his tongue brushed my lower lip and I parted them, he brushed his tongue across mine, dancing for domination, his teeth nipped my bottom lip and I moaned again. I needed more.

His hands reached up and cupped my cheeks as his lips covered mine, kissing me so deep. I grabbed the back of his head, needing him closer, he leaned my head back, deepening the kiss. His lips left mine, trailing kisses down my jaw towards my neck and I whimpered. I needed his mouth back on mine. I could feel his breath on my neck as he laughed at my greediness.

He kissed my throat and then licked it before moving back up towards my jaw. "So needy." He murmured before his lips found mine again.

This was really happening, I was kissing Gabriel Anderson. I let another moan escape and he groaned in response, he broke the kiss and I stared up at him. His thumb stroked my cheek. "You're killing me with those noises Mel."

CHAPTER TWENTY-SEVEN

I needed more.

I needed him.

I swallowed, having him look at me like that was everything I wanted, and it was everything I needed. "I want…"

He kissed me again. "Want me where honey? Use your words."

"I…" I couldn't say it.

He leaned in and licked my bottom lip. "Say it." He whispered.

I exhaled. "I want… I want you… inside of me."

He groaned and dived back in catching my lips. He kissed me like his life depended on it, pulling down the straps of my dress, he pulled the fabric down, groaning again as he encountered my bare breast.

He leaned in, wrapping those lips around my sensitive bud. My knees buckled, struggling to stay upright. His teeth grasped it before he soothed it with the swirl of his tongue. He sucked me in his mouth before moving to the other. I didn't know I could feel this much pleasure from just my breasts. I moaned, leaning into his mouth. He released me with a pop and came back up, kissing me again. He reached under the hem and pulled the dress above my head, leaving me in just my black lacy underwear.

He took a step back, staring at my body like he had never done before, like no one had done before. His fingers grazed the hem of my underwear, and he leaned in resting his mouth next to my ear. "Were you going to show him this?" Him? Shawn? I had completely forgotten about Shawn. All my thoughts were consumed by Gabriel. Was I going to show Shawn this? I shook my head. "Good." He murmured.

His hands reached inside, parting me and I gasped. "Jesus. You're so fucking wet." He grunted. "For me." I nodded, it was all for him. No one else had made me feel like this.

His finger grazed my clit and my knees buckled. "Oh God." I breathed out. They travelled down until he plunged two of them inside of me, deep. I hissed at the tight fit and he retrieved them.

"Did I hurt you?" He asked.

I shook my head, keeping my eyes closed.

"Mel are you a virgin?" He asked.

Was I a virgin? That was an interesting question. Technically you had to be penetrated to lose your virginity and that I was, but did I have sex? No.

I looked up at him. "No, it's just… it's been a long time."

"How long?"

"Five years?"

"What?"

I nodded. I didn't want to talk about this, not now, not when his fingers were deep inside of me, surrounded by my arousal.

His lips crashed into mine and he kissed me, long and deep. "We don't have to do anything."

"No." I almost shouted. "I want to." I assured him. I wanted this more than anything. I had done nothing but dream of this and it was finally happening.

He kissed my jaw. "I'll take care of you, Mel." He whispered, before pushing his fingers back inside of me, not as deep this time, allowing me to stretch around him. His thumb grazed my clit, rubbing slow circles on it.

"I've wanted you for so long." He panted, his voice husky with lust. "You have no idea how many times I fisted my cock thinking about you, thinking about this." His movements quickened and my nails gripped his shoulder, this was…too much and not enough at the same time. "Fuck, you're dripping." He murmured before taking my nipple in his mouth. I gripped onto him, grinding into his hand until I felt myself clench around his fingers.

"I've thought about you too." I heaved, breathless and dizzy, full of desire. So many nights I had thought of him. So many times, I didn't let myself indulge in the fantasy of me and Gabriel and now it was happening.

"You have?" He asked. I nodded, moaning when he hit a spot that almost blinded me. "Did you touch yourself thinking about me?" I nodded again, husking out a whispered 'yes' and he grunted, curling his fingers inside of me.

"Did you cry out my name?" I shook my head. "Why not?" He asked, frowning at my confession.

I squeezed my eyes shut, the pressure was building in my core, and I couldn't hold it. I writhed my hips against his hand and his other hand reached up, pinching my puckered nipple. "Why not?" He repeated.

"Because." I moaned. "I was trying to keep quiet." Zaria and I shared a wall. I couldn't exactly scream Gabriel's name every time I made myself come, thinking about him.

He leaned in, kissing me deep and hard. "Don't. it's only me and you. I want you to cry out in pleasure when I make you come. The only one you think about." He punctuated his sentence with a hard kiss as his thumb worked faster on my sensitive clit.

"Please." I panted.

The pressure was so intense, I saw stars. I opened my eyes, staring down at his gorgeous face, his eyes dark and lustful burning into mine as his thumb accelerated on the swollen bundle of nerves. "Gabriel, Oh god." I cried out, coming around his fingers. My legs gave out, but he held me up by the waist as it subsided. He kept going until I came down from my orgasm. His fingers pulled out of me, and I was suddenly very aware of the fact I was practically naked, and he was still in his clothes.

I pulled his shirt up, I needed to see him, to feel him. He threw the t-shirt over his head, across the room. I brought my hands up his chest, rubbing them over his pecks and his tattoos, I've always wanted to feel him underneath my fingertips and now I was. I wanted this moment to last forever, I didn't care what happened later or tomorrow, all I wanted was now. I ran my hands down his arms and then back down his chest reaching his belt.

His hand came over mine, stopping me. I looked up and he shook his head. "Let me take care of you." He said. Stepping closer, his lips pressed against mine as he grabbed my ass in his hands. "Hold on, baby." He murmured in between kisses. He pulled me up and I wrapped my legs around him, he was walking…somewhere. I didn't care where, I was too focused on how his mouth worked me, sucking on my tongue, biting my lip.

He set me down somewhere hard and cold, and I opened my eyes, seeing that I was sat on the kitchen island. He broke the kiss trailing down my neck, down my breasts and my stomach, leaving little soft kisses all over my body. His mouth reached the hem of my underwear and he looked up at me, waiting for the green light. I swallowed and nodded.

He pulled them down my legs and flung them to the floor. He looked up at me for a while, shaking his head. The look in his eyes was enough to have me clenching around nothing. "You're so fucking beautiful." He growled, dipping his head to kiss my stomach before leaning down and parting me with his tongue. My head flew back, and his tongue brushed my clit, flicking it.

My hands reached into his hair, he had barely any to grab on to and I let out a frustrated groan. His mouth left my swollen bud, making its way down to my entrance, he plunged it deep inside, lapping up my juices. He continued that way, alternating between dipping his tongue inside of me and abusing my clit until I was a writhing mess underneath him, gripping the back of his head. "Gabriel." I panted. I was a wreck already sensitive from coming mere minutes ago, and I was somehow close, already.

"I know baby." He murmured. "You taste so fucking good."

Oh my god. I couldn't take it anymore. I let go of his head, letting my back hit the cold kitchen island. "Gabriel." I called out as I shuddered, coming on his tongue. He dipped his tongue inside of me again, licking up every last drop.

When he raised his head, his beard was covered in my arousal and the sight of it almost made me come again. He rushed towards me, kissing me, hard. I could taste myself on his tongue, it was the hottest thing I had ever experienced. When he pulled away, I licked my lips, loving my own taste, knowing he had enjoyed that as much as me.

"Fuck, Mel."

I nodded. I couldn't speak, not after that.

He grabbed the back of my thighs, lifting me up again, I wrapped my legs back around his waist burying my face in the crook of his neck.

"My bed or yours?"

"Yours." My voice was muffled, my face pressed up against his body. I wanted to be buried in his sheets, have his smell surround me whilst he devoured my body. Not even my fantasies could have prepared me for this moment, what Gabriel was doing to me, beat anything I could have concocted in my imagination.

His lips found mine, walking us into his bedroom, he closed his door, sitting me at the edge of his bed. He pulled back, looking down at me as he stood above me. His hands reached for his belt, and I licked my lips.

"Let me." I said, palming his crotch over his jeans. He grunted at my touch and dropped his hands.

I hastily undid his belt, pulling down his jeans to his knees. He kicked them off, standing in only a pair of black boxers that did nothing to hide him. He was big. I gulped, if his fingers hurt, how was I going to fit his cock inside of me?

He must have sensed my apprehension, because his thumb pulled my chin up to look at him. "It will fit." He reassured me. But how did he know? What if he didn't fit or what if it rejected him, what if —

"Mel." Gabriel whispered, snapping me out of my head. "Stop overthinking this. I'll take care of you, I promise."

I promise.

That was a big statement, one that I wasn't sure Gabriel could declare without knowing for sure. But for some reason, I trusted him. I loved him and I trusted him. I bit my lip, I was nervous, but I knew Gabriel would take care of me. I nodded and he kissed me, pushing me back onto my back until I was laying on the bed.

He broke the kiss and I whimpered, he laughed shaking his head as he walked away. Where was he going? He opened his nightstand and pulled out a condom. *Oh, right.*

I watched as he pulled his boxers down and kicked them off, rolling the condom on his hard length, I swallowed. He was even bigger than I expected. I buried my face in my hands. I wanted this to feel good for him, I wanted to make him feel like he had made me feel but I didn't want my pain to be the cause of that pleasure. What if I couldn't take it?

I felt my hands being pulled away from my face and Gabriel's mouth found mine, kissing me for a second, letting all thoughts flee. He was kneeling above me on the bed, this was it. I was going to have sex with Gabriel. I was going to have sex. Period.

I gasped when I felt his cock prod my entrance. He leaned down, taking one nipple in his mouth as he pinched the other. That feeling was better than any pain I would face. He pushed in slowly and I bit my lip, it hurt. "You still with me?" He asked, breathlessly. I nodded and he continued pushing into me until he was completely seated inside of me. He stayed there, mumbling curse words under his breath, waiting for me to stretch to accommodate for his size.

"You good?" I was so full, this was unlike anything else. The feeling of Gabriel inside of me was more than I could imagine.

I nodded. "Yes." But he stayed still inside of me. "Are you going to move?" I asked him.

"Mel, I need a fucking minute, you're so fucking tight if I move, I'm going to bust."

I laughed. The thought of Gabriel not being able to help himself because of me was something I never expected.

His eyes narrowed. "You think it's funny."

"Maybe." I teased.

He leaned in licking my bottom lip. "I'm going to make you regret that." He whispered before he pulled out, only leaving the tip in, and thrusting in so fucking hard I had to grip the sheets, almost coming on the spot.

"Holy fuck." I breathed out.

He laughed.

I opened up, wrapping my legs around him. His hands reached down, gripping my hips as he pumped in and out of me. I dug my feet into his ass, pushing him deeper inside of me.

"Fuck." He growled. "Mel, you're driving me fucking crazy."

Good. He knew how I felt about him now, everything he did made me wild, I needed him to be in this like I was. I felt my walls clench again and I threw my head back, crying out his name.

"Look at me Mel. I want you to look at me when you come on my cock." I did as he told and he leaned forward catching my lips with his, this angle made his pelvis grind into my clit and I moaned into his mouth, digging my nails in his shoulder. The intense feeling inside my core took over and I moaned.

"Oh god... I'm going to come again." I cried out, squeezing my eyes shut.

"Open." My eyes snapped open. "Focus on me, come for me, baby."

His words launched me over the edge, my pussy gripping his cock in a chokehold inside of me. He continued pounding into me until my legs were shaking underneath him. I was coming down from my orgasm, and my inner walls were still pulsing around him.

"Fuck, me." He growled, slowing down his movements.

"That's what I'm doing." I teased.

He smacked my ass, lightly and I yelped. "Don't test me, woman." He plunged deep inside of me, my head hitting the mattress. I covered my face with his pillow, crying out into it. This felt so fucking good, and it was Gabriel. Gabriel was worshipping my body like I was made of gold.

He pulled out of me, flipping me over until I was laying on my stomach. He slowly pushed into me again. "I want another one." He panted. Another what? Another orgasm? I just had one, I couldn't possibly come again before him, it was too much.

"I... I can't." I cried.

"You can." He said. "And you will."

He was presumptuous. How the hell was I going to—

Oh, my fucking god.

Gabriel reached down, pinching my clit between his fingers before rubbing it with his thumb. I could feel another orgasm crest and I cried out. "Gabriel, please." This was too much. My forehead was covered in sweat, but I needed more. Harder, faster.

"Mel." He grumbled. "You feel so fucking good." He slowed his movements, plunging deep inside of me, hard. One thumb on my clit, the other holding me by my hips. "You were made for me." He grunted.

I turned my head over my shoulder, looking back at him. His eyes were rolled to the back of his head as he bit his lip. The sight made me clench. "Oh God." I whimpered. "Harder."

He gave my ass a light squeeze. "Anything for you." He didn't need to go any longer.

He thrust deep inside of me, hitting a sweet spot that made me clamp around him, coming on his cock. "Fuck. Fuck." I cursed.

"Ah, shit." He groaned, coming with me. His back arched as his movements turned frantic, until he stilled, cursing as he came.

We were both hot, sweaty and panting wrecks by the end of it. He crashed down on the bed, coming down from his orgasm. Several seconds went by, the room filled with us trying to catch our breaths. When it was all done and finished, my mind went into overtime, once again. What the hell just happened? Me and Gabriel just had sex! Great, mind-blowing sex. What did it mean? How were we going to go from here?

"What just happened?" I whispered.

Gabriel found my hand and squeezed it, bringing his other hand to cup my cheek. He pressed a light kiss to my forehead and whispered. "Don't overthink this, Mel. I'm right here with you." I turned my head to face him, and he leaned down, covering my lips with his. He kissed me until nothing else mattered, but his lips.

"I'll be right back." He muttered. He stood from the bed and left the room, leaving me lying on the bed, naked and alone. I fought the tears daring to arise. This felt just like the last time, the first time. I knew this was different but being left alone here made me relive those moments where I felt used, dirty and abandoned.

A minute later Gabriel came back into the bedroom, he was here. He didn't leave, he didn't think I was disgusting and left. The tears spilled out of me, I couldn't help it. Great, now Gabriel was going to be repulsed by me, he just had sex with me, and I was crying.

"Hey, hey." Gabriel soothed, brushing back my hair out of my face. "What's wrong?"

"I thought you left." I sobbed.

"Honey, I'm right here. I was just bringing a hot towel to wipe you down." He pulled out the wet towel, showing me what he had been doing. Of course, after sex people usually took care of whoever they fucked. I was an idiot. I was an unexperienced idiot who cried after receiving mind blowing orgasms.

"Mel, lie back." He kissed my forehead, and I did as he told.

He pressed the warm towel to my thighs and brought it up, cleaning me up, taking care of me. *Don't cry.* He would think I was crazy. After he cleaned me up, he pulled my arms until I was sat on the bed.

"Mel, what happened? Were you…hurt?"

His expression was pained, he thought someone… God no. "No, nothing like that." I reassured him. "It's just…" I sighed. "It's complicated."

He nodded, pressing a soft kiss to my lips. "You can tell me whenever you want, I want you to trust me."

I loved him, and the worst of all, was that I trusted him deeply. I trusted him with my heart and now my body. "I do trust you." I took a deep breath, if I was going to have to relive this moment, I needed to stay calm.

CHAPTER TWENTY-EIGHT

"My first time was in college." I started.

The only person who knew this story was Zaria. Gabriel had to know how much he meant to me, how much I trusted him to be able to tell him this.

"I went to a party with my roommate, Stella. She kind of reminded me of Zaria. She was fun and wild and loved to socialize and party, the complete opposite of me. I had declined her offers lots of times before, but this time I felt… I felt like a loser, stuck in my room whilst everyone else went to the frat house." I breathed and looked up at Gabriel, his hand was rubbing my knuckles as he held onto my hand, urging me to carry on. "We got there, and I told her I didn't know anyone there, the only person I really talked to was Stella. She assured me she wouldn't leave my side and would introduce me to some people. By some people, she meant guys, but I didn't know that."

I hated reliving this, but I trusted Gabriel. "She matched me up with the first guy she found, who was playing beer pong and introduced us, leaving me with this stranger I had never met whilst she disappeared. He asked if I wanted to play beer pong and I said yes, we were on the same team against some other guys and we ended up losing. He pulled me to the side, asking me questions like: 'why have I never seen you here before?' and 'are you in a sorority? I'm sure I would remember your face.'" I took a deep breath and looked up at Gabriel.

"I'm right here." He said.

I nodded and continued. "I told you that in high school no one showed interest in me and that was true so hearing these things from him was a new world for me, I was interested, very much so, just for any attention. He ended up taking me upstairs and we made out, he took off my clothes and…" I squeezed my eyes shut, trying not to cry.

"I'm technically not a virgin because he did penetrate me but… I didn't tell him I was a virgin. I thought he would be repulsed by it, and I just wanted someone to pay attention to me, I wanted to just get it over with. When he pushed in, he noticed I was in pain and he immediately pulled out, my blood was on him, and he looked at me like I was a pile of trash."

My voice was shaky, I could barely understand myself. I exhaled and pressed the heel of my hand to my eyes. "He said 'I don't fuck virgins' and left. He left me there naked and alone and abandoned after I was vulnerable with him. I was so embarrassed. I didn't technically have sex, he pulled out of me and left me there. I gave him my virginity and he was disgusted by me. I just…"

Gabriel pulled me into his arms, pressing his mouth to my hair. "You're not disgusting. That guy was a fucking asshole. If you don't want him to count, then he doesn't fucking count, you got that?"

I pulled back, sniffling. "What do you mean?"

"I mean." He kissed me. "I can be your first."

"But… you're not."

"I might as well be. I'm the first guy to make you come, I'm the first guy to shove deep inside of you I have the imprints of your pussy burned into my cock." I couldn't help the laugh that escaped. "He doesn't deserve to be your first, it barely even counted."

Gabriel being my first would make everything better, I could forget that horrible night and make it an almost. Gabriel was my definitely. I nodded. "Okay."

He leaned in, kissing me again, softly. God, I was deeply in love with this man. But I still didn't know what it meant, what we just did… what did that mean for us? Was there an us? What if he just wanted a friend with benefits situation?

"I can hear you thinking in there." He said, against my lips.

"Sorry I… I'm just confused."

"About?"

"This." I gestured between me and him. "Us."

"Mel, what do you want to ask me?"

A lot.

But for now… "What does this mean? Are we dating or is it just a one-time thing or—?"

"Fuck, no." He interrupted. "One time thing, are you kidding? I wasn't joking when I said you were made for me. I fucking mean it, you're mine, in every sense of the word, no one else gets you, no one else gets to even look at you, you got that? You're never going to think of Shawn or any other guy again."

That was good enough for me, all I wanted was him. Since I was fourteen all I ever wanted was him.

"What about Zaria?"

"Fuck." He ran a hand through his beard. "I didn't think about that."

She had made it very clear that she didn't want us together, even when she thought that was an impossible thing to happen.

"We'll keep it a secret." I told him.

His eyes widened. "You're okay with that? Lying to her?"

"No, but what else are we going to do?" Was I okay with lying to my best friend of ten years, hell no. But I was used to it, every dirty thought I had about her brother, I kept secret, maybe she wouldn't find out about this either, until we could finally muster up the courage to tell her. We had *just* gotten together, what if in a week we broke up and it was all for nothing?

"OW." I cried. Gabriel had pinched my nipple between his fingers. "What was that for?"

He held his hands up, laughing. "Sorry trevi, you seemed to like it before and I couldn't help myself, your tits are in my face and it's turning me on. You're so beautiful."

I smiled at that, his compliments would never get old, hearing those words about me come out of Gabriel's mouth was all I ever dreamed but never thought would happen. My smile dropped when I felt the pain twinge in my nipple, I narrowed my eyes at him. "Okay, first of all, that was in the heat of the moment, not when they're sore, and second of all, you can't call me trevi now that we're dating."

He grinned, his smile reaching ear to ear. "You love that nickname, don't pretend you don't." Before I could answer him, he pulled me into him, pressing his lips against mine. I could get used to this.

Both our eyes widened at the sound of keys jingling outside of the apartment. We broke the kiss and stood up. "Shit." I whispered. "What are we going to do?"

Gabriel ran a hand down his face. "Stay here." He ordered, putting on a pair of sweatpants. I obeyed. I looked around for my clothes but remembered Gabriel had taken them off in the hallway, along with his own.

"Gabriel, my clothes." I hissed. He nodded and ran out of the room.

"No, you can't come in." He yelled.

"Why not?" Zaria called back.

"Um..." *Think faster.* "Mel's upset and she uh... vomited all over the apartment, I've been cleaning it up."

"Since when do you call her Mel?" She slurred. Oh god, she was drunk. I covered my face with my hands. "And if she's upset, I should see her, she doesn't even like you." She scoffed. I crinkled my nose, I hated lying to my best friend.

Gabriel's head popped into the room, waving his hand, ushering me out of his bedroom. "C'mon." He whispered.

I followed him, making my way out of the room, the apartment was clothes free, I didn't know where he had hidden them, but I didn't have time to think, I rushed to my room, closing the door behind me. I sat on my bed, realizing I was naked. I reached for my robe, wrapping it around my body. I could hear Gabriel and Zaria talking, she must have gotten into the apartment by now.

I jumped when a knock hit my door. "Come in?" I didn't know if it was Zaria or Gabriel. My shoulders tensed when Zaria came stumbling into my room.

"Hey." She said, her eyes glazed over.

"You're drunk." I pointed out.

"What?" She yelled. "No? I'm fine." She tripped on her foot, falling onto the floor.

I couldn't help but laugh, I loved drunk Zaria. "Z." I called out, dragging her to sit on my bed.

She sighed. "Stop worrying about me. I'm fine, what happened with *you*?" She poked my arm on that last word, putting emphasis on it.

I didn't know what to say. Nothing was wrong with me. I was the happiest I had been in a very long time, and I couldn't tell her anything about it.

"Was it Shawn?" She asked. "What did he do? I told you to call me."

"You're drunk."

She scoffed at me. "No. I told you, I'm *fine*." Her voice went up multiple octaves higher on the last word. "I'm not leaving until you tell me what happened with Shawn." She said, her eyes fluttering closed.

I sighed. She probably wouldn't remember this tomorrow anyway. "He was an asshole, rich guy who thought he was better than everyone else, so I left." I felt a little guilty speaking about Shawn like that when I didn't know if that was really him. I stood him up today and didn't even call to cancel.

"But Gabriel said you threw up?" Crap.

"Oh… uh, yeah. I… ate some bad fish." She nodded like she understood. My heart clenched. My best friend was drunk and still asking about me and I was lying to her. "Okay, let's get you into bed." She replied with mumbles I couldn't understand.

I made sure Zaria was in bed, tucked in, propped up on her side in case she threw up. I had even taken off her makeup, but her ten-step skincare routine would have to wait until the morning.

I stepped out of her bedroom, seeing Gabriel on the couch, facing me.

"Hey." He whispered.

"Hey."

"She asleep?" I nodded. He patted the couch, gesturing me to come to him. I bit my lip, walking over to him.

Not having to hide how I felt was the best thing about this, I could be as cheesy as I wanted, I could ogle him forever because he was mine. I reached the couch and he pulled me into him, sitting me on his lap. He brushed my hair out of my face and kissed me. It was heaven. His lips were soft and perfect, I could sit here and kiss him forever. I sighed when we pulled away.

"Good?"

I nodded. "Perfect." I nuzzled into his chest. His hand rubbed up and down my back. This was what was missing. Him, Gabriel. This felt like…home.

CHAPTER TWENTY-NINE

Gabriel and I had been dating for two days.

Two long days with no touching.

Zaria had been home sick since she had come home from the club. Somehow, my lie had become her reality and she ended up getting food poisoning from the takeout we ordered for her hangover cure. Fish tacos from one of her favorite spots. I had the chicken tacos, which unfortunately meant it was the fish tacos that had made her sick. Gabriel scorned us about ordering takeout every day when he could just cook for us.

I loved taking care of people, I wanted them to feel safe and loved and know that they wouldn't have to worry, someone was looking out for them, so taking care of Zaria was the obvious thing to do.

However, that meant that I spent the past two days by her side, which meant that I hadn't gotten the chance to be alone with Gabriel since. Every interaction we had was in front of Zaria, so we returned to 'hating each other' whenever she was around.

If we were friendly to each other and Zaria got suspicious, there would be no way of covering it up, this way she thought we still hated each other, and she didn't have to know that we gave each other mind blowing orgasms.

"I'm fucking sick of watching this, trevi." Gabriel groaned. He was sat on the couch with me, with Zaria sat in the middle, of course. She was our 'buffer' so we wouldn't break out into arguing. The irony.

"I don't care, we're watching this. If you don't like it, eat a dick." I knew he was lying. We were watching Legally Blonde, one of mine and Zaria's comfort movies, though Zaria was barely paying attention, but I remembered Gabriel telling me he liked this film. I bit my lip to hide my smile, I loved knowing little quirks and facts about my boyfriend.

Oh god.

Boyfriend.

I had never had a boyfriend before and now Gabriel was mine. All mine.

He didn't retort my insult. That was weird, usually he would spit back something even worse, and we'd keep going back and forth.

My phone buzzed on my thigh, and I grabbed it, unlocking it.

Gabriel: I'm going to fuck your mouth for that comment.

I licked my lips. I could almost taste him on my tongue. I was dying to fit him inside of my mouth. I wanted to make him feel good. My phone buzzed notifying another message.

Gabriel: Hard.

Oh my god. I pressed my thighs together, feeling my arousal pooling in my underwear. Sexting. This was new.

Gabriel: Are you wet right now?

I looked up at Gabriel, he was staring right at the tv acting like nothing was happening. Zaria was oblivious, resting her head on her brothers' shoulder, her eyes fluttering closed, she was clearly tired from spending the night up crouched by the toilet. I felt guilty. My best friend was feeling horrible, and I was sexting her brother. What kind of person does that? I was usually the type of person who didn't care about anything else other than helping the person in front of me. Gabriel had spun my head. I bit my lip, I couldn't help replying.

Me: Yes.

I gulped when I pressed send. I had never sexted before. I had no idea what to write, did he want me to make it up or just let him go with it? My leg jerked at the buzzing.

Gabriel: Don't worry. I'll take care of your sweet pussy later.

I groaned, slapping my hand over my mouth when I realized, I had let that sound slip. Zaria's head jerked towards me, her eyes were barely open, but her brows wrinkled in confusion. I looked up at Gabriel who was smirking, still not making eye contact with me.

"I uh, I don't feel good, I'll be right back."

I stood up from the couch, bursting into my room. "Calm down." I muttered to myself. I paced around my room trying to get it together. Jesus how could a text get me that turned on. My panties were ruined, and I quickly discarded them. My phone lit up again and I eagerly read the text.

Gabriel: You need to be less obvious than that, Mel.

"I know." I hissed at the screen, knowing he couldn't hear me. I didn't reply, I was a mess. I needed to keep my hormones in check before Zaria found out.

It had been two days, she couldn't find out now. I didn't even know what this meant. According to Gabriel we were dating but what if we didn't work out or worse, what if Zaria found out before we were ready to tell her, and she hated me. I couldn't lose her over this. Gabriel was all I ever wanted but Zaria was my best friend. For ten years she had been there for me through everything, every birthday, every failed date, every time I cried over something, every panic attack. Everything.

I couldn't let her down. I needed to know what this thing between me, and Gabriel meant. I needed more time with him. What if all he wanted was sex? He said that this wasn't a one-time thing, but he never said anything about us being together for longer than a fling. And here I was using words like boyfriend.

I ran a hand down my face, taking deep breaths in. I needed to talk about this with him. My phone buzzed again, I took one more deep breath before looking.

Gabriel: I can't stop thinking about you. About all of the ways I want to fuck you and all of the places I want to kiss you. How to make sure you think of nobody else but me.

I bit my lip, resisting the urge to moan. Ugh, why was he doing this to me? I was so turned on and I couldn't do anything about it anytime soon. Fuck, who knew words could be so hot. Everything Gabriel did was hot.

Gabriel: Come back out here. If you behave, I'll give you a reward later.

My smile spread wide. What kind of reward? I hoped it was the dirty kind. I didn't have to think twice. I opened my door and sat my ass on the couch. I didn't know what reward he would give me, but my pussy clenched to find out. For the rest of the movie I sat in silence, trying to get all thoughts of Gabriel and his body out of my mind.

My phone buzzed again, and I debated on looking. What if I couldn't control myself? Curiosity took over and I picked up my phone.

Gabriel: I think she's asleep.

I looked to my right, seeing Zaria laying on Gabriel's shoulder, her mouth wide open and her eyes closed. She was definitely asleep. I got up from the couch, picking up her feet and placing them on the couch, covering her with the blanket, and Gabriel carefully dropped her head on a pillow, standing up. His eyes locked on mine, and he gestured to my room.

Gabriel and I walked quietly to my room, closing the door, slowly. As soon as we were alone, he pulled me into his mouth, sliding his tongue deep inside my mouth, caressing my tongue with his. It had been two days since Gabriel and I kissed, and I could still taste him on my lips. But being reminded of how he kissed was nothing like I expected it, he was hard then soft, he kissed me fast like he would die without this and then slow like he had all the time in the world.

When we broke the kiss, my lips were swollen, and his eyes were glazed over. "I fucking missed you." He grunted. Lifting me up by the back of my thighs. He was so strong, he liked to pick me up and man handle me, and I didn't mind it at all. I wrapped my legs around his waist holding on tight as he dived in, catching my lips again.

I gasped when my back hit the bed, he left my lips, kissing my jaw, my neck and then sucked on the base of my throat before his mouth worked down my body, sucking my nipple through the material of my tank top and my head fell back, succumbed by pleasure. He lifted my tank top, kissing my stomach and then the underside of my breast.

His hands teased the hem of my shorts, looking into my eyes, waiting for approval. I nodded, biting my lip and he grinned. Pulling down my shorts to my knees, he groaned at the sight of my bare pussy. My underwear was soaked when he sent me those texts, so I had discarded them. He threw my shorts across the room and gave me a long lick, parting me.

"I promised you a reward." He said, his hot breath teasing my skin. "You were good, now let's see how hard you can come." I was so close, and he had barely touched me. "Can you keep quiet?" He asked.

I shook my head, I would be screaming by the time this was finished. He opened my nightstand, picking out a pair of my red, lacy underwear. He bunched it up and held it out to me. I furrowed my brows. He wanted me to put underwear on?

"Open." He said. I opened my mouth, and he shoved the underwear inside. "Be a good girl and scream into those." My eyes snapped shut, waiting for him to do whatever he wanted to my body.

His head dipped between my legs, flicking his tongue over my already swollen bud. His fingers found my entrance and he pushed two of them inside, deep. I was still getting used to this, I squirmed, from the uncomfortable feeling. He didn't move his fingers, allowing me to get used to it but never removed his tongue from my clit. His tongue swirled around it before sucking it into his mouth. I moaned, loud.

"Every time you make noise, I'll spank you. You need to be quiet. Can you do that for me?" He asked, ending his question with a long flick of his tongue across my pussy. I nodded, my eyes still closed, lost to the feeling of Gabriel's mouth on me.

His fingers started moving inside of me, pulling out and pushing them back in before curling them, finding that spot that made me see the stars. I buried my face in my hands, trying to stifle my moans. I must have not done a good job of keeping quiet because I got a spank to my ass, which only made me moan more. I never would have thought pain would be something I liked, but with Gabriel, I liked everything.

His tongue focused on my clit, abusing it until I was shaking, and my pussy was clamping down on his fingers. Holding them in a vice grip, trapping them inside of me. "Fuck." He grunted. My legs were shaking as I rode the orgasm, his hand rubbing back and forth on my thighs, whilst his other one was still inside of me, letting me ride his fingers until I subsided from my orgasm.

His fingers pulled out of me, and I whimpered at the loss. I loved the feeling of being full. I opened my eyes and sat up on my elbows, removing the panties still stuffed in my mouth. The sight of him on his knees between my legs almost brought me overboard. He looked me dead in the eyes before bringing his fingers, the ones that were inside of me, into his mouth, wrapping his lips around them.

His eyes closed, as if it was the best thing he had ever tasted before pulling them out. My mouth dropped open at the sight. He licked his lips, lapping up my juices and I licked my own, pulling him by his t-shirt, I wanted a taste too. I brought his lips to mine and licked the remains of my arousal from him. He groaned into my mouth, and I moaned into his. How did I ever go so long without this? Without him?

He pulled back and stood up. My eyes level with his erection through his sweatpants. I licked my lips again. I wanted to taste him. I palmed his dick through his pants, and he thrust into my hand, throwing his head back. I had never done this before, and I didn't want to mess it up. I wasn't sure if I should tell him or just go with it.

I pulled his sweatpants and boxers down and off, his cock springing free, long and hard. He pulled his shirt off. Gabriel was naked. Butt ass naked, in my room. His hands wrapped around the base of his cock as he stroked himself, his tip dripping. I brought my hand over his and copied his movements. He groaned, releasing his hand. I stroked him, squeezing tighter when I approached the tip. I needed to taste him. I scooted forward on the bed, bringing my tongue over his dick. I licked the tip before sucking on it. He was big, I needed to work through this slowly. I wrapped my lips around his cock inch by inch. Gabriel thrust inside of my mouth, slowly until he was so deep that I gagged.

"Slowly." He whispered. "Relax your throat." His thumb brushed the tear that had escaped from gagging on him. I leaned my head back and opened my throat as much as I could. His hands tangled in my hair, pushing himself into me until he was seated inside of my mouth. "I'm going to fuck your mouth now." His voice was shaky as if he wouldn't be able to hold back any longer.

I pressed my thighs together, I was so fucking wet. He pulled out of me before thrusting his hips, feeding every inch into my mouth. He did exactly as he said, he fucked my mouth with earnest, I stroked my tongue around him whilst he held my head between his hands, thrusting into me. His eyes were glazed over, and I knew he was close, I tightened my throat, gagging on him, his movements quickened, jerky and relentless.

"Fuuuuuck." He grunted. It was the only warning I got before his thick cum hit the back of my throat, coating my tongue with it. He pulled out of my mouth when he came down from his orgasm and I swallowed, licking every last drop.

He tilted my chin up and stared down at my tear-filled eyes. "You're so fucking perfect." He murmured before smashing his lips into mine. I could still taste myself on his tongue and he could taste himself on mine.

I wanted more. I wanted him inside of me again, I didn't want to go any longer without this. I wrapped my fingers around his softening cock and stroked him.

He groaned, pulling away from our kiss. "Mel." He said, shaking his head. "I want this too but…" He turned to look at the door and then back at me. "I want my time with you." He removed my hands from him, he was already semi hard, and I smiled. "I want to kiss you slowly, fuck you for hours until we can't breathe."

"I'm pretty breathless right now."

He tilted his head, smiling at me. That smile. "Smart ass." He said. "I'm serious. Zaria could wake up any minute and find us."

I sighed, letting my head hit the mattress. "Okay."

He leaned in, kissing me. "I'm going to take a shower."

I grinned, maybe we could take one together. He must have read my mind because he narrowed his eyes at me. "Separately." He warned.

He pulled his t-shirt over his head, then put on his sweatpants, covering up his body and I frowned. Gabriel saw my face, upset at the fact he had covered himself and grinned before turning around, walking to the door. He shook his head. "Trouble, trouble trouble." He murmured under his breath before leaving my room.

I couldn't help but smile. I wasn't sure if this was just sex to him but the way he looked at me made me think it was so much more. I was in love with him. And I could finally have him.

CHAPTER THIRTY

I never knew life could be this good.

That I could be this happy. Gabriel had done that. Having him in my life had been the best thing that had happened to me. My life had been nothing but work and home, I never allowed myself to get close to anyone before, not like how I'd gotten close to Gabriel. He knew more about me than any other person did, and I was okay with that.

I didn't have a problem with letting him into my life, allowing him to see every part of me, the good, the bad and the ugly, because he had seen them all and for some strange reason, he still wanted to be with me.

It had been a week since he kissed me. Seven days ago, the man I was in love with kissed me and wanted me, the way I wanted him.

Gabriel and I nursed Zaria back to health and she was her chipper self, again. After the first date she had with the barista, where she came home drunk, she vowed never to have a first date at a bar again. I scoffed at her, knowing that was bullshit. But somehow, she had remembered the date with the barista, Trey, and planned another date, which I assumed went well, as she only came home the next morning.

Gabriel and I still hadn't talked about what this meant, and what it would mean for the future. Was this a relationship? When would we tell our families, Zaria included?

A knock on my bedroom door startled me. "Yes?" I asked.

The door opened and Gabriel poked his head through the door. "Can I come in?" He asked, grinning. My stomach fluttered with the knowledge that Gabriel couldn't help but smile whenever he saw me.

I smiled, nodding. He approached the bed and I relaxed. Whenever he was near me all I felt was bliss, happiness, love.

"Get dressed." He whispered.

"Why?" I whispered back.

"Because." He said, leaning in for a fleeting kiss. "I'm stealing you away." He kissed me again before pulling the covers off leaving me exposed in a tank and shorts, I was shivering. It was the middle of fall, at eleven at night. Where the hell were we going?

I got out of bed and threw on a sweatshirt and replaced my sleep shorts with denim shorts. I wrapped my hair up into a messy bun and glanced behind my shoulder, watching Gabriel watch me.

"Damn." He muttered, under his breath.

I turned back around, bringing my hands to my face. I was smiling so hard, my cheeks hurt. I gasped when I felt Gabriel behind me, wrapping his hands around my waist, pulling my back flush with his chest. He pressed his hips against the curve of my ass, letting me feel his erection. "Hey, girlfriend." He said. I could hear him grinning.

My stomach fluttered at the word 'girlfriend'. "Hey boyfriend."

He turned me around and pulled me in for a kiss, sliding his tongue inside my mouth, tasting me, savoring me. When he pulled back, his eyes were hazy, and a smile spread on his stupid, beautiful face.

He pulled me into his chest, laying a kiss on the top of my head. He sighed. "I fucking missed you, Mel."

"You saw me this morning." I reminded him.

He laughed. "Yeah, and I fucking missed you then too."

I didn't need him to explain. I understood what he meant, Zaria was always around us, and we had to keep our distance, so even living in the same apartment, it still felt like we were miles apart.

His cock prodded my thigh, thick and ready for me. I leaned into him, wrapping my arms around his neck. "Mmm, someone's trying to get my attention."

He leaned down, pressing his lips against mine. "You've always had my attention." He whispered against my lips before pulling back. He cleared his throat. "Stop distracting me, trevi." He said, interlocking his fingers with mine, leading us out of my bedroom. "We've got to go."

He opened the door, poking his head through it. "All clear." He whispered.

We left the apartment, making our way outside. He opened the car door for me, and I got inside. "Where are we going?" I asked him when he finally got inside.

"Be patient, Melissa. You'll see when we get there."

I exhaled. I was very impatient. I wanted to know where we were going. What if I didn't dress appropriately for whatever he had in mind. I didn't know where he was taking me at this hour, but my stomach fluttered with anticipation. This was a date. My first official date with Gabriel and I was dressed in an old sweatshirt that belonged to my dad.

I rolled down the window, feeling the cold fall air hit my skin. I turned on the radio, connecting my playlist to it. The music playing from the speakers filled the car, I tapped my foot along to the beat.

"Not this again." He groaned.

I smiled. "Stop whining." I told him. "If you don't like Ariana Grande, I'm afraid this relationship won't work." I crossed my arms across my chest.

He smiled. "Cute, trevi." Turning his head, to face the road, he ran a hand down his face grunting. "Fine." He conceded. "You can listen to whatever you want." I smiled. He narrowed his eyes at me. "But on the way back, I choose the music."

"Deal." I grinned. I loved his music, so I would win either way.

He was glancing back at me any chance he got, as if he couldn't believe I was here with him. I got that feeling. It all felt surreal. "Focus on the road." I told him. "You'll get us killed."

He grinned back at me. "I can't help it. You're distracting."

I rolled my eyes at him, secretly loving how happy and cheery he was with me. "Stop flirting with me and drive."

He grabbed my hand, bringing it up to his mouth. He kissed my knuckles. "Never." He whispered against my skin.

I leaned my head back onto the head rest, looking out of the window. Night life was so beautiful in the city, and I never appreciated it as much as I should have. The palm trees swinging in the air, the city lighting up the dark sky. I closed my eyes, listening to the wind hitting my ears as the music played.

"We're here."

I snapped my eyes open, seeing the car had stopped. "That was fast." I mumbled.

He laughed. "I think you dozed off." He said, kissing the top of my head.

I opened the car door, stepping out. I squinted my eyes, looking around. I couldn't make out where we were. It was darker here. We must be away from the city.

He disappeared behind the car, opening the trunk. I walked towards him, feeling the ground squish beneath my feet. I peered down, seeing sand covering my shoes. "The beach?"

"Yeah. You like it?" He extended his hand, and I took it, interlocking it with mine as we walked deeper in the sand. He held a folded-up blanket in his other hand.

I shrugged. "I've never been to the beach at night." I admitted. I had never been to the beach much. Period. It was crowded and busy, it overwhelmed me, so I stayed far away in the summer.

He smiled, nuzzling in my neck, he kissed the top of my collarbone. "Then let's go." He whispered.

CHAPTER THIRTY-ONE

I leaned into Gabriel, walking deeper into the beach. We stood for a while, looking out at the ocean, it was still, quiet, relaxing. I inhaled breathing in the salty smell. It had been so long since I was at the beach, willingly. I smiled at myself remembering the family beach trips, my dad swimming in the ocean with me clung to his back.

Gabriel unraveled the towel, lowering it to the sand. Inside was a pizza box and two cans of soda. I sat down, tucking my knees in my chin, cradling my legs against my stomach.

"Pizza? Is this a date?" I asked him, my smile reaching my ears.

He lowered himself to the towel, beside me and leaned in leaving a soft kiss on my lips. Those lazy soft kisses would be the death of me. "Yes. Honey. The first of many."

"Technically the diner was our first date. According to you."

He smiled. "You didn't count it, but I sure did."

I always thought of love and what it would feel like. Sometimes I liked to think it felt like listening to a Taylor Swift song, other times I wondered if it felt like when you watched a really good chick flick or how you felt at Christmas time. A blissful feeling of happiness and contentment.

And looking at the man next to me I knew now. I knew that love felt like all of that and more. Love is bittersweet. Love is a mixture between feeling butterflies any time he looked at me, and sheer euphoria and calmness whenever he was around. But it was also heartbreak and years of pining for him, wanting him to look at me like he looked at me now.

I tucked my knees beneath my chin, cradling my legs against my stomach. "Wow." I mumbled. Looking to my right I could see a clear view of the golden gate bridge, lit up in the depth of night. It looked beautiful.

"It's my favorite place." He said, "Remember I told you I come to the beach often?" I nodded. I remembered everything he told me. I kept all the information I knew about Gabriel locked tight in my mind as if it was a treasure to know it. "This is the one place I can think and breathe clearly. Especially at nighttime." He continued. I leaned my head on his shoulder, relaxing into him and he wrapped his arm around me, pulling me closer.

"I prefer sunsets, but I can see why you like it at night." I smiled at him.

"Whenever I feel stressed or I need some quiet, I come here." He replied.

I closed my eyes, zoning in on the sound of the ocean crashing against the sand. "I can see why you come here, it's peaceful."

He nodded. "I came here a lot in high school actually."

I scoffed. "With girls most likely."

He smirked, looking down at me. "Jealousy looks good on you, honey."

I smiled, weakly back at him. I *was* jealous. I envied those girls who got to come here with Gabriel, cuddling him and kissing him like I was doing now.

He placed his thumb on my chin, lifting my head to his, he leaned down, kissing me. "I wish I could have brought you here." He whispered.

Me too.

But I knew why he couldn't. He didn't even like me in high school. I didn't know what had changed or when it had changed, but I finally had him, and I wasn't going to question it.

I couldn't help but smile. I was happy. For the first time in a long time, I was happy. My heart felt like it was going to burst any minute, but this time it was a good feeling. Love could be a bitch, but it also felt like the best thing in the world.

Gabriel would be leaving soon, moving into his own apartment. Who knew when or how often we'd see each other? I needed to appreciate these moments for as long as I could.

"The last time I was at the beach, it was with my dad." I said, reminiscing on the times he would drag me out of the house in summer, wanting me to at least get some fresh air. I was a homebody by nature, I could have spent days, even weeks holed up at home. Even now, I always preferred to stay at home. If it wasn't for Zaria, I wouldn't leave my apartment, for anything other than work.

"You loved your dad, huh?"

I nodded. My dad had always been my hero. "He was the best father." Wetness pooled in my eyes, and I blinked it away. "He taught me everything a little girl should know. How to ride a bike, how to swim, he taught me how to be strong and to be proud of who I am." I smiled, letting a tear drop down my face. "Cancer took him away from me." I whispered. "When my mother left, he stayed, for me."

I shook my head. "Did you know that she left because she wanted to move to Spain?"

Gabriel didn't reply, he just squeezed my hand.

"My dad told me that was why she divorced him." I continued. "Not that she would have stayed either way. My dad said she had already hired a divorce attorney and had the papers drawn up, before even talking to my dad about it, about why she wanted to leave."

I wiped a tear from my cheek, taking in a deep breath. "He could have gone. He could have packed up his life and moved us to Spain. But he stayed, for me." I shook my head. "I can't believe he chose me. He was in love with her, did you know that? Even after she divorced him and left us, he loved her, and he gave that up, for me."

"You're worth it," He mumbled, kissing the top of my head.

I shook my head. "I don't think I was. He got sick shortly after. He could have spent those last few years with her."

I closed my eyes remembering my dad, withered and sickly, nothing like the strong man I used to know. I felt so guilty leaving for college, leaving him in the hospital. I wanted to stay. Those first months were the hardest, I barely went out, barely ate, and spent all my available spare time on the phone with him and visiting him until he died.

"You are worth it. Your mother made the choices she made. She gave up on him, and on you. He didn't give anything up by deciding to stay. That's not your fault and it never was." I snuggled into him closer. I knew what he was saying. I knew that my fathers' choice to stay wasn't my fault. It was his choice. But I couldn't help but feel guilty that I had kept him here, alone… and sick.

"That's why your family is so important to me. They're like my second family."

"They are." He kissed the top of my head. "You are family. We'll always be here."

I bit my lip, tears streaming down my face. "And when they find out about us?" I asked. "How do you think they'll react, especially Zaria?"

He sighed, pulling me into his lap until I was straddling him. His hands were cold against my skin as he cupped my face, stroking his thumb across my cheek. "Are you happy? With me?" He asked.

It had only been a few days, but this was the happiest I'd ever been. He didn't know I had been wanting this for years. For him to look at me like he was looking at me now. For him to kiss me and hold me and love me like I loved him.

I nodded, smiling, my face wet underneath his fingertips. "So happy."

He brought his lips to mine and kissed me, slow and soft. "Then whatever happens, happens." He said, tucking a strand of hair that escaped from the bun, behind my ear. "My parents love you, they'll be happy for us." He kissed my jaw. "And Zaria will just have to deal with it."

My stomach dropped. Zaria was too important to me. His family might accept us, but I was worried that Zaria wouldn't. Especially when she found out that I was lying to her, she would feel betrayed. "I don't want to lose her." I whispered, closing my eyes.

"You won't. Zaria is my best friend, and she's yours. There's no way she won't be happy for us if we're happy."

"Then why doesn't she want us together?"

He shrugged. "I don't know, Mel. Maybe because she thinks I'll never be more than a player who can't commit to a woman." He ran a hand through his beard, laughing. "I mean, I did break up with my first girlfriend after only six months."

"Why did you?" I blurted out. I was always curious about Gabriel's relationship. He had never committed to anyone, never settled down and then suddenly he was in a relationship and four months later they had moved in together.

He shook his head, and I furrowed my brows. "Why don't you want to tell me?" Did he really love her that much? Did the relationship ending affect him so much that he couldn't talk about it? I swallowed the lump in my throat. Gabriel loved her. Would he ever love me one day? Was I worth it for him? I was nothing but complications for him.

"I promise I'll tell you another time. I just want to be here with you for a minute longer." He whispered against my neck before catching my bottom lip between his teeth, sliding his tongue in my mouth. Tasting and sucking on my tongue.

I moaned into his mouth, wrapping my arms around his neck. Kissing Gabriel was addicting. I craved this. Him. Everything he had to offer me. I grinded my hips, gasping when I felt his erection beneath me, providing the friction that made my eyes glaze over. I worked my hips into his harder, faster.

He groaned in response, grabbing my hips and rolling them against him. His mouth left mine, trailing kisses down my neck and jaw. "Oh my god." I gasped. I leaned forward, grinding faster, his cock rubbing against my clit through my shorts. He didn't stop until I shook and panted, moaning into his neck.

I pulled back, bringing my lips to his. I could still feel his hard length digging into me. I reached down, palming him through his pants. He groaned. "Fuck. I haven't got any condoms."

I bit his jaw. "I'm on birth control."

He pinched his brows together, looking confused. He was probably wondering why I was on birth control if I wasn't having sex. I waved a hand. "Period issues."

He nodded. "I'm clean."

I smiled. I trusted him and I wanted to feel him inside of me, more than I wanted anything. I wanted no barriers between us. I reached my hands down his pants, but his hand came over mine, stopping me. "Let's go to the car, I don't want sand in my ass crack."

I laughed. "Good point."

We rushed to the car, I needed him. Now.

He opened the back door, getting into the back seat, gesturing for me to climb in. He pulled me up until I was straddling him again. He unbuttoned my shorts, pulling them down and off. He cupped my pussy, still covered by my pink thong. He nuzzled my neck, his hot breath hitting my skin. "I'm starting to see why you like pink so much."

I giggled, pulling down his pants. I lifted my knees to remove my panties, but he stopped me. Ripping them clean off my skin, throwing them onto the dashboard. That was so hot I couldn't even be mad that he had ripped my favorite underwear. He stroked his length lazily, before positioning it at my entrance. I was dripping, anticipating the feel of his cock thrusting in me, I didn't even realize I was bucking my hips seeking for him until his hand came up on my waist, squeezing it. He smirked at me, and I bit my lip, waiting impatiently for him. I moved my hips again, the tip of him sliding inside. I gasped.

"Fuck." He groaned, under his breath. I lowered myself to the hilt. His eyes closed, his hands squeezing on my hips begging me to stay still until he could compose himself. Knowing what I was doing to him drove me crazy. I felt my pussy contract around him and he groaned, bringing his forehead to my chest. "If you keep doing that, I'm not going to last very long."

"How promising." I teased.

He pulled back, his tongue poking the inside of his cheek, smirking at me. He shook his head. "You do great things to a man's ego."

"Your ego's big enough."

He ran his thumb on my lower lip. "Not as big as my dick."

"Speaking of…" I looked down at where we were connected. "Can I start moving now?"

He responded by lifting my hips and dropping them. We both groaned at the friction and fullness, having him inside of me without any barriers between us felt incredible. I was certain I wouldn't be able to hold out much longer.

I lifted my hips, slamming down on him again and again. The car filled with the sound of our skin slapping together, my moans and pants and his groans in my ear. I grinded my hips against his, his pelvis hitting my clit, right where I needed him. "Gabriel." I cried out as I came, milking his cock, squeezing him tight with my pussy.

"Say that again." He growled.

"Gabriel. Gabriel. Gabriel." I panted, breathlessly. He held my hips in place, thrusting up into me until he came inside of me. Shuddering at his release.

When we both came down from the high, he kissed me, soft and slow.

"We forgot about the pizza." He murmured, letting out a small laugh.

I kissed him back. "All I need is you."

His eyes locked with mine, even in the dark they were captivating. "There's no one like you." He whispered.

It felt like *I love you.*

CHAPTER THIRTY-TWO

I couldn't get rid of the smile on my face. All day I had been smiling, my cheeks hurt, my heart hurt, but in the best way possible. Last night was perfect. Only me and Gabriel. I felt at peace whenever I was with him, like everything in my head quieted down when he was around.

I think Allie suspected something. She'd be crazy not to, Allie took one look at me and started clapping. She knew, I didn't confirm it, but she knew what had happened. She said I had the 'after sex glow' which again, I didn't respond to.

I couldn't hide my emotions that well, and I tried, I really tried. Especially whenever Zaria was around, I didn't even dare look at Gabriel, I knew as soon as his eyes locked onto mine, I would look like a lovesick puppy, and Zaria would know.

It was crazy that less than two weeks ago, I dreaded going home. I hated the fact that I would have to see Gabriel and interact with him, but now I was rushing home to see him.

I reached into my purse, pulling out my keys as I was approaching my apartment. I looked up and stilled. The smile that had been there all day was now gone. My heartbeat accelerated against my chest, faster and faster. Nothing would ease this. I blinked, making sure I was seeing right.

It was her. She was really here. I spent so much time trying to erase her from my memories, not wanting to miss her. I convinced myself I didn't need her, and I didn't miss her. I convinced myself that I didn't even remember what she looked like, but seeing her here, now, I could never forget.

Her skin was darker than I remembered, probably because she spent the last thirteen years in Spain, as far as I was aware. Her hair was a lighter brown than mine, cut just below her shoulders.

I always wondered if any part of me resembled her, especially now that I was an adult. Her lips. I had her lips, and her nose. My dad had more of a bigger nose, and I hoped that at least I had my mother's nose. I wanted something to attach me to her. It was weird how we were connected, but she was a complete stranger to me.

She glanced around the street, trying to look for someone. Was she trying to look for me? How did she even know where I lived? Her eyes found mine and I held my breath, wondering what she was going to say, why she was here. But her eyes left mine and continued looking around. She looked right past me as if I was a ghost.

I let my eyes drift closed, feeling tears start to rise. She didn't even recognize me, not that I was shocked. It had been thirteen years, the last time she saw me I was a kid. But I would never forget my mother, I would never forget her beautiful face, as hard as I tried, and she didn't even recognize me.

I took a deep breath in. Fuck it. I needed to do this, to be rid of her completely. I needed to know why she was here.

I approached the apartment building, where she was stood. Her eyes lifted seeing me approach, I kept expecting her to realize, to know it was me, but she just smiled at me as I got closer, like she would to a stranger.

"Mom?" I asked.

Her eyes met mine, once again, but this time she knew. Her mouth dropped and widened as she looked me up and down, finally taking in her daughter, who she abandoned thirteen years ago.

"Melissa?" She asked, warily. One thing I couldn't remember was her voice. I had forgotten how her voice sounded and now I wish I hadn't ever heard it, because how was I supposed to go the rest of my life without hearing it again.

Her voice was like honey, sweet and thick and she had an accent, which she probably always had, seeing as she was from Spain. I couldn't remember if she had an accent or not when I was younger, my dad barely had one, only when he rolled his r's.

"Is this really happening?" I blurted out, speaking out loud instead of in my head. I didn't know if this was just some sort of hallucination or if she was really here.

"I'm sorry, is this a bad time?" She asked.

I didn't know whether to cry or laugh. "As good as any considering you're thirteen years too late."

She dropped her eyes, shaking her head as if I said the wrong thing. The only wrong thing I did was acknowledging her, I could have walked right past her, and she wouldn't have known.

"Melissa, can we talk. Please."

I wasn't really interested in what she had to say, what could she say to me that would erase those years that she was gone? "Talk."

"Somewhere private."

I sighed. I should've just told her to leave. I didn't need this. I didn't need her, not anymore. But some masochistic need inside of me, needed to hear her out, or at the very least to be around her, to be near her, just for a little while.

I walked inside the apartment building and she followed. We entered the elevator in silence, only the sound of our breaths filling the space. What would I say to a woman who left me? Who decided one day that I wasn't worth it, I wasn't worth the hassle it took to be a mother and left.

The elevator doors opened, and I walked to my apartment, with my mother following me. My hands were shaking as I held the keys in my hand and inserted it into the door. I shouldn't be nervous around my own mother, but once again, she was a stranger to me. The door opened and I entered, letting the door open so she could walk in.

She looked around the apartment, taking in the place her daughter was living in, the daughter who she knew nothing about.

"Nice place." She said, running her hands over the kitchen island. "I don't know if you remember, but I was a real estate agent, just like your dad." She chuckled. "That's how we met."

She was laughing. Like nothing had happened, like this was a regular day. This wasn't show and tell, I didn't want to sit here and talk about my life. If she wanted to know, she would have been a part of it.

"Yeah. I know." I responded, flatly.

She turned to face me, gulping as she looked at my eyes. "How is he?"

Now I wanted to laugh. How could she not know? Did she never check up on us? On me?

I sighed. "Dead. You want some coffee?" I walked over to the kitchen, where the coffee pot sat. I hated the taste, but Zaria was a coffee addict, and Gabriel was no different.

"What?"

"Do you want some coffee, or do you prefer tea?" I asked her, filling up the coffee pot with water.

"Your dad is... dead?" She asked, her voice sounding distressed. I could bet she wasn't feeling as much as I did when I lost him. When I lost the only person in this world who gave a crap about me.

"Yes." I replied, with no emotion in my voice. "Five years ago." I opened the jar with the coffee beans. I had never done this before, you just add coffee and water right?

"How?"

"Cancer."

She gulped. I was turned away from her, but I heard her gulp. I should have been a little more sympathetic, especially since this was the first, she was hearing of it. But I lost all will of being sympathetic when I remembered that she was the one that abandoned us. She got to start over and leave us behind as if her husband and daughter were just a bad night in college she wanted to forget.

"When?" She asked. her voice almost a whisper.

I poured the coffee beans into the filter, as I'd seen Zaria do and started the pot, staring at it to avoid looking in the eyes of the woman I dreamed about, but had no memory of.

I closed my eyes, gripping the counter to keep me afloat. "He started getting sick when I was around seventeen and he died in my freshmen year of college."

"You went to college? What did you major in?"

"English." I didn't take my eyes off the boiling water as if looking at her would acknowledge that this was really happening.

"You were always so smart. What's your job?"

I couldn't take any more of this. Her coming in here, acting as if nothing was wrong and she could just waltz right back into my life like she didn't forget about me.

I haven't forgotten, no matter how much I wanted to. I haven't forgotten what it felt like to grow up without a mother, not buying gifts for Mother's Day, having to celebrate my birthday without my mother because she didn't want me, she didn't think I was worth it.

"Teacher." I said, turning around to face her. "Are we done with the twenty questions?"

Her face dropped. My gut clenched, even now I felt sorry for her, I felt guilty for what I said to her and for how I acted. I shouldn't, I should keep her at a distance, I shouldn't let her in, but seeing her face disappointed in how I spoke to her, just made me want to reach out and hug her. Hug my mother.

Her eyes dropped to the ground. "I deserve that." She looked back up to face me and swallowed. "I'm sorry Melissa, I don't know what to say."

Then why did you come here?

"There's nothing you can say to fix this. you left." I shook my head, a tear dropping down my face as I quickly wiped it away. I will not be vulnerable in front of this woman, I will not cry. "I was a kid and you left."

She took a step closer, then stilled. Like she wanted to approach me, to comfort me but she realized I was nothing but a stranger now. "I didn't leave you. I left your dad."

I laughed, bitterly, my eyes filled with tears. I begged myself not to let them drop, I was sure she could see the wetness in them, they were probably red and puffy, but I would not lose a tear over her.

"Really?" I asked. "Because for the past thirteen years, I haven't had a mother, so tell me again how you didn't leave me."

She sighed. "Melissa, I didn't come to talk about the past. I came to talk to you about the future."

I blinked away the tears. "I don't want to talk to you at all, so why don't you say what you came here to say so we can get this over with."

"I'm getting married." I blinked at her. This was why she was here? "And I want you to come to the wedding."

My chest started to ache, she didn't care about those years she lost with me, she didn't even want to apologize, she just came here to invite me to her dumb wedding so I could see she was fine without me.

"In Spain? Do you still live there?"

"Yes." She said, the edge of her eyes wrinkling as she smiled, like she smiled at me outside of my apartment building, like I was a stranger.

"Why now?" I blurted out.

"What?" She asked, her brows furrowing.

"Why now?" I repeated. "You had so many years to reach out. Why now? You didn't care about me before, so what's different now? Why do you want me at your wedding?"

"Because you're my daughter." She replied, like that would fix everything. She didn't care about her 'daughter' for over a decade and now, when it's convenient, I was her 'daughter' again.

"Really? Because how I see it, I don't have a mother."

"I'm family."

I shook my head. *No, you aren't.* "You say you're family, but where were you when I hurt? When I needed someone, when I needed you? You weren't there."

"Melissa, please." She begged, her eyes brimming with tears. *Please Sofia, don't lose tears because of me, you never cared before, don't start now.*

"I have nothing else to say to you." I walked over to the door, ready to kick her out of my life for good. My heart was pummeling out of my chest, the anxiety was building up, too intense to see anything, if I had a panic attack in front of her, I would scream.

Before I reached the door handle, she stopped me. Her hand on my shoulder. "You have a sister."

I turned around, blinking at her, unable to form words. A sister?

"Isabella." She said.

I didn't say anything. What could I say to that?

"She's two." She continued when I stayed silent. "Please come and meet her."

I shook my head and said the only words that were getting louder and louder in my head. "So, you've replaced me."

She frowned. "No." She said, shaking her head. "It's not like that."

"You abandoned your family, to start a new one. Isn't that right?"

She didn't reply and I knew why. Because that was exactly what she had done. She left us and started over in a new country with a new life, a new husband and now a new daughter, so she didn't need the old one anymore. Her silence was enlightening, without speaking she said so much, I almost smiled. Almost.

"Just leave. Please." I opened the door and waited for her to step out and accepted that this would be the last time I would ever see her again.

She took a step forward, her head dropped low as if she couldn't look at me. "What about your sister?" She whispered when she made it to the door.

I had a sister. I couldn't let that go, and I wouldn't abandon her and forget she existed like my mother had me. "I would like to meet her. But not now." The thought of having to see my mother again made the pain in my chest astronomical. I pressed down on it, trying to not call attention to the fact that she was breaking my heart all over again. "Maybe in the future. But I don't ever want to see you again."

"Melissa."

I shook my head, stopping her. "You had your chance to make amends. It's too late now. Get out of my apartment and don't contact me again."

She walked out. Out the apartment, out of my life, out of my heart. Without so much as an apology or a reasoning for leaving. She didn't even say the words 'I miss you'. *Well, I've missed you mom. So much. And I'll never see you again.*

As soon as the door closed, the ache in my heart became too big not to notice. I took deep breaths in, but nothing helped. I pressed my hand to my chest, willing my heartbeat to slow down. I dropped to the floor, my vision blurred, my breathing erratic. I couldn't catch air, I couldn't breathe, I couldn't see. The room was spinning as my hand pressed harder on my chest.

"Hey, hey, I'm here, breathe slowly." I heard Gabriel say. I felt his hands brush the hair back from my face, cradling my face in his hands. beads of sweat trickled down my forehead as my breathing slowed down and my vision became clearer. I inhaled and exhaled deep and slow, coming down from the panic attack, relaxing even more when Gabriel's face was above mine, looking at me with so much care and anguish.

"Gabriel?" I said, breathlessly.

His lips smashed into mine as he kissed me like he was scared to lose me. I'd had many panic attacks, some alone and some with Zaria but this one was the worst one I had. My mother. I argued with my mother. That was the last time I would ever see her again. God, I wanted to crawl up until I could forget this ever happened.

"I'm right here, baby. Focus on me."

I did as he told me to. I focused on his beautiful face looking down at me, his eyes were clearer than ever to me.

"You're okay, Mel." He whispered, more to himself than me, almost as if he was saying the words to comfort himself, not me. He pulled me closer to him, holding me and I never wanted him to let go.

I love you. The words were right on the tip of my tongue as I leaned in to kiss his forehead.

"Who was that?" He asked as he stroked my arm.

He probably saw her walk out of the apartment, I hope he hadn't heard anything.

"My mother." I replied.

He squeezed me tighter. *Please don't ever let me go.*

CHAPTER THIRTY-THREE

Waking up with Gabriel was something I never thought would happen.

Zaria was still at Trey's house which meant she wouldn't be home until later tonight, after work.

After what happened yesterday, I needed to tell Zaria. She was too important to me, and Gabriel was too important to me. I didn't want to lose either of them and I needed to do this the right way.

I knew how amazing Gabriel was, no matter what I used to think of him before all of this happened between us, I knew he wouldn't hurt me, and he would always make me happy. He was a successful, driven man who made happier than I had ever been in my life.

And I didn't want him thinking I wanted to keep him a secret because I was ashamed of him or thought he wasn't good enough for me. It was the opposite. I was afraid he was too good for me and selfishly I wanted to keep him, even if I thought I didn't deserve him.

My leg was wrapped around his waist as his face snuggled in my breasts. I held back the giggle as I kissed his forehead. Cuddling was never something I thought I'd like. I liked my space, my privacy, but with Gabriel, there was no such thing as too close. I needed him as close to me as possible.

"Mmm." He mumbled, stirring as he woke up. His eyes fluttered open, and he smiled as soon as he saw I was in his bed, wrapped around him.

"Morning." I whispered.

"Morning, baby." He rasped, his morning voice making me smile. He leaned in to kiss me and I pressed my hand to my mouth to stop him, his brows wrinkled in confusion.

"I haven't brushed my teeth." I mumbled behind my hand.

He groaned. "I don't fucking care." He rasped, ripping my hand away from my mouth and ravaging my mouth, kissing me deep and hard. I could so easily get used to this. "You're so beautiful in the morning." He mumbled against my skin as he kissed my neck.

I picked up my phone from the nightstand groaning when I saw I needed to leave soon. "Gabriel." I moaned when he bit my nipple. "We don't have time for this, I need to leave in fifteen minutes."

He kissed the base of my throat before pulling away. "Fine." He sighed. "I need to be at work in half an hour, too." I pulled back the sheets, hopping off the bed.

I left his bedroom, running to the bathroom. I needed to get last nights' stench of sex off my body before teaching a bunch of 6th graders.

I pulled my towel off, climbing out of the shower, dressing as quickly as I could. There was no doubt that I would be late. I opened the bathroom door and walked out, grabbing my purse and putting on my shoes.

I gasped when I felt a hard smack on my ass. Looking back, I saw Gabriel behind me grinning as he stared at my ass whilst I was bent over putting my shoes on. I grinned back at him. He was wearing nothing but a pair of black boxers and that was tempting me to continue what we didn't finish in the bedroom this morning. He was too distracting for my own good.

I stood up and pushed him back. "Stop distracting me and get in the shower."

He was strong, so the only reason I was able to push him back was because he let me, he was smiling down at me. God, that smile was intoxicating. I never wanted to go a day without seeing it, without being the reason he smiled so brightly.

"I'll be thinking of you." He winked as he walked inside of the bathroom, closing the door behind him.

I groaned at myself, thinking of him in the shower stroking himself to the thought of me. Should I just skip work and hop back in the shower with him? I shook my head, he *is* distracting.

My head jerked back when I heard a knock on the door. My brows wrinkled in confusion. Zaria was probably at work by now and Gabriel was in the shower, who else would come here?

I opened the door and my stopped in my tracks. My breath caught in my throat, at the sight of her.

Fuck, I forgot how beautiful she was. The dress hugged her figure, the blue fabric a contrast to her pale skin, complimenting the blonde hair draping down her back, long and straight. She stood tall in her six-inch heels, looking down at me, her blue eyes twinkled with a smile pasted on her face. "Hi, is this Gabriel's apartment?"

My eyebrows dropped slightly. She didn't remember who I was? Of course, not. Why would she, we only met once, and she was oblivious to me, as most people are. I was the one obsessing over Gabriel's new girlfriend. How beautiful she was, how I would never be like her, confident, outgoing, funny.

She was the type of person who turned heads whenever she entered a room, as opposed to me who hid from the attention and spotlight as much as possible.

"Um… Yes, hi Lucy, I'm Melissa, Zaria's best friend."

Her eyes dropped down my body, widening as they took in my clothes. She was in a tight blue dress at seven in the morning, and I was in jeans and a green top. She finally made her way back to my face, her smile not quite reaching her eyes. "Yes, of course."

"What can I help you with?" I asked. Why was she here?

"I just came to talk to Gabriel, I've been texting him and I wanted to talk to him in person." The corner of her lips tilting up.

I frowned. She'd been texting him? Why would he be texting his ex-girlfriend if they broke up? I felt so stupid. This whole time we spent together, he was still in contact with her. Did he want to get back together and what we had was just a fling until he moved? I bit the inside of my cheek to stop my eyes from welling up.

He didn't even want to talk about her at the beach, I misread the situation as him being heartbroken over her, but maybe that wasn't it at all. Maybe he didn't want to talk about his breakup with her because he wasn't planning on staying broken up.

I pressed my hand to my chest, this time it was my heart that was hurting. I loved him and he was using me as a pass time until he got back together with his ex?

Before I could even process this, Lucy's eyes drifted behind me, her eyes widening, and I knew that she was looking at Gabriel. I closed my eyes for a second, taking in a deep breath as I turned to face him. He had just stepped out of the bathroom, with only a towel wrapped around his waist. His eyes weren't on me. He was staring right back at Lucy.

I felt my heart break. Even after everything, she would always be the one he noticed first. His eyes drifted to me and then back to Lucy. He shook his head, approaching the door.

His eyes were locked on mine as I swallowed hard, pasting on a fake smile. "Your girlfriend just came over to get back together with you." I stepped to the side of Lucy as she entered the apartment, hastily making my way out.

"Wait, Mel." Gabriel called out behind me.

"It's fine. I'm going to work, have fun."

I rushed to the elevator, quickly pressing the door to close. I saw Gabriel running towards the elevator and pressed the button even faster. *Please close before he gets here.* I didn't want to hear any bullshit excuses. The proof came out of the horse's mouth itself, he was still texting her enough that she clearly thought he wanted to get back together with her. Was he flirting with her in those texts? Was he calling her baby when he called me that?

"Mel, wait, let me explain." Gabriel's face came in view as the elevator doors closed.

I let my back hit the wall as I exhaled, hard, blinking away the tears that dared to fall. I wasn't going to cry over this, I knew what I was and what I wasn't. I was a distraction to pass the time, I wasn't a fun person who he'd want to spend time with. I wasn't an easy person to have around, I was moody, quiet and antisocial.

He was leaving in less than two weeks anyway, if he ever found an apartment to move into. If not, he could always move back in with his girlfriend. I needed to forget about him, I was never going to be enough for him and I knew it, too bad I let myself believe otherwise.

CHAPTER THIRTY-FOUR

Gabriel, Gabriel, Gabriel.

That was all my mind was focused on today. I only had myself to blame for all of this. What did I think was going to happen? Gabriel hated me for years. He just got lonely and wanted some company and that was what I was to him, nothing more.

I dreaded going home. I didn't want to see him or talk to him, I didn't want to hear whatever excuses he was going to use to explain why his ex-girlfriend was there to get back together with him or why he'd been texting her.

I walked, slowly to my car. There was no reason to rush, nothing waited for me back home except for a pile of bullshit and confusion. Maybe I could go to the café or a bookstore. I didn't have to go home just yet, if I could avoid him for as long as possible, it wouldn't be a problem.

Zaria would be home soon anyway, he wouldn't be able to talk to me in front of her even if I had to sleep in her bed, so he didn't come knocking on my door when she went to sleep then so fucking be it.

"Hey, Melissa." My back straightened when I recognized that voice. He had stayed away from me since the dance, barely saying two words, it had worked.

"Hi Chad." I said back, walking hastily to my car.

"Woah there." He laughed. "Wait up, I came out here to talk to you." *Why?*

I looked around at the parking lot, it was pretty empty at this time, only a handful of cars sat out here, and no one was around. "What about?" I asked, warily.

He stood in front of me, licking his lips as he looked down at me. I swallowed the lump in my throat. "I was just wondering how things have been with your boyfriend, I haven't seen him around."

He doesn't exist. Not anymore.

"Well, he works, too so he's not exactly hanging around at a middle school." I said, laughing nervously.

His hands came up to my car windows, trapping me with his body. "What are you doing?" I asked. What the fuck did he think he was doing.

"See, what I think, is that he isn't real." He licked his lips again. "I think you just wanted to play with me, make me chase you, isn't that right?"

No.

I shook my head. "I don't want to play with you, I have a boyfriend. Let me go." I snapped.

He just laughed, not letting me escape as he came closer and closer. I closed my eyes, wincing. I always knew Chad was creepy, but I never thought he would do something like this. Why was nobody around? I could scream for help, and no one would hear me.

My hands came up, trying to push him back but he wouldn't budge. I pushed harder but he just groaned. He was turned on by this? What a creep.

"Let me fucking go." I seethed.

His head leaned down as his hands grabbed my face, he was going to kiss me? Fuck no!

I turned my head to the side, avoiding his lips as I bit down, hard on the hand that was still cupping my face.

He hissed. "You fucking bitch." His eyes were black as he tried to lean down again. I snapped my eyes closed, I bit him, and it did nothing. I couldn't push him off me. I waited, waited for him to kiss me. I couldn't do anything to stop him, I just wanted it to be over. My hands were still pressed against his chest, pushing him as hard as I could but it was no use.

I heard a groan and then something hit the floor. I opened my eyes and blinked at the sight in front of me. Chad was on the floor, his hand covering his cheek as blood dripped from his lip. What?

I glanced to my right seeing Gabriel, staring down at Chad as his chest rose and fell, his hands curled into fists by his side. His lip curled as his teeth bared. He was furious. I had never seen him like this.

He didn't even look at me as he made his way over to Chad once again. He picked him up by the collar of his shirt and pulled him up, slamming him against the door of another car. "If you ever put your hands on my woman again, I will fucking kill you. If you touch her, look at her, if you even think about her, I will find you and make you taste death, you got that?" Chad's face contorted as blood dripped down his face. he nodded at Gabriel. Gabriel pushed him against the door again before pulling away, letting him fall to the floor. "Fucking pig." He hissed.

Gabriel turned to face me, walking over to me as his jaw clenched. His hands came up to cradle my face. "Are you okay?" He asked.

I just wanted to cry. Not because of Chad... ok a little because of Chad, but mostly because Gabriel did this for me, and all I could think of was Lucy. Were they back together?

A tear dropped down my face as I nodded. His thumb brushed it away as his eyes scanned my face.

I yanked my face away from his hands and pulled away, he stepped back letting me go. Chad was gone. He must have run away when Gabriel was checking up on me. Good fucking riddance. I wanted to thank Gabriel, I wanted to kiss him and thank him for saving me, for taking care of me, but I couldn't.

I reached inside my purse, pulling my car keys out. I reached to open the car door, but Gabriel's hand wrapped around mine. "I'm taking you."

"My car's right here."

"And mine is right there." He pointed to the far end of the parking lot where his black rover sat.

"Why are you here?"

"Because you ran away from me this morning and I wanted to talk to you."

I bit the inside of my cheek. "There's nothing to talk about. I don't want to talk to you." Maybe it was petty, but I didn't care, I needed time to think about this, to process it.

His hand tightened around mine, as he pulled me away from my car, walking over to his, instead. "That's too fucking bad, we're talking."

I rolled my eyes. "There's nothing you can say to me, you're getting back together with your ex, that's fine. We both knew I was nothing but something to pass the time with."

He stopped abruptly, his eyebrows wrinkled. "What the fuck are you talking about?" He groaned as he ran a hand down his face, shaking his head. "I'm not having this conversation with you here, let's go, Mel."

"My car's right here, dipshit, I can't just leave it." He smiled. He actually smiled at the nickname I used to call him when he still hated each other.

"We'll come pick it up later, now get in."

I crossed my arms over my chest, not opening the car door.

He sighed. "Trevi, get your ass in the car or I'll put you in myself."

I scoffed, "I'd like to see you try." I knew he could. I couldn't fight him off even if I wanted to, but I wasn't going to just get in voluntarily, I didn't want to sit with him, I didn't want to talk to him.

He shrugged, making his way to me. My eyes locked on his as he smirked. He opened the car door and I stayed still as he waited to see if I'd go in. I didn't.

"You're a pain in my ass." He mumbled as he picked me up, effortlessly and dropped me in the seat of his car.

"Then why are you here?" I hissed. If I was such a pain in the ass for him, why did he want to talk to me? He could just move on with his girlfriend and forget about me.

He smirked as he licked his bottom lip. "I guess I like to torture myself."

I rolled my eyes. So, I was torture now? Lucy comes back one day and suddenly I'm an inconvenience.

CHAPTER THIRTY-FIVE

"I don't want to talk to you."
I shoved the keys into my apartment door, Gabriel trailing behind me.

The door opened and I rushed inside. Before I could make my way to my bedroom, his hand wrapped around my elbow, stilling me. I sighed. I just wanted to be alone, why couldn't he just let me do that?

"Mel." He breathed out. "Let me talk to you." He sounded defeated, like he didn't know what else to do to make me listen. I didn't want to sit here and hear him talk about his ex-girlfriend, but the strain in his voice made me want to hear him out.

I turned to face him, crossing my arms. "Fine, talk."

He exhaled, running a hand through his hair. "I'm not getting back together with Lucy."

I scoffed.

"Don't." He warned me. "Let me finish."

"That's bullshit, she said you've been texting her." I jutted in, not letting him continue.

He nodded. "I have been texting her." I closed my eyes, hearing him admit it hurt. "But not for the reason you think." I looked up at him. Why else would he be texting her about?

"Her father owns the building I wanted to purchase for my restaurant." He explained. "She called me the other day saying he backed out of the deal because he didn't want to associate with someone who broke his daughters' heart." His eyes locked on mine as he scanned my face.

"I had been texting her to apologize for what went down when our relationship ended, but not because I wanted to get back together with her, I was trying to convince her to talk to her father and explain the situation more clearly." He shook his head. "I didn't want to hurt her, the reason I ended it had nothing to do with her and she knew that."

He took his phone out of his back pocket and handed it to me. "Here. You can see for yourself."

I hesitantly took the phone from his hands, seeing the lock screen. My heart picked up and I looked up at Gabriel, my jaw dropped. It was the picture of us I had sent to Zaria. "Your lock screen."

He licked his lips, rubbing the back of his head. "Yeah, I kind of hacked into Zaria's phone to get your number and sent myself that picture."

I shook my head, looking down at the phone with the image of us on it. I was speechless. How long did he have this picture as his lock screen? I cleared my head and went into his messages, seeing Lucy's name and clicking on it.

It checked out. Every message was either about the restaurant or the business with her father. I locked his phone and handed it back to him. So, he wasn't planning on getting back together with her, then why did he end it? He could barely talk about her, it seemed like he was heartbroken over her.

"I ended it because of you." He explained, reading my mind.

Huh? My eyes shot wide open "Me?" I asked. How was that possible. He broke up with Lucy before he moved in here and he still hated me at the beginning.

He nodded. "I love you." He whispered, approaching closer to me. "I've loved you for a long time."

My heart flipped. "You… that's not possible. You hated me."

He shook his head, his hands cradling my face. "I never hated you, not from the first moment I saw you."

What?

I shook my head. "You barely talked to me, you insulted me and argued with me all the time."

His eyes looked deep into mine as he smiled. "The day I met you, I was instantly attracted to you." He admitted. "You had your hair all curly and wild spread across your back, and you wore a blue sundress even though it was fall. You were so shy and quiet, and I couldn't stop staring at you. But you were my sister's best friend, and I was a dumb teenager. I didn't want a relationship and I knew that was what you deserved so I tried to push you away when you were near, I didn't want to become your friend or make you think I was interested, or it would have just made you get false expectations."

I sucked in a breath, hearing him admit this was too much. I shook my head. "That's such a dumb excuse." I said. Maybe it wasn't the right thing to say when he had just admitted to being in love with me, but it was all my brain was thinking.

He shrugged. "Like I said, I was a dumb teenager."

But he carried on for years. "You're not a teenager anymore." I pointed out.

He nodded, looking embarrassed. "You're right. I thought if I kept it up, it would be easier, but it wasn't. I didn't want to admit to myself that nobody even came close to you. That

I couldn't feel for anyone what I felt for you and Melissa... I feel for you. So much."

I gulped. It was everything I wanted to hear, and it was too much to take in.

"But the more you came over, the more I wanted you, and I hated it, so I thought if I couldn't keep you away, I could make you hate me, then you wouldn't be tempted around me, and maybe I could make myself hate you too."

I swallowed. "Did it work?" Did he end up hating me like I did him? This whole time I thought he couldn't stand me, but he actually liked me?

He shook his head, leaning down for a fleeting kiss. "I told you, I could never hate you. You have no idea how hard it was to pretend to hate you when I didn't, not even a little bit."

He tucked a strand of hair behind my ear. "I fell in love with you when I was eighteen." My eyes snapped closed. Eighteen? How did I not know this? How was that possible?

"I knew I couldn't have you, so I stayed away, kept up the facade and tried to move on." His jaw clenched. "But nothing worked. No one even came close,"

"Lucy did." I whispered. He had moved in with her, that obviously meant he loved her.

"No." He whispered. "I tried to forget you, but you're unforgettable. All I could think of was you, every fight we had I loved because if I couldn't make you love me, I could make you hate me and any feelings you had for me meant you cared. Even if those feelings were that you wanted me to drown in the ocean."

He laughed and I smiled. "I moved in with her because I wanted to believe it." He shrugged. "Maybe if everyone thought I loved her and was in a committed relationship then I would think it too, I wanted to prove to myself that I wasn't just good enough for a night."

"Then why did you break up?"

He kissed me again, quick and fleeting. "Because I couldn't love her. Not like I loved you. I was a fucking coward for pushing you away, I realized that when I came here and saw how much you actually hated me."

His eyes closed for a minute and when he opened them, they burned into mine. "You couldn't even stand to be around me. I saw then how much I'd actually hurt you. I couldn't sleep for days after that. I never wanted to hurt you like that, I just wanted you to stay away from me so I wouldn't be tempted into having you when I knew I wasn't worthy of you."

I laughed, wetness pooling in my eyes. He wasn't worthy of me? He was everything I'd always wanted.

"I knew then I had to fix this, I didn't care if I got too close to you, I didn't care about any of it. I tried to keep it platonic but you're irresistible." He smirked at me.

I closed my eyes, processing everything he had just told me. He never hated me, only hated the fact that he was in love with me and couldn't stay away. I looked up at him, smiling down at me. His lips crashed into mine, kissing me slowly.

I pulled back from the kiss. "I'm nothing like Lucy." I told him.

He smiled. "That's a good thing."

I shook my head. "I mean I'm not like her or you. I'm not fun or social or even like going out. You said yourself that I stay home more than your grandma. I can't even go out clubbing without almost having a panic attack." I sighed. "Why would you ever want a life with someone like that?"

His jaw clenched. "I wish I never said that. I was just spewing shit to make you hate me. I don't ever want you to think there's something wrong with you or that I wouldn't want to be with you."

He cradled my face, rubbing his thumb across my cheek as he stared deep into my eyes. "I love you as you are. Exactly as you are."

I shook my head again. I didn't even love me sometimes, how could he?

"I know it's hard for you to love and trust. Especially because of your mother, but let me try Mel. All I want is to love you with everything I have."

I nodded, looking up at him as a small smile spread across his lips. I could do that. I could love and trust him.

"I love you." He whispered against my lips. My grin spread wide, my cheeks heated beneath his fingertips. He loved me.

"I—" Before I could tell him, I loved him back, his lips found mine again ravishing them as he proved to me how much he loved me in this one kiss.

"I love you too." I breathed out when he pulled back from me. His hands were still caressing my face as he looked deep into my eyes with nothing but *love*.

"I know." He said, rubbing his thumb on my lower lip. "I'm pretty lovable." He grinned like a kid in a candy store.

I rolled my eyes. "You just ruined that." I told him but he just laughed as he brought his lips to mine once again.

CHAPTER THIRTY-SIX

"What do you want to know?"

"Everything." I beamed.

Gabriel was mine. My boyfriend. He loved me. And I loved him.

Never in a million years did I think I'd be here straddling Gabriel on the couch, with my arms wrapped around his neck as we got to know each other, for real. No fake date, just me and him talking about our lives.

"What did you want to be if you weren't a chef?" I asked him.

He shrugged. "I've always been interested in cooking but if I wasn't I'd probably have gone to college for football."

I nodded. He was a really talented football player. I even saw a few of his games that Zaria would drag me to.

"What about you? What's your dream job?"

"I already have it. I love being a teacher. I really feel like I make a difference in their lives, I can inspire and create a positive influence in their lives so they feel like they can count on someone even if it's a teacher."

He smiled. "Those kids are lucky they have a teacher that looks like you. Do any of them flirt with you?" He asked, grinning.

I rolled my eyes. "Seeing as they're eleven, no."

His hands tightened around my waist. "I had a crush on a teacher when I was eleven."

My brows shot up. "You did?"

He nipped my jaw. "If they looked like you, I would."

"Mmm, your dirty talk is out of this world." I teased.

He smacked my ass, grinning when I let out a small moan. "Stop being a smartass."

I laughed. "Ok, ok, um… what's your biggest fear?" I asked.

"Honestly… losing my parents. I know it has to happen eventually but thinking about not having them around breaks my heart." His eyes weren't on mine, he was staring through me, his throat bobbed, holding back from getting emotional. I understood more than anyone, losing my dad was one of the hardest things I had to go through, it was when the panic attacks started and not having a mother who comforted me during those times, was even harder.

I leaned down, cupping his face and kissed him, letting him know I was here for him, no matter what.

"What else?" He asked, smiling weakly at me.

"Mmm…." I trailed off in thought. "Ooh, what's your biggest flaw?"

He grinned, licking my bottom lip. "My huge cock."

I rolled my eyes. "Hilarious… of course you had to ruin it."

He laughed and then shook his head. "Ok, seriously, um… maybe putting other peoples' needs ahead of mine most of the time." He smiled. "It's why I thought I could push you away so that I wouldn't hurt you or Zaria, even though it killed me to stay away from you." He shook his head, sighing. "I can't believe I finally have you."

I snorted. "Took you long enough. You obviously have no game seeing as it took you ten years."

He grinned, wrapping his arms tighter around my waist as he dropped my back to the couch, hovering above me. "You want to see game?" He said, grinding his erection against me. I moaned. "I'll make you come so hard you'll forget your own name."

I shook my head. "We're supposed to be getting to know each other." I said, breathlessly as his teeth scraped the skin on my neck.

"Are you going to let me eat this pussy or are you going to continue talking?"

I moaned, arching my back. God, I wanted to. But no. We couldn't do this now. "Gabriel, please." I gasped when his mouth pulled my nipple. "I want to know you."

"You do know me." He said, kissing up my neck, landing on my lips.

"I'm being serious." I looked into his eyes, and he sighed, sitting up and pulling me onto his lap, straddling him once again.

His hands sneaked under my tank top wrapping around my waist. "I've never had a boyfriend. This is new to me."

He kissed me. "This is new to me too."

My brows wrinkled. "But you had a girlfriend."

He shook his head. "She wasn't you." His lips found mine again as we kissed until we were breathless.

I smiled so wide, closing my eyes. My cheeks hurt from smiling, I was so happy but in the back of my mind I felt like I was betraying Zaria. He must have seen the change in my face because he sighed.

"She'll get over it." It was creepy how well he knew me.

He didn't know that. Not for sure. She could resent me and feel like I betrayed her trust, I lied to her and did the one thing she was scared would happen. I fell for her brother. If she ended up resenting her brother because of me, I'd never be able to live with myself. She was his best friend, they had a strong bond, and I couldn't be the one to break it.

"What if she hates me?"

"She won't." He reassured me. "She loves you. This won't change that.

"But what if —"

"Please shut up and kiss me." He interrupted.

I giggled. "I love hearing you beg." I leaned in bringing my lips to his, lingering on his soft lips. His tongue traced my bottom lip, and I parted my lips allowing his tongue to slide in my mouth, dueling with mine as I wrapped my arms around his neck.

Gabriel's hands shifted down to my hips, pushing me into him in a figure eight motion.

Yes please.

I grinded my hips on his, feeling his bulge under the thin fabric of my shorts. His lips left mine as he trailed down my jaw, nibbling on the hollow of my neck that had me throwing my head back as his hands on my hips grew more aggressively, rocking me into him.

His hands left my hips as I mindlessly rocked into him as he ravished my jaw, neck, leaving small kisses down to my cleavage. He cupped my ass, squeezing it. I let out a small moan and he groaned, smiling against my skin, lifting his head, bringing his lips back to mine.

"Let me take you out on a real date." He said, his voice strained as if he was in pain. "I want to see you in a tight dress, knowing you're all mine when I walk in with you on my arm." His thumb traced my lower lip as he looked deep into my eyes. "I want to talk to you for hours about anything and everything and then kiss you for everyone to see."

I wanted all of that.

I nodded, my hips rolling slowly over his. "Yes, I'd love that." I replied. "I want everything with you."

He smiled at me, so brightly. I loved being the cause of that smile. I had seen it many times, but I had never been on the receiving end of it. All this time I thought he hated me, when in reality he wanted me, like I had once wanted him.

He pulled me in, kissing me fervently like he would die without this.

"What the fuck."

I pulled away from Gabriel, stilling as I heard Zaria's voice. Fuck. Fuck. Fuck.

I glanced up, seeing her standing at the door, her eyes wide open as she stared down at me and Gabriel, blinking fast as if she was imagining the whole thing.

"Zaria, oh my god." I stood up from Gabriel's lap. Running a hand through my hair as I looked back at my best friend. Her face made my stomach twist with guilt. She looked so... betrayed, disappointed. I shook my head. "You weren't supposed to find out like this." I didn't even know how she was supposed to find out. But not like this, not now. This was all wrong. I wanted a redo.

I walked over to her, but she threw her hand up, urging me to stop as she looked at me with sadness in her eyes. I did that. I was the cause of the pain she was feeling. I had never felt shittier in my life.

"Sis, let's talk about this." Gabriel said. Her eyes shifted from me to him as she shook her head.

"I don't even know what to say right now." She dropped her hand as she balled it into a fist at her side. "I don't know if I feel more betrayed by my brother or my best friend."

I closed my eyes, a tear falling down my cheek. I was a horrible friend. Not only did I lie to her, but I had come between her and her brother. I didn't want to be the cause of her pain or make her feel betrayed by her own brother because of me. I was her best friend, I was supposed to stand by her no matter what. I was supposed to be the cause of her happiness and laughs and smiles, not her pain.

"Z, I'm so sorry." My voice wobbly as I glanced up at her, through tear filled eyes. She looked at me, and then back at Gabriel before shaking her head.

"I just… I need to get out of here, I don't even know what just happened."

With that, she turned and walked out of the apartment, closing the door.

CHAPTER THIRTY-SEVEN

The temptation to smash my phone was high.

It had been a whole day and no text or call back from Zaria. I didn't know what else to do. I couldn't exactly track down her location, I wouldn't even know where to begin to look.

"She's not answering my calls." Gabriel told me.

I threw my phone out of my reach, luckily it landed on the couch pillows. If I broke my phone before Zaria had a chance to call me back, I would break down. "She hates me." I whispered, letting the tears fall down my face. I buried my face in my hands, muffling my cries.

Gabriel kissed the top of my head, rubbing my back as I cried out. "She doesn't hate you, Mel. She's just processing it. I mean the way she found out was probably shocking for her."

I groaned into my hands remembering how she walked in on me straddling her brother, practically grinding all over him. This wasn't how she was supposed to find out. I needed time, maybe a month before we told her, and definitely not when I had my tongue down his throat.

I jerked when the sound of my ringtone played. I reached for my phone, seeing Zaria's name on the screen. Wiping the tears on my face, I answered hastily. "Z?"

I heard a sigh on the other end of the phone. "Meet me at the café."

I nodded, stopping when I realized I had nodded to myself as she couldn't see me. "When?" My voice came out wobbly and I cleared my throat.

"Now? If you can."

"Yes, I'll be there." Anything to talk to my best friend. At least try and explain it to her. Having Gabriel there would probably make me more comfortable with this whole thing, but it had to be me alone. I had to talk to her about this and be honest with her, one thing I hadn't been, not for our whole friendship.

The phone hung up and I looked up at Gabriel, a small smile played on my lips. "Zaria wants to meet me."

He leaned down, his thumb wiping off the tears from my face. His lips brushed mine. "I told you, she just needed time. Do you want me to go with you?" He asked.

I shook my head. It needed to be me. If we were there together, she could feel overwhelmed and run again.

♡

"How did this happen?"

I shook my head, not knowing how to answer that. How did this happen? Did it happen last week, or did it happen ten years ago? I didn't even know the answer to that. "I don't know." I told her, honestly. "I had a crush on him when we were teenagers, but then I thought he hated me, so I hated him back." I sighed. "But it turns out he never hated me, he told me he fell in love with me when he was eighteen and tried to push me away because of how important you were to him."

"Eighteen?" Zaria gasped. "So how long has this been going on?"

"No, no." I reassured her. "I thought he hated me until two weeks ago. We became close... trying to be friendlier for your benefit—"

"Oh, don't try to blame this on me." She cut in.

"I'm not, I just... You wanted us to stop arguing so I tried to be friends with him, for you Z. I always had a crush on him, I just didn't let it affect me because he was an asshole. But then we became friends and we got closer and the more I got to know him..."

"You fell in love with him." She finished for me.

I nodded, meeting her eyes as she smiled. She was smiling?

"M. I'm happy for you, I am. I know how you've never had luck in the past with trusting people, especially any guys, after that jerk at college, and if you love my brother and he makes you happy then that's all I want for you." She reached over to squeeze my hand. "I just... I felt betrayed. Both my best friend and my brother had lied and were sneaking around behind my back, and I didn't handle it well. I can't believe I told you not to fuck my brother." She laughed. "I mean, who does that?"

She shook her head. "I just didn't want him to hurt you. Gabriel has never been in a committed relationship. He went from hook up to hook up and I thought if you got together, that he would break your heart and you wouldn't be able to be around him, even more than before, which meant you wouldn't want to be around me."

I swallowed the lump stuck in my throat. Hearing Zaria speak about Gabriel like that knowing he struggled to be taken seriously by anyone and just thought of as a player made me sad for him. I knew who he was, with me. He was caring, thoughtful and gentle. Words I never thought I would use to describe Gabriel at the start of the month.

I squeezed her hand back. "I love you Z. I never wanted to lie to you or betray you in any way. And I never wanted you to resent Gabriel because of this, because of me."

She laughed, her smile shining so brightly. "I'm going to have to get used to you defending Gabriel instead of ranting about how much he pisses you off. But that would never happen. If I could forgive him for burning my Bratz dolls when I was six, I would definitely forgive him for this, and you too M. That's what family does. They argue, they make up and all is fine again."

Hearing her refer to me as her family meant more than she would know. I confided in her about what happened with my mother, I and how I stood up to her. I told her about Gabriel following me to my date and our first kiss. I told her how he took care of me when I was moody and menstruating, and how I had fallen in love with him. I told her everything about us.

She groaned. "I just realized, now that you're dating my brother, I won't get to hear about your sex life."

I chuckled. "I can promise you, Z. Even if I wasn't dating your brother, I would never tell you that."

CHAPTER THIRTY-EIGHT

Nothing is sexier than a man cooking.

Especially when he's shirtless, and when he looks as good as Gabriel Anderson.

"Can you stop ogling me, Mel. I'm supposed to be teaching you."

"Huh?" I looked up, meeting his eyes. His lips are pulled in a smirk as he looked down at me, shaking his head. I was leaning against the kitchen island, my head propped up on my hands as I stared at him cooking... whatever he was cooking.

"C'mon. It's your turn."

I sighed, lifting myself off the island, making my way to the stove. "Why do I need to learn how to cook when I could just watch you instead?" I beamed at him.

His lips spread into a smile. "Cute, trevi. But I'm leaving next week, and you can't live off take out and grilled cheese sandwiches."

Why not?

"Because we both know your bank account can't afford all those food deliveries, and grilled cheese? Not exactly the healthiest thing." It was like he could read my mind. Always knowing what I was thinking.

I lifted my brow at him. "Are you calling me fat?" I teased.

His hands looped around my waist as his hands shifted to my ass, grabbing it. "Never." He murmured into my neck as he kissed my jaw, lightly. "I just want you to live a long, long life with me."

I couldn't help but smile. My heart hurt so much I pressed at my chest. I wanted nothing more than a future with Gabriel, marriage, kids. I wanted everything with him.

I rolled my eyes. "You sound like Zaria." She would scold me for eating too many grilled cheese sandwiches, going off about the sodium content and the health factors that went with it.

He shrugged. "Can't help it. My dad's a doctor, he's been instilling this into us for years."

I sighed. "Okay. What are we cooking?" I asked.

"Chicken stir fry, it's just vegetables and chicken, easy enough."

I nodded, stepping to the side as Gabriel spent the next twenty minutes teaching me how to cook the chicken and vegetables, tempting me with sexy cooking language like 'sautéing'. It didn't hurt that he was shirtless and just in sweatpants. That was one way of incentivizing a student. He guided me, teaching me how to cut the vegetables, how to season them, how long to cook them for.

"Like this?" I asked, looking behind my shoulder, catching Gabriel staring at my ass whilst licking his bottom lip. He nodded, a small smile appearing on his lips as he approached me closer, wrapping one hand around my waist and the other, he placed on top of mine, as I mixed the stir fry in the pan, his hand moving with mine.

He pressed into me from behind and my eyes closed as I felt his hard bulge poking against the seam of my leggings. His lips found my neck as he kissed and licked, scraping his teeth on my skin before sucking it into his mouth, tasting me like a starving man. I whimpered. "Dinner." I mumbled.

"I'd rather eat you." He growled, his breath hitting my skin, making me tremble.

Fuck the stir fry. I spun around, wrapping my arms around his neck as I brushed my lips with his, kissing him hungrily. I ran a hand through his hair, landing on the back of his neck as I pulled him deeper into me. Who knew cooking could be so erotic?

"Ew, gross."

I broke away from the kiss, glancing at Zaria stood in the doorway, her face contorted in disgust. I laughed into the crook of Gabriel's neck. It had been over a week since she had found out about us, but she still hadn't gotten used to it.

"Don't fuck in the kitchen, please. It's where we eat." I looked up at Gabriel as we smirked at each other. *Oops.* Zaria groaned. "You already did, didn't you?" She laughed. "You know what… don't answer that. I'm going over to Trey's. M, we still on for Friday?"

"Yes. There's a new season coming out." I grinned. Our tradition of reality shows and take out was back and I couldn't be happier.

"Uh, am I invited?" Gabriel asked.

Zaria shook her head. "Sorry bro, you have Melissa all day every day. Friday is our thing, consider yourself uninvited."

Gabriel frowned. He had become as obsessed as us with California Girlz. But I needed my girl time with Zaria, no matter how much I loved Gabriel, best friends needed time together. "Fine." He sighed.

Zaria laughed at Gabriel's sour mood and walked out of the apartment. I smiled at Gabriel, leaning in to kiss him before pulling away.

I opened the freezer, pulling out the strawberry ice cream I had stashed away.

Gabriel shook his head. "You have such a sweet tooth. You haven't eaten dinner yet."

I shrugged. "I wanted to celebrate."

His brows wrinkled. "With ice cream?"

I smiled as I nodded. I had used ice cream as a comfort food for so long, whenever I was stressed or sad, a bowl of ice cream would drown those feelings, at least for a little while. But I had so much to happy about, for once in my life, I wanted to mark it in some way.

"Celebrate what exactly?"

"You, me, us." I grinned at him. "Your restaurant, my new therapist. Everything good in our lives." The anxiety attacks had calmed a lot since I had started attending therapy last week, and the fact that I was beaming with joy every day might have a thing or two to help with that.

I opened the tub, scooping out two large spoonful's of ice cream.

"Do you like strawberry ice cream just because it's pink?" Gabriel asked, watching me as I dug into my ice cream, licking my lips when it dribbled down.

I giggled. "No. It was my dad's favorite, I guess I just got used to it as a child." I shrugged. "I like it because it tastes good." I glanced down at my bowl, and maybe a little because it was pink.

He groaned as I ate another spoonful. "It's disgusting."

I made a show of it, moaning as I licked the spoon clean. I glanced up at him, finding him smirking back at me. He definitely wanted to finish what he started in the kitchen. "If I remember correctly, you said you liked it when you tried it."

His exact words were *best thing I've tasted.* How could he hate it now?

He leaned in, holding my chin between his fingers as he licked my bottom lip with his tongue, cleaning up the ice cream the dribbled down. "It wasn't the ice cream I was talking about, trevi." He whispered against my lips before pulling back with a shit eating grin plastered on his face.

All those little moments from before were irrelevant in my eyes. Every conversation, every argument, every day we spent together, all meant something completely different to Gabriel than it had to me.

All these years I felt like a nuisance and invisible. I wanted him to see me, to notice me, to feel something other than hatred even if at the time it was all I thought I felt for him, and he had. This whole time he was in love with me, and I made myself believe I hated him, because I thought he hated me too.

But we were here now. Together, finally. After so much lost time, I wouldn't waste another with him.

For so long, I had felt unwanted by Gabriel, by my mother, by every other person who didn't want to be around me, given my less than vibrant personality. Being an introvert did that to you. I could remember being nineteen at college, barely being able to order a cup of coffee on my own without having a panic attack, and how far I had come.

I confronted my mother for fucks sake. My own mother, after years of hoping and wishing I would understand why she left me, I confronted her. Even if I would never know the answer to that, I was content with my decision.

At least she was happy, with her new family in Spain and her new husband, I guess I still wanted happiness for her, even if I wasn't included in it.

Everyone deserved to be happy. And in the longest time, I finally was. Gabriel made me smile like I had never done before, he took care of me and made me feel loved.

"Are you happy?" He asked me.

I grinned, tucking my head into his chest. "The happiest."

CHAPTER THIRTY-NINE

ONE YEAR LATER

I glanced around the restaurant, still closed to the public filled with family and friends, and I all I could think was, he did it. He opened his own restaurant. My boyfriend was now a chef and a business owner, and I had never been prouder of him.

"Melissa, sweetie." Naomi called out as she entered the restaurant. I smiled walking up to her and Terry, greeting them both in an embrace.

"Hey." We hugged and when I pulled back, her hands cupped my face, scanning it.

"You look beautiful." She said, sounding stunned.

"Thank you." I smiled, weakly, my face still cradled in her hands.

Her hands dropped from my face, but her eyes continued scanning my features. "Have you been using a new skincare? Your skin is glowing."

"Oh." I laughed, nervously. Compliments were always hard for me to accept. "No, same old stuff." I assured her. I wanted to tell her my skin was probably glowing from being so happy. I couldn't remember a moment in my life where I'd felt pure bliss, but everyday was like that for me.

She smiled back. "I can't tell you how happy I am that you'll be living close by." I finally decided what to do with the house my dad had left me in the will. It meant so much to me and my dad when I was growing up. It was the place that held all of our memories, all of our holidays and birthdays and summers. All the good and the bad was filled in that house, and I didn't want to get rid of that.

So, Gabriel and I took the plunge and moved in together, remodeling and fixing the house to our taste. Which meant that Zaria was living alone... for two weeks before Trey moved in with her. I suggested for her to move to a different apartment, as that one had two other bedrooms that would be unused, but she refused, saying that when she would move out, it would be to a house she bought.

She looked really happy, especially with Trey. I worried about her, moving so quickly with someone new, but he's made my best friend happier than ever, so I approved. I wanted nothing but for her to feel like I did every day.

"Me too." I told Naomi. Terry had excused himself and walked over to the bar. I looked towards the bar, seeing Allie and Charlotte stood by, having a drink and laughing at whatever they were talking about. I would bet that they were already a little drunk.

A loud noise snapped my head to the right, seeing Gabriel's friends stood around, yelling at the tv as they watched a football game. I had met them many times and I loved his friends. They were all funny and loud, very loud. My cheeks heated, smiling as I looked around the room. Everyone was here, everyone who mattered to us and loved us, were here.

My feet were hurting, lately I'd been getting tired. It was probably because of the heels I decided to wear today, and I still needed to do something. I looked around, looking for Gabriel. I didn't see him around, I didn't know where he was but hopefully, I managed to do what I needed to do without him finding out.

I walked around the back, into the kitchen, seeing Jim there stirring a pot on the stove. Jim was Gabriel's sous chef and tonight was the grand opening. Gabriel had opened the restaurant for family and friends only.

"Hey Jim."

"Hey Melissa." He said, barely glancing back at me.

He was the only one in the kitchen, which meant Gabriel wasn't here either. "Where's Gabriel?" I asked.

"He went out with Zaria."

I didn't even see him leave, but I hadn't seen Zaria either. "Oh, well, I actually came to look for you."

"Me?" That caught his attention. He spun around, his eyes wide as he looked at me with confusion, wondering what the hell I would talk to him about. Jim was new, seeing as this was the first time the restaurant was opening, which meant I had spoken to him exactly three times, this being the third.

I nodded. "I need your help. Gabriel's birthday is next week, and I suck at cooking."

He laughed, shaking his head. "I'm aware."

Great. Gabriel must have told him about my horrible cooking skills, it annoyed me how much it amused Gabriel that I couldn't cook, almost as if he loved that about me. But that was about to change, I wanted to learn, I wanted to cook my boyfriend breakfast for his birthday.

I narrowed my eyes at him. "Whose side are you on Jim?"

"Uhh…. My boss since he pays my bills."

I sighed. "Fine. But can you help me? I want to cook him breakfast. At first, I thought about baking him a cake but that seemed too complicated so I thought breakfast would be a good start."

He nodded. "Can you make eggs?" He asked me.

I winced. "Only if you want them burnt."

He laughed, again. "How about pancakes?"

I shrugged. I had never made pancakes before. "Maybe? I mean, it's kind of like a grilled cheese, right? You put it in the pan then flip."

"Sure." He laughed. "Maybe we should start with something simpler."

♡

"Okay. I want to show you something." I smiled up at him.

"What is it?" Gabriel asked.

I shook my head. "Before you get too excited, it's nothing. Really."

"Then why are you smiling like that." He asked, rubbing two fingers over my lips, my smile was so wide my cheeks hurt.

I gave his fingers a light kiss, wanting to pull him closer to me, but my hands were currently behind my back hiding my surprise. "Because *I'm* excited. But to you, this will probably mean nothing." I suddenly wanted to erase the last half an hour, I wanted to forget about this. Maybe he would even think it was stupid. What kind of adult didn't know how to cook? I was making a big deal out of nothing.

"Okay, show me." He smiled.

I brought my hands in front of me, holding the egg in my hands.

"An egg?" He asked, his brows furrowing. I wanted to hide. This *was* stupid.

"A boiled egg." I gulped, the smile completely vanished from my face.

He stroked his beard, wondering what the hell I was doing with a boiled egg in my hand.

"Well," I explained. "I asked Jim to help me cook, but he said he didn't want to be the cause of your restaurant burning down on the first day it opened, so he settled on showing me how to make a boiled egg, how long to cook it for, that sort of thing."

"You asked Jim, when you could have asked me?" He frowned.

I reached up, cupping his face. "I wanted it to be a surprise." I dropped my head. "But now that I think about it, it's dumb."

He took the egg out of my hands, looking at it. "It's perfect." He said, beaming down at me.

I narrowed my eyes. "You haven't even cut it open yet." I only made one egg and I didn't know if it was the right texture inside.

He placed the egg on the counter behind him and slid his hands to my waist. "Doesn't matter, you made it." He smiled against my skin, leaving soft kisses on my jaw.

"Jim helped." I told him. I didn't want all the credit, I mean most of the time Jim was telling me what to do, step by step.

"Fuck Jim." He breathed out, licking my throat, before his lips crashed onto mine.

He slipped his tongue inside my mouth, making me moan into his. His hands drifted to my ass, giving it a light squeeze before he gripped my hips, and pulled me up and sat me on the counter. He spread my legs and stepped in between them. His hand trailing up my thigh getting closer and closer to the place that was weeping for him.

"We can't." I panted, already breathless from his kisses. "Your family is out there." I said.

"Our family, baby." He whispered against my lips.

I groaned, pulling him into me until I felt his hardness through my panties. I worked his belt off and pulled his pants and boxers down in one swift motion until his cock sprung free, the tip wet and ready. I spread my legs wider, feeling the cold metal underneath my legs. Good thing I wore a dress, today.

He didn't even pull off my panties, which somehow made it so much hotter, he pulled them to the side, running his fingers down my seam, over my clit, making sure I was wet enough for him. I was dripping, I could feel my arousal coat my thighs and I canted my hips, seeking for him.

He wasted no time, bringing his erection to my wetness, rubbing the tip over my clit, making me whimper. His lips covered mine, to stifle my cries and when he pushed inside me, he swallowed my muffled moans, groaning into my mouth.

"Gabriel." I breathed out, trying not to make too much noise. The kitchen was open, anyone could walk in.

"What do you need honey?" He asked me, bringing his thumb to my swollen bud as he continued thrusting inside me, gripping my thighs for support.

"Harder." I whispered, throwing my head back, feeling the orgasm build and build inside my core.

He thrust deep, hard until I moaned so loud, he covered my mouth with his hand. I shook and trembled as his cock hit a spot that made me convulse in pleasure.

"Oh fuck." He groaned, when my walls tightened around him, making him thrust with abandon, speeding up his moves until he stilled, spilling inside of me.

He breathed out, coming down from his orgasm, as I tried to catch my breath. His hand cupped my breast, squeezing it and I winced.

"Are you okay?" He asked, pulling back with a straight face.

I nodded, reassuring him I was fine as I pulled him into a kiss. "They're just feeling sensitive." I told him. It was probably my period, coming in.

He buttoned up his pants, stepping in between my thighs, gripping my waist. I looked up at him, smiling at his beautiful face. Who would have thought I would ever be here, with him, happier than ever?

"I'm so proud of you." I beamed.

"I couldn't have done it without you."

"That's not true." I frowned. I loved him for saying that, but I had nothing to do with it. "This was all you, you didn't need me."

He shook his head. "Mel, you have no idea how much I need you. You're it for me. You're my life, my happiness, my love."

My heart fluttered, feeling so full. "Keep saying sweet things to me and I might never let you go."

He smiled, cupping my face and leaning in until our noses touched. "That's the plan." He whispered before leaving a soft kiss on my lips.

I never wanted to let him go.

EPILOGUE

Gabriel

I glanced at my watch. Where was she?

I told Zaria to bring her here at five. What was taking so long? If my sister ruined this, I would shave her head in her sleep. The sun was setting soon, she wouldn't be here in time. She loved the sunset, it needed to be done now.

I wiped my arm across my forehead, wiping off the sweat. Fuck, why was I so nervous? This had been twelve years in the making. I glanced around looking at the candles spread out next to the pool. The rose petals surrounding them. Everything was perfect, why was I stressing?

Only Melissa could do this to me. No one else made my heart thump so fast it felt like it was going to explode out of my chest. No one else made me laugh like she did. I couldn't help but grin at the thought of my beautiful girlfriend.

How she nearly burnt down our house when trying to surprise me with birthday pancakes. How when she found out she was pregnant the first words she said to me was 'why couldn't we be seahorses?'. I would carry all of the babies in the world for her if it was possible.

This woman had ruined me, I was so hopelessly in love with Melissa Trevisano since I was eighteen years old. At this very pool, in this very house. The moment she had pulled me into the water, I knew. She was the only girl I wanted. And twelve years later, that hadn't changed.

I fell more and more in love with her every day. Every song she sang, even though she wasn't the best singer, every time she ate that godawful strawberry ice cream and moaned to entice me into eating it. Everything she did had me captivated.

I had been too much of a coward back then, letting everyone else's assumptions about me reign true, allowing everyone else's feelings to come before mine. Hell, I could still feel the blow to my chin I got, when I threatened some kid to stay the fuck away from Mel. She was my girl, she just didn't know it yet.

What I had told her was true. There were guys fighting over her in high school, what she didn't know was that one of them was me. It took me way too long to finally claim what was mine all along and now that I finally had her, I was never letting go.

It was like whenever I watched a great film and I wished I could experience it for the first time again, to experience everything from fresh eyes. I would do that in a heartbeat with Mel. I didn't regret a single moment in my life because all of it led me to her, and I would do it all over again.

I groaned, growing impatient. Glancing back at my watch. Sunset was coming soon. I ran a hand down my face, willing my breath to stabilize. I couldn't do this if my voice was shaky.

My breath hitched as I witnessed my beautiful girlfriend walking towards me. She had a blindfold on, Zaria guiding her around the pool. I ground my teeth together, maybe the poolside wasn't the safest option for someone who was six months pregnant. Fuck.

I approached her, interlocking her small hands in mine as I pulled off the blindfold. She blinked, adjusting to the light. She was fucking breath-taking. Pregnancy had made her even more beautiful, and I couldn't help smiling at the thought of my little girl in there. I reached up, cupping her face in my hands. Bringing my lips to hers. I kissed her soft and slow. We had all the time in the word. "Hi." I whispered.

Her eyes were glazed over when I pulled away from the kiss "Mmm, hi." She mumbled back, smiling like she had just witnessed a unicorn. Fuck, those smiles would be the death of me. I would never get over how she looked at me, like I hung the moon for her, like I was the source of her happiness. And I wanted nothing more than that.

For so long, I had been the cause of her pain and scowls and now I got to see every laugh, every smile, every snort she made. I was a lucky motherfucker. I couldn't help but laugh as I stroked her cheeks with my thumbs. She was mine. After so long, so much anguish and disappointment with my life, I had my honey. My sweet girl.

Her eyes finally left my face as they glanced around the pool, taking in the candles all spread around, surrounded by rose petals, her eyes widening as she looks at the pool, realizing where we were.

Yes baby.

We were at the exact place I had fallen in love with her. I was right here when I realized I would have done anything to make her happy, but at the time I didn't think I was worthy of her. I didn't believe that now, I think we deserved happiness, we deserved each other. I only wished I would have realized it sooner. So much time spent without her in my arms, gone. I wouldn't make that same mistake again.

I wanted every day with her until death, and every day after that. She was the love of my life, the only one who would ever make me this happy every day. And this was the perfect place to do it. Away from everyone, only the two of us. I knew Mel wouldn't react well to a public proposal, the attention and people staring at her would only end up in a panic attack and I wanted this to be only the best of memories for her.

"Mel." I whispered. "Ten years ago, I was sat in this very pool, with an annoying Italian girl who clawed her way into my heart." I smiled at the sound of her laugh. "It took me a long time to go after what I wanted, but now that I have you, I'm never letting you go." My hands left her face, grabbing onto her hands.

I dropped down to one knee, smiling at the sound of her gasp. "You're the only woman I have ever loved. The only woman who has made me a sappy shit and got me hooked to those crappy reality shows." Her laugh vibrated through the air as tears streamed down her face.

I reached into my pocket, pulling out a black velvet box. Zaria had helped me pick it out a little over five months ago, before we found out she was pregnant. I put it off, deciding to propose after the baby arrived, with the restaurant opening up, there were more and more reasons to delay it.

But I had made that mistake once, and I wasn't going to make it again. I wanted Melissa to be my wife. To have all the time in the world with her, for however long we had.

I opened up the box, revealing the gold ring. Her hands flew to her mouth as more tears fell down her face. She made no attempt to wipe them away, so enraptured by this moment to do anything else.

"I promise to make you laugh every day. I promise to make you as happy as you've made me. I promise to love you more and more every day. I'll love you when we stay home and watch tv and I'll love you when you endanger our lives by cooking." Her laugh escaped out through her tears. "I promise to love you when we argue, because I know I'm the only one who you allow to see that side of you." I smiled, remembering all the arguments we got into. And since then, every time we argued and she yelled at me or called me dipshit, all I could do was smile because I knew she loved me.

"I'll love you when you bring our baby girl into this world." I stroked her belly, so beautifully round. "And I'll love you when we're old as fuck and you can't walk without a cane."

I looked up at my beautiful girlfriend, wanting this moment to last forever. "I want you in my life forever, for as long as we live, I want to be yours and I want you to be mine. Will you marry me, Melissa Trevisano?"

"Yes. Yes. Yes" She cried out, wrapping her arms around my neck. I stood up, wrapping my hands around her waist as her lips crashed into mine, resisting the urge to wrap her legs around my waist. Mel being six months pregnant and being next to a pool, it would be too dangerous, and my girls were the most important thing to me.

"I love you." She whispered into my mouth as we kissed.

"I love you."

My girl. Twelve years and a lot of tribulations but we were here. Together.

The End.

Thank You

If you are reading this somewhere in the world, I would just like to say thank you. Thank you for purchasing and reading Love me or hate me.

I hope you had a great time reading this book and that you enjoyed it, and hopefully this book could act as an escapism to some.

As a romcom lover and the biggest enemies to lovers fan, I enjoyed every minute of writing Melissa and Gabriel's story, and I am so excited to share it with the world.

Please leave a review if you enjoyed the book and be on the lookout for any future book releases.

About the Author

Stephanie Alves is a Portuguese / English twenty-two-year-old from England.

When she's not writing, she's either reading or watching rom coms.

She loves her family and her two adorable dogs, and loves to read about happy endings!

Printed in Great Britain
by Amazon